The story, all names, characters, and incidents portrayed in this production are fictitious. No identification with actual persons (living or deceased) is intended or should be inferred.

First paperback edition: June 2025

Book cover by DreamStudio

ISBN   978-1-9680273-8-4 (5x8 paperback)

The Survivor's Compound

Part III
Desperate Survivors

M.P. Hendy

Table of Contents

Chapter 27

The Negotiator's Gambit

The dust swirled around the Behemoth as Eric expertly backed the armored vehicle into its usual spot near the work shed. Josh and Lily hopped out, their faces grim. Lynn followed, her hand shaking slightly as she gripped Josh's arm. The absence of Lynn's parents spoke volumes. The rescue mission had not gone as planned. "What happened?" David asked, his voice carrying the weight of unspoken fears.

Eric started, his expression troubled. "We found Lynn's parents' house. It... it looked too good. Generator running, house clean, cleaner than normal, according to Lynn. Too perfect." Lynn nodded, tears welling in her eyes. "It was like they were expecting us." Then Josh spoke, his voice surprisingly steady. "We found something else, David. Lynn's flat tire from two months ago? It wasn't just a puncture. The tire was shot. Deliberately."

The revelation hung heavy in the air. David's mind raced, connecting the dots. The ambush on Summer's convoy, the sabotaged tire... it was all orchestrated. Someone had been manipulating events from the shadows, patiently setting the stage. Lily spoke next, her voice small and laced with fear. "Daddy, they knew I was with them. They left a letter in Grandma and Grandpa's mailbox. It...it was meant for you."

With a heavy sigh, David requested, "Show me the letter." Lily, her eyes wide with worry, produced the crumpled paper. David scanned the message, his gaze lingering on the mention of Lily. "They want to negotiate," he stated, breaking the tense silence. "They haven't attacked us in over a month. They could have just killed Lynn's parents. Instead, they send a letter. They could have staged an ambush when you guys were at their house. They want something."

Jennifer scoffed, her voice laced with anger. "Negotiate? After everything they've done? David, they ambushed Summer! They tried to lure you out with Lynn! They're the same people who posted our location online!" "Indeed," David agreed, tilting his head slightly. "But their methods have shifted. Direct attacks have given way to manipulation. Why?" "Maybe they realized they can't win a straight fight," Aidan offered, his voice thoughtful. "They lost a lot of people at the ambush." "Or maybe," Elena interjected, a glint in her eyes, "they're trying to get close. They want to use you, David, to gain access to our resources, our technology."

David considered this. "A plausible hypothesis. But still... risky. They know my capabilities. They know what I'm capable of doing to them. There are easier ways to get resources." Tanya stepped forward, placing a calming hand on his arm. "David, whatever their reason, we can't just ignore this. Lynn's parents are in danger."

David's gaze softened as he looked at Tanya. "You're right. We can't abandon them. But we also can't walk blindly into a trap." He turned to the assembled group, a strange mix of apprehension and determination swirling in the room. "I'm going. But I'm not going alone." A murmur rippled through the room. Tiffany spoke first, her voice laced with concern. "David, that's insane! You're the most valuable asset we have! We can't risk you!" "And that," David countered, a hint of steel in his voice, "is precisely why they want me. They think if they can get me, they can control everything. But they underestimate the team I have built."

He began to assign roles, his decisions swift and decisive. The house was locked down. Some stayed behind, a shield against potential threats. Others, carefully chosen, would accompany him. The choices were difficult. Jessica, pregnant and wanting to help, was denied. Kris, despite her apparent reluctance, was ordered to go.

As the Behemoth rumbled back to life, David felt the weight of responsibility settle upon his shoulders. This negotiation was more than just a meeting; it was a gamble with the lives of those he cared about, a dance on the edge of a knife in a world where trust was a forgotten luxury. The stakes were high, and the consequences of failure were unimaginable. The journey into the unknown had begun, and with it, the desperate hope for a resolution that wouldn't shatter what little peace they had managed to build.

Elena smoothly maneuvered the Ford Transit van into position behind the Behemoth, its headlights cutting through the darkness. The van was less imposing than the Behemoth, but no less capable, filled with the equipment and expertise they would likely need. David gave Elena a nod of acknowledgement before turning his attention to the back of the behemoth.

David grabbed his radio. "Eric, lower the ramp." His voice was calm, but edged with steel. A moment later, a low hydraulic whine filled the air as a massive steel ramp unfolded from the back of the Behemoth, extending towards the ground like a mechanical tongue. It was an impressive sight, even for those who saw it regularly.

Turning to Elena, David gestured towards the ramp. "Alright, Elena, drive up." Elena, ever the professional, nodded curtly and expertly guided the Ford Transit up the ramp and onto the back of the Behemoth. The fit was snug, but secure. Once the van was parked, David hit the radio again.

"Eric, ramp up." He watched as the ramp retracted then folded back, holding the van safely in place on the trailer of the Behemoth. The absurdity of the situation wasn't lost on David. Here he was, in the middle of a post-apocalyptic Texas night, preparing to roll out in a behemoth of a vehicle carrying a transit van, piggy back, all because someone was trying to use Lynn's parents as bait. He couldn't help but appreciate the irony.

"Alright," he said, his voice cutting through the tension, "anyone else need to use the facilities before we move out?" The question, despite its mundane nature, broke the heavy atmosphere. Kris, perched in the back of the van, responded. "Master, are you suggesting we might not have potty breaks on this little adventure?" David raised an eyebrow, a flat smile playing on his lips. "Kris, I'm suggesting that if you need to relieve yourself, now is the time. We're not exactly stopping for scenic overlooks."

Summer shook her head. "Smart man. Best to be prepared." Lily, halfway out of the top of the van like a prairie dog, just looked down at her father with wide eyes. "Let's give them hell, Daddy."

Satisfied that everyone was as ready as they could be, David turned to Eric, who was already behind the wheel of the Behemoth, the engine rumbling like a slumbering giant. Lynn sat beside him, her face pale but determined. "Let's roll," David said, climbing into the passenger seat. The Behemoth lurched forward, the sheer power of the machine evident in the way it effortlessly pulled the weight of the Transit.

As the Behemoth lumbered onto the abandoned highway, crushing debris under its massive tires, David glanced back at the Transit perched precariously on the trailer. He could practically feel Kris's eager energy vibrating through the metal. Suddenly, a small cough broke the rhythm of the engine. David frowned. He turned around to face the passenger area, and sure enough, there she was: Jessica, tucked away in the corner, looking like a guilty puppy.

Her big, blue eyes pleaded with him. "Jessica," he said, his voice a low rumble that barely carried over the engine's roar. "What are you doing here?" Jessica squirmed. "I… I wanted to come." David sighed, pinching the bridge of his nose. This was not ideal. Not at all. "Jessica, you're pregnant. This isn't a sightseeing trip." "I know, Daddy," she said, her voice a whisper. "But I haven't been on a mission yet. Everyone else gets to go. And… and I don't trust Kris."

David's lips twitched. He understood her jealousy. Kris's enthusiasm was… intense. And Jessica, despite her sassy exterior, was deeply sensitive. "You don't trust Kris? Why?" Jessica twisted her fingers in her lap. "She's… too eager, Daddy. And she asks too many questions. Not like, 'how do you do this?' questions, but like… 'why do you do this?' questions. Like she's trying to figure you out."

David raised an eyebrow. He hadn't noticed anything particularly out of the ordinary. He was used to people being curious, fascinated even. But Jessica had a keen intuition, honed by her own quick wit and a healthy dose of sass. "And?" he prompted. "And," Jessica continued, leaning forward conspiratorially, "she's too smart to be acting so… stupid. Like she's playing dumb so you'll overlook her."

David considered this. Kris was definitely intelligent. He'd seen flashes of brilliance in her observations and insights, despite her often ditzy demeanor. And she had been unusually attentive lately, hanging onto his every word. "She's trying to learn, Jess," he said, but even to his own ears, it sounded weak.

Jessica scoffed, a flash of her usual fire returning to her eyes. "Learn? Daddy, she's not trying to learn about you. She's trying to get the Cliff's Notes version of David. So she can… I don't know… manipulate you better? Earn your trust faster? It's like she's… cheating." "Cheating?" David chuckled, but the sound was devoid of humor. "That's a bit dramatic, isn't it?" "Maybe," Jessica conceded, shrinking back a little. "But I just… I don't trust her. And I don't want her near you. Or our baby." She placed a protective hand on her stomach.

David appreciated Jessica's perceptiveness. He gently took her hand, feeling the warmth of her skin and the subtle swell of her belly where their child was growing. "I understand your concern, Jess. I do. And I appreciate you telling me. You're very important to me, you know that, right?" Jessica nodded, her fiery gaze softening under his attention. "I know, Daddy. And you're important to me. That's why I'm saying something."

He stroked her hand, his mind already analyzing Kris's behavior with a newfound scrutiny. The apocalypse had clarified things, stripped away social niceties, and amplified survival instincts. People were rarely subtle about their motivations anymore. Yet, Kris's act was too heavy-handed, too… calculated. "You don't like her calling me Master, do you?" David asked, stating the obvious. He'd noticed the subtle shift in Jessica's demeanor whenever Kris used the term.

Jessica wrinkled her nose. "It feels… fake. And it's insulting. Plus, this whole super-submissive thing? It's… weird. We respect you, we love you, but none of us do that." David sighed. "I'm not easily fooled, Jess. I'm aware of her… affectations. But I'm also trying to be open-minded. Everyone copes with this new world in their own way." "Coping shouldn't involve trying to manipulate my husband," she retorted, her protective instincts flaring again. "And it definitely shouldn't involve giving me creepy stares when you're not looking."

David's jaw tightened almost imperceptibly. "Creepy stares?" "Yeah," Jessica confirmed. "Like she's… measuring me. Judging me. And it's not just me. I've seen her do it to Tiffany and Summer too."

The pieces were starting to fall into place. Kris wasn't just trying to curry favor with him; she was sizing up the competition. And that, frankly, concerned him. "Alright, Jess," he said, squeezing her hand. "I hear you. I'll be more careful. I promise. But I need you to do something for me." Jessica looked at him expectantly, her eyes filled with concern. "Anything, Daddy." "I need you to stay in the Behemoth tonight," David said, his voice low. Jessica's brow furrowed. "What? But I want to be there. I want to help. I'm pregnant, not helpless."

David pulled her closer, his gaze intense. "I know you're not helpless, Jess. You're one of the strongest people I know. But you're also carrying my child. And this… this feels different. It feels like a trap. Too neat, too orchestrated. I can't risk you being in the thick of it." "But…" She started to protest, then stopped, seeing the worry etched on his face.

She hated being sidelined, but she understood. He was trying to protect her, and his concern was… endearing. "Fine," she relented reluctantly. "But I'm not happy about it. And I expect a full debriefing." "Of course," David said, relief washing over him. He knew she wouldn't like it, but he needed to know she was safe. He was already feeling the weight of responsibility for her and the baby, a weight he embraced wholeheartedly. That's what he did. He took care of his people.

He cupped her face in his hands, his thumbs gently stroking her cheeks. "Thank you, Jess. You're the best." "I know," she said with a hint of her usual sassy sarcasm, though her eyes softened. "Just… be careful, okay? And don't let Kris get any ideas."

David chuckled, a genuine, warm sound that eased some of the tension in the air. "I promise. I have no intention of letting anyone get any ideas. Especially not tonight." He leaned in and kissed her, a slow, lingering kiss that conveyed all the love and reassurance he couldn't put into words.

As they turned onto the road leading to Lynn's parent's house, Eric lowered the ramp on the back of the Behemoth. The ramp groaned under the weight of the Ford Transit as Eric expertly worked the hydraulics. David scanned the horizon, his gaze sharp and calculating. The night was their ally, cloaking their approach in a blanket of darkness. But darkness could also conceal enemies, and David wasn't about to let his guard down. Not for a second.

With a practiced hand, Elena reversed the Transit off the ramp, the tires biting into the asphalt. Lily squealed with delight, bouncing in her seat, while Summer calmly watched through the side mirror. Kris, eyes gleaming with anticipation, fidgeted beside Grace.

As Eric lifted the ramp, the behemoth rumbled onward, its massive frame eating up the road, while Elena skillfully maintained a safe distance behind, keeping the Transit's headlights dimmed. David had drilled them all on convoy tactics, and Elena, always a quick study, had mastered them.

David hopped out of the Behemoth with a surprising agility. He strode purposefully towards the gate, the gravel crunching under his boots. This whole situation reeked of a trap, a meticulously crafted snare designed to capture him. And he knew, with chilling certainty, that whoever was behind it was counting on his predictable altruism. "Alright, ladies, gentlemen," David said, his voice a low rumble that cut through the night. "Let's dance."

He wrestled with the cattle gate, its hinges protesting with a rusty groan. The Behemoth lumbered through, its sheer size dwarfing the modest suburban landscape. Elena, with a flick of her wrist and a knowing smirk, mirrored the Behemoth's passage with the Transit. The gate clanged shut, sealing them into what could very well be a kill zone.

Immediately, Lily and Grace sprang into action. Moving quickly through the shadows as they circled the property on both sides. David, meanwhile, adopted a casual gait, strolling alongside Lynn towards the front door. He even managed a reassuring pat on her arm, though his eyes missed nothing. Kris shadowed him like a nervous coyote, her eyes fixed to David. Josh, bulkier and more imposing than he remembered, brought up the rear, his gaze sweeping across the property, his hand resting on the pistol holstered at his hip.

The house itself was… unsettlingly normal. Too normal. The porch light flickered cheerfully, casting long, distorted shadows. The property lacked its signature empty flower pots and looked suspiciously perfect. And the air hung heavy with the scent of freshly cut grass — an anomaly in a world where gasoline was more precious than gold. "Stay sharp," David murmured to Kris and Josh, his voice barely audible. "Something's not right."

Lynn, her face etched with worry, fumbled with the doorknob. "Mom? Dad? It's me, Lynn!" A moment of agonizing silence stretched, punctuated only by the chirping of crickets. Then, the door creaked open. Standing in the doorway was Clarence, Lynn's father, looking even grumpier than David remembered. He squinted through the dim light, his face a roadmap of wrinkles and disapproval. Behind him, Margaret, Lynn's mother, peered over his shoulder, her expression a mixture of relief and apprehension.

Clarence's gruff voice sliced through the night. "Lynn? What took you so dad gum long? And who are all these people?" He squinted harder, recognition finally dawning. "Well, I'll be… David? And is that Josh? You've gotten bigger, boy." He stepped aside, waving them in. "Come in, come in, before the mosquitoes carry you off. Margaret, look who's here!"

Margaret bustled forward, her social worker instincts kicking in. "Lynn, darling! We were so worried! And David, how lovely to see you again." Her gaze lingered on David, a flicker of something unreadable in her eyes. She then noticed Josh and smiled warmly. "Josh, it's so good to see you. You've grown into such a fine young man."

David nodded politely to Margaret and Clarence, ushering Lynn inside. He knew this house like the back of his hand. He'd spent countless Thanksgivings and Christmases within these walls in his past life, a lifetime ago. The smell of old pot roast and bug killer was a familiar, almost comforting scent. Yet, tonight, it felt…wrong.

"You should have called," Margaret chided gently as she led them into the living room. "We've been so worried sick after the grid went down. Just vanished!" Clarence grumbled again, shuffling towards his recliner. "Phone lines are down, woman. Can't call nobody."

David scanned the room, his mind racing. He noted the pristine condition – not a speck of dust, the furniture meticulously arranged. It was too perfect, too staged. "We tried to get here sooner, but the roads are…difficult," David explained smoothly. The grid going down had changed everything, turning familiar routes into treacherous obstacles.

Margaret's smile seemed a touch too wide, her eyes darting around as if searching for something, or someone. "Well, we're just so relieved you're all safe. Where's your wife, Josh? Lily, wasn't it? We were so eager to see her."

David stepped forward, his voice calm and reassuring, a stark contrast to the razor-sharp calculations happening behind his eyes. "She's taking her time, Margaret. You know how girls are. She'll be in shortly." He subtly touched Lynn's arm, a silent signal. There was an unspoken agreement between them; something was amiss, and they needed to tread carefully.

Clarence, oblivious to the tension, settled into his recliner with a groan. Lynn knew this routine. Turn on the TV, complain about the news (even though there wasn't any anymore), fall asleep within twenty minutes. But tonight, the TV remained off, and Clarence seemed unusually alert. The comfortable predictability of her childhood home had been replaced by an unsettling unease. "So, David," Margaret began, her voice laced with a sweetness that grated on Lynn's nerves. "These…men who helped us after Lynn left. They were so kind. Said they were friends of yours."

David's expression didn't flicker. "Did they say their names, Margaret?" He knew he hadn't sent anyone. The situation was rapidly escalating beyond mere awkwardness. Margaret glanced quickly, almost imperceptibly, at Kris, perched beside David. "I…I don't recall. But they assured us they were looking after us on your behalf." "Interesting,"

David murmured, his gaze hardening. "Because I haven't sent anyone. It seems we have some uninvited guests using my name." The implications were clear: someone was manipulating her parents, and that someone was likely dangerous.

A tense silence descended, broken only by Clarence's heavy breathing. Lynn felt a prickle of unease intensify. She knew her parents, or at least, she thought she did. But something was off. Their eagerness, Margaret's overly solicitous tone, Clarence's unusual alertness…it all painted a picture of elaborate deception. It wasn't just unease anymore; it was a cold, creeping fear. "Clarence," David said, turning his attention to the older man. "Did you happen to check the mail today?"

Clarence blinked, his brow furrowed. "Mail? What for? Post office ain't running." "Just a precaution," David pressed. "Did anyone ask you to check it or put something in it?" The persistence in David's voice hinted at something deeper, a suspicion that resonated with Lynn's own growing anxieties.

Clarence shifted uncomfortably, his eyes darting to Margaret. "Well…I did go out a few hours ago. Nice young man asked me to see if anything came through, then told me to drop off a letter."

Before David could respond, a gentle knock sounded at the front door. Lily, ever the picture of composed efficiency, didn't wait for an invitation. She opened the door and stepped inside, her eyes scanning the room before settling on Clarence and Margaret. Her mere presence exuded an aura of control and quiet competence which heightened the sense of foreboding.

Clarence and Margaret stared back, dumbfounded. They clearly didn't recognize the beautiful young woman standing before them. "Good evening," Lily said, her voice polite but firm. "I'm Lily, Josh's wife, and David's daughter." She offered a small, professional smile. "It's lovely to finally meet you both."

Clarence's jaw dropped. "Josh…is married?" He looked at Lynn, a mix of confusion and disbelief plastered on his face. He seemed genuinely surprised, as if the world he knew was crumbling around him. Margaret, used to his shenanigans, simply rolled her eyes. She offered a strained smile. "Well, if it isn't Lily, we've heard so much about you from Joshua. Please, come in, dear. Let me get you something to drink. Coffee, perhaps?"

Lily inclined her head politely. "Thank you, Margaret. Coffee would be wonderful." She stepped further into the room, her movements fluid and graceful despite the tactical gear she wore. A Sig Sauer P365 nestled discreetly on her hip, and an M4 rifle hung casually from her shoulder. The juxtaposition of girlish charm and paramilitary readiness was jarring, especially to Clarence and Margaret, who looked as if they were witnessing something beyond their comprehension.

Clarence, still sputtering, pointed a trembling finger at the M4. "What…what's with the gun? You going hunting?" Lily's smile didn't falter, but a hint of steel entered her eyes. "Security," she replied simply. "We take it very seriously." Margaret bustled towards the kitchen, her voice a little too bright. "Oh, don't mind Clarence. He's just…old fashioned. I'll go put on a pot. Black, right?" She glanced back at Lynn, who nodded tightly, her heart pounding in her chest. The charade had gone on long enough.

As Margaret disappeared into the kitchen, David stepped forward, his gaze sweeping over the room, taking in every detail. He stopped in front of Clarence, his expression unreadable. "So, Clarence," he said, his voice calm but carrying an undercurrent of authority. "This 'nice young man' who asked you to check the mail… Can you describe him?" The question hung in the air, a prelude to what Lynn feared was coming: a confrontation that would shatter the illusion of normalcy and expose the dangerous reality lurking beneath the surface.

Clarence wrung his hands, his eyes darting between David and Lily. "He was…clean cut. You know, like a salesman. Lots of tattoos, said he was just helping out, making sure we were safe." Before Clarence could elaborate, a gruff voice echoed from the back of the house, "Everything alright out here? I heard voices gettin' loud."

The thin, wiry man, covered in tattoos sauntering into the living room immediately disrupted the already fragile peace. His presence, a stark contrast to the comfortable domesticity, hung heavy in the air. "Name's Boyd," he announced, his raspy voice cutting through the silence. "Just making sure these good folks are comfortable. We're here to help, after all."

David, ever the pragmatist, sized him up instantly. He noted the calculated sweep of Boyd's gaze, the subtle challenge in his eyes, and the instinctive movement towards the potential weapon concealed at his lower back. "Helpful of you, Boyd," David replied smoothly, masking his suspicion. "We appreciate your…assistance. Especially considering how vulnerable Clarence and Margaret were after Lynn left." He allowed the unspoken implication to linger, a silent accusation hanging in the air. "Tell me, Boyd, who exactly sent you to look after them?"

Boyd's dry chuckle was devoid of warmth. "Just some concerned citizens. Heard they needed a hand, that's all." The flimsy excuse was barely believable, a smokescreen barely concealing a hidden agenda.

Interrupting the escalating tension, Margaret entered from the kitchen, a tray laden with steaming mugs in her hands. "Coffee, everyone?" she chirped, her voice noticeably strained. She began distributing the mugs, her hands surprisingly steady despite the palpable unease. "David, dear, I hope you like black; if not, I can get you some cream and sugar." She offered a mug to Lily. "Lily, honey, a little cream and sugar for you." Then, turning to Boyd, her eyes narrowed almost imperceptibly. "Boyd, you take yours with that artificial sweetener, right?"

Boyd's eyes betrayed a flicker of surprise, a minute reaction that David didn't miss. "Thanks, Margaret," Boyd mumbled, accepting the mug. "You remembered." "Of course, dear," Margaret replied, forcing a saccharine smile. She passed a mug to Clarence, then to Kris. "And extra sugar for you Kris, hope you enjoy," she said as she retreated back to the supposed safety of the kitchen. The slight emphasis on Kris, and the seemingly innocent addition of sugar, hinted at a subtle message, a hidden communication within the unfolding drama.

David took a slow sip of his black coffee, his gaze locked on Boyd. He recognized Margaret's attempt to diffuse the situation, but the polite facade was crumbling. "Let's cut the pleasantries, Boyd," David stated, his voice hardening. "We both know you didn't stumble across Clarence and Margaret out of the goodness of your heart. And you didn't spend the last month and a half guarding them just to be a good Samaritan. So, why am I here? What do you want?"

Boyd's forced smile vanished, replaced by a calculating glint. He swirled the coffee in his mug, the silence becoming a palpable force. "Alright, alright," he conceded, raising his hands in mock surrender. "No need to get all paramilitary on me." He took a deep breath, his gaze sweeping around the room before settling back on David. "It's simple, really. I know about your place. Your little fortress. And I want in."

A disbelieving chuckle escaped David's lips. "You 'want in'? You think after all this, after the charade, the manipulation, the blatant setup, I'm just going to welcome you with open arms?" Boyd leaned forward, his voice dropping to a conspiratorial whisper. "Not just in. But as a partner. An equal."

Lily snorted, nearly choking on her sugary coffee. Josh, ever protective, placed a hand on her back, his eyes narrowed at Boyd. Kris, however, remained impassive, that faint smirk still playing on her lips, hinting that she knew more than she was letting on. David raised an eyebrow, intrigued despite himself. "A partner? What makes you think you have anything to offer?"

"I know things, David," Boyd said, his eyes gleaming with unsettling intensity. "Things you need to know. About who's been pulling the strings, about the people who want what you have. I'm not just some random thug, David. I'm a survivor. A strategist. And I'm damn good at what I do."

David steepled his fingers, considering Boyd's words. "Let's say, hypothetically, I refuse your generous offer of partnership. What then, Boyd? Do you unleash your hidden army? Do you threaten Lynn's parents again? What cards do you hold that you think will sway me?"

Boyd chuckled, a dry, humorless sound. "No armies, David. No direct threats. I'm not stupid enough to go to war with you that way. My cards are…subtle. Let's just say, I know things about your little community. Vulnerabilities. Weaknesses. Things you might not even be aware of." He paused, letting his words sink in, the threat hanging heavy in the air. "Information, David. Information is power. And I have plenty of it."

"A 'strategist'?" David echoed, a hint of playful disbelief lacing his voice. "Last I checked, 'strategists' generally don't rely on kidnapping elderly people to get my attention. It seems a tad…unrefined, don't you think?"

Boyd's smile tightened. "Collateral damage, David. Sometimes, the ends justify the means." "Ah, yes, the old 'ends justify the means' argument," David sighed dramatically. "A classic. Tell me, Boyd, is that the same justification you used when you helped build my apartment bunker? The one you clearly intend to compromise, considering you know its existence? Or is it just convenient now?" He paused, letting the implication hang in the air like a bad smell. Clarence visibly stiffened, while Margaret choked on her tea. Lynn shifted nervously. "David, what are you talking about?"

Chapter 28

The Price of Betrayal

Before David could answer, a sharp rapping echoed from the living room window. Four distinct knocks. Tap, tap, tap, tap. David's eyes flicked to the window, recognizing the signal instantly. Grace.

David's gaze lingered on the window for a split second, the four knocks from Grace echoing was the "all clear" signal, his team's way of saying the perimeter was secure, no hidden threats lurking in the shadows. David felt a surge of relief mixed with amusement. Here he was negotiating with a tattooed schemer who thought he was playing 4D chess, while his own people had already checkmated the board.

David rose from his chair, the wooden legs scraping against the floor in a way that sounded comically deliberate, like a vaudeville act. He unholstered his sidearm and laid it on the table with exaggerated care, then removed the wakizashi and set it beside. "There we go," he said, his voice laced with mock solemnity. "Can't have a proper handshake with all this hardware getting in the way. Wouldn't want to poke an eye out."

Boyd blinked, his intense gleam faltering for a moment. The man was all sharp edges and faded ink, but David could see the gears turning behind those eyes. Boyd had been so sure of his "subtle" cards, but now he looked like a poker player who'd just realized his bluff was called.

David extended his hand, a grin tugging at his lips. "Alright, Boyd, you win. Let's partner up. Someone with your... strategic flair could be useful. After all, in a world without Netflix, a good plot twist is hard to come by." Boyd hesitated, then grasped David's hand, his grip firm but uncertain, like a man shaking hands with a wolf he'd just invited into his den. "You mean it? No tricks?" David shook his head. "No more tricks."

Lynn gaped at David, her jaw practically scraping the floor. One moment, he was radiating silent menace, the air thick with unspoken threats; the next, he was offering a partnership, all smiles and disarming charm. It was like watching a cobra suddenly offer a cup of tea. "David, what are you doing?" she blurted out, unable to contain her incredulity. "He's been lying, manipulating... probably trying to kill us! And you're offering him a job?"

David turned to her, his blue eyes twinkling with amusement. "Lynn, relax. Hasn't anyone ever told you to keep your friends close, and your enemies closer? Besides," he added with a wink, "I'm a sucker for a good villain origin story. Boyd here clearly needs a redemption arc."

Boyd, still holding David's hand, looked like he was trying to decide whether he'd just won the lottery or been sentenced to community service. He glanced at Lynn, then back at David, a flicker of unease in his eyes. Maybe partnering with David wasn't going to be the cakewalk he'd envisioned.

David's suggestion hung in the air, thick with unspoken implications. Lynn still looked like she wanted to set Boyd on fire, and Clarence and Margaret were staring at the unfolding scene with a mixture of confusion and dawning horror. "Come on, Boyd," David said, releasing his hand and clapping him on the shoulder with a little too much enthusiasm. "Let's talk shop. You know, strategy, world domination, the usual topics."

David led Boyd into the guest bedroom behind the living room. A moment later, David left the room, closing the door behind him. David clapped his hands together. "Alright folks, pack your stuff, time to leave." Lynn stared at him, aghast. "What about Boyd? You were only in there… for like… a second!"

David sighed dramatically, running a hand over the back of his head. "Oh, Boyd? Well, let's just say he won't be coming with us." A collective gasp rippled through the room. Margaret whispered, "David, you didn't…"

David held up a hand, his expression a carefully crafted mix of innocence and exasperation. "Look, he threatened my family, explicitly. He knew about our fortress, our plans. He was a loose end, a liability. And frankly," he added with a shrug, "he was really cramping my style." Clarence, surprisingly, chuckled. "Good riddance to bad rubbish. Guy had shifty eyes." Margaret shot her husband a disapproving look, but a faint smile played on Clarence's lips. He'd never liked Boyd.

Lynn, however, was still struggling to process what she'd just heard. "But…you just offered him a partnership! You shook his hand!" "Think of it as a theatrical gesture, Lynn," David replied smoothly. "A dramatic irony moment, if you will. Besides, I needed to get him somewhere… private. Look," he said, his voice turning serious, "this world is different now. We can't afford to be naive. Boyd was a threat, and I neutralized it. End of story."

David's gaze turned, glacial and unwavering, towards Kris, who was standing at the edge of the living room, clutching a ceramic coffee mug depicting a cartoon armadillo. The mug shook in her hand, rattling against her teeth. "Kris," David said, his voice dangerously soft, "care to explain why Margaret knew your coffee preferences when you've never met before?"

The color drained from Kris's face, leaving her looking like a porcelain doll that had been dropped in a bucket of bleach. The armadillo mug slipped from her grasp and shattered on the floor, the sound echoing in the suddenly silent room. Josh winced, automatically grabbing Lily's hand, who stared wide-eyed at the broken pottery.

Kris didn't answer, instead, she took a shaky step forward, her eyes wide with a mixture of fear and desperation. "Master... I..." "Don't 'Master' me, Kris" David snapped, cutting her off. He rarely used that tone, and it sent a shiver down everyone's spine. Even Clarence stopped smirking. "Start explaining. Now."

Kris burst into tears, abandoning any pretense of composure. She rushed toward David, stumbling over the broken pieces of the mug. "Master, please! I'm so, so sorry! I didn't mean for any of this to happen!"

David sighed, a sound that seemed to carry the weight of the world. He watched Kris approach, her face streaked with tears, her small frame shaking with sobs. He knew, intellectually, that she was manipulative, that her histrionics were likely calculated.

He held out his arms, and Kris practically hurled herself into his embrace, burying her face in his chest. He wrapped his arms around her, a familiar warmth spreading through him despite the ice in his gut. He patted her back gently, like he would a child. "Shhh, Kris, it's alright," he murmured, the lie tasting bitter in his mouth. "Just…tell me what happened." Kris hiccupped against his chest, her words muffled. "Boyd…he…took advantage of my…. He knew I was insecure. He said he could help me."

David's grip tightened almost imperceptibly. "Help you how, Kris?" "He…he said if I gave him information about the ranch, about your family, he'd… he'd talk to you. He'd tell you how much I care. He said he could make you see me the way I wanted you to." She sniffled, pulling back slightly to look up at him with tear-filled eyes. "I just wanted you to include me, Master. I just wanted you to love me like you love Jessica."

"A liability can never be trusted," David murmured, his voice barely audible amidst Kris's pathetic wails. He continued to hold her, her slight form trembling against him, her pleas for forgiveness a broken record in his ears. He felt a familiar wave of something akin to pity wash over him. He knew what it was like to be overlooked, underestimated. He knew what it was like to crave connection, to yearn for acceptance. He could almost understand Kris's desperation, her misguided attempts to gain his affection. Almost.

But understanding couldn't excuse betrayal. Not after everything. Not after the lies told, the unwavering trust his family placed in him. Kris's actions weren't just a breach of loyalty; they were a direct threat to the safety and security of his entire community.

He tightened his embrace, a subtle shift in pressure that wouldn't be noticeable to anyone but him. He felt Kris stiffen slightly, her sobs momentarily ceasing as if sensing a change in his demeanor. "Master?" she whimpered, her voice laced with a renewed sense of fear.

He didn't respond. Instead, he increased the pressure, the muscles in his arms coiling like springs. He channeled all his focus, his strength, into the simple act of holding her. It was a slow, deliberate squeeze, a controlled application of force that bypassed the immediate breaking point.

He felt the delicate bones in Kris's ribcage begin to creak, a subtle symphony of destruction playing out against his chest. He registered the slight gasp that escaped her lips, the widening of her eyes in dawning horror. He smelled the faint metallic tang of blood, a sign of internal trauma. "I'm…so…sorry…" she choked out, her voice a mere whisper.

David remained silent, his expression unreadable. He continued to squeeze, the pressure building steadily, relentlessly. He felt the bones in her spine begin to buckle, the delicate network of nerves screaming in protest. He heard a soft, wet cough, and felt the warm trickle of blood seeping through his shirt.

It was over quickly, silently. Kris's body went limp in his arms, her final, desperate breath escaping her as her eyes glazed over. He held her for a moment longer, the weight of her lifeless form a heavy burden.

He gently lowered her to the floor, laying her out with a strange tenderness. He straightened her limbs, smoothed her hair, and closed her eyes. He might be a pragmatist, a survivor, a leader who made difficult choices, but he wasn't a monster. He could acknowledge the humanity, however flawed, that had once resided within Kris's small frame.

Standing up, he brushed off his shirt, a faint smudge of blood the only evidence of what had just transpired. He met Lynn's wide, horrified eyes. He knew he would have to explain. He knew there would be questions, doubts, perhaps even condemnation. But he also knew that he had done what was necessary. A liability could never be trusted, and Kris had become the most dangerous liability of all.

"Margaret?" David said, turning his attention to Lynn's mother, bypassing Lynn's shock entirely. Margaret was staring dumbly at Kris's corpse. Clarence just staired, a statue of confused grumpiness. "You recognized Kris. From before?"

Margaret blinked, her eyes fluttering like a trapped bird. "Yes…yes, I did. It was…a week or so after the blackout. After Boyd showed up. He was…introducing himself, trying to be helpful. And she was there. With him." "Here?" David pressed, his voice calm, devoid of accusation.

Margaret nodded slowly. "Just outside. They were…talking. She seemed…ambitious. Yes, that's it. Ambitious. She kept glancing at the house. At us." Lynn gasped. "She was…reconnaissance? Even then?"

David ignored Lynn's outburst, his mind already several steps ahead. He cataloged the information, cross-referencing it with every detail he possessed. Kris's ambition, her presence with Boyd, her knowledge of his ranch even before they "rescued" her family. It all painted a disturbingly clear picture.

"She knew," David stated, more to himself than anyone else. "She knew exactly who we were when we found them on the road. Mark and Janet, their kids…they were all pawns." He looked at Lynn, the grief and horror battling on her face. "I picked them up fleeing Austin two months ago. How did she know to be there?"

Lynn shook her head, tears welling in her eyes. "I…I don't know. I just…it doesn't make any sense. Why? What did they want?" "Me," David replied flatly. "They wanted me. Boyd couldn't beat me head-on. He tried ambushes, he tried to use you and now, your parents as bait. Kris was his last, desperate gamble. A long-term infiltration.

David's gaze flicked to Josh, standing silently near the doorway, his expression unreadable. "Josh, do you remember the route we took when we picked up Mark and his family?" Josh's brow furrowed in concentration. "Yeah, we had to detour a couple of times. There was a large pileup down the highway just past the main city, we had to exit south of Austin. Then, further on, a bridge was blocked by a tractor trailer, so we had to take a back road." David nodded grimly. "Those weren't accidents. They were placed there, intentionally. To force us onto specific routes."

He pinched the bridge of his nose. "We scouted the route to Austin several times before we picked up Mark and his family. Boyd probably had someone staked out at a point along our most likely route. He knew we had a preference for it. She knew we were altruistic and would stop to provide aid." He turned back to Lynns parents. "I need you both to pack a bag," David said, his voice brooking no argument. "You're coming with us."

Clarence, ever the contrarian, grumbled, "Where in the hell we goin'?" "That's something we'll discuss back at the ranch," David stated. "Everything will be explained there." He paused, letting the weight of his words sink in. "But understand this: you have two choices. You come with me now, or you stay here. And if you stay here, your chances of surviving this…apocalypse…are minimal, at best."

Margaret studied David's face, searching for any hint of deception. She saw nothing but grim determination. "David's right, Clarence," she said quietly, laying a hand on her husband's arm. "We're old. We can't survive out here on our own. We'll go with him."

Clarence harrumphed, but didn't argue further. He knew Margaret was right. He might be stubborn, but he wasn't stupid. Besides, the thought of seeing his daughter and grandson again, under somewhat safer circumstances, was appealing. "Alright, alright," he grumbled. "Give me a minute. I need my dentures and my medication." David nodded, a hint of amusement flickering across his face. "Take your time. Lynn, can you help them gather what they need?"

Lynn reflexively sprang into action and started moving toward the guest room in search of her old photos. After carefully sidestepping Kris's body, she casually opened the door, stepped into the guest room and stopped dead. Boyd was on the bed, alright. Just… very, very still. His head was at an unnatural angle, supported by the pillow, and his usually ruddy complexion was now a disturbing shade of purple. His neck… well, his neck didn't look like a neck anymore. It resembled a poorly executed sculpture made of Play-Doh, the kind a toddler might inflict on an unsuspecting action figure.

Lynn immediately winced, a wave of nausea washing over her. She'd completely forgotten Boyd was in there. The image was both disturbing and, in a strange way, comforting. David would kill to protect them. A shudder ran down her spine. She forced herself to focus, closed the door gently, and plastered a smile on her face. "Everything's fine," she said, a little too brightly. "Just...looking for family photos."

Clarence shuffled out and Margaret followed, her brow furrowed with concern. Lynn busied herself grabbing her father's bag of medications. David, ever observant, noticed Lynn's forced cheerfulness and the subtle tremor in her hands. He understood the lengths she was going to protect her parents from the brutal reality. He appreciated it, and filed it away.

Outside, the night air was crisp and cool. Eric was perched on the hood of the Behemoth, holding his rifle. Jessica lounged in the driver's seat, humming a tune. Elena and Summer stood a short distance away, whispering conspiratorially. Grace, ever the watchful observer, sat on the front porch, her gaze sweeping the surroundings.

David meticulously supervised the loading process, ensuring everyone was comfortable and secure. He paused beside Summer and Elena, his gaze softening. He enveloped them in a hug, a prolonged, almost desperate embrace. "Something's wrong," Summer murmured, her voice barely audible. "Very wrong," Elena added, her eyes searching his. "What happened in there?"

David simply shook his head, his expression unreadable. "Later. We need to get them back to the ranch. I'll explain everything then." He squeezed their hands, a silent promise, before turning his attention back to the task at hand.

Jessica, nestled in the driver's seat of the Behemoth, watched David climb in, his movements unusually stiff. "Everything alright, Daddy?" she asked, her voice soft and laced with concern. She reached out, her small hand covering his much larger one, seeking to ground him. The term of endearment, usually playful, now carried a genuine weight, a plea for him to confide in her. David squeezed her hand, his grip firm but gentle. He met her gaze, his eyes a swirl of emotions, grief, anger, regret. "Not really, Jess," he admitted, his voice low and gravelly. "But I'll tell you later. Just...drive. Get us home."

He didn't elaborate, and Jessica didn't press. She understood his need to compartmentalize, to focus on the immediate task at hand. He would reveal everything in his own time. Eric, oblivious to the silent exchange between David and Jessica, cranked the engine of the Behemoth, then glanced back at David, a question in his eyes. "Let's go, Eric," David said, his voice regaining its usual authority. "Get Lynn's folks back to the ranch." He leaned back in his seat, closing his eyes. The weight of what he had done pressed heavily on him.

As the Transit followed the Behemoth onto the highway, Summer tapped Elena on the shoulder. "Where's Kris?" she asked, her voice a mix of curiosity and apprehension. "Did she get in the Behemoth with David?" Elena glanced towards the Behemoth. "I don't think so. I didn't see her. Maybe she's still inside? I thought she was right behind us." Summer frowned. "I haven't seen her since we got to the house. That's weird, right?"

Josh, who was sitting in the back with Lily, overheard the conversation. He exchanged a quick, uneasy glance with Lily. Neither of them said anything. Lily busied herself with braiding a strand of Grace's hair, while Josh stared out the window, pretending to be engrossed in the passing darkness. The image of David hugging Kris, the sickening crack…it was burned into his mind. He didn't want to think about it, let alone talk about it. And judging by Lily's silence, she felt the same way.

The drive back was unsettlingly quiet, without a single word spoken. As the Behemoth and the Transit arrived back at the ranch, Tiffany, Jennifer and little David waited, while everyone else was asleep. "David, I'm glad you all made it back," Tiffany said, offering an affectionate hug. David didn't respond, but after kissing her cheek, he immediately grabbed Clarence and Margaret's bags.

Lynn, still pale and shaken, led her parents towards her apartment, her steps hesitant. Clarence grumbled about the whole ordeal, while Margaret kept glancing back at David, her eyes filled with a mixture of gratitude and something akin to…pity? David ignored her gaze, focusing on the task at hand: getting everyone settled and safe.

Once Lynn had her parents safely inside their apartment, David followed her out into the hallway. "Thank you," she said softly. "For everything." David simply nodded.

"Get some rest, Lynn," he said. "We'll talk in the morning." He turned and walked back towards the main house, leaving Lynn standing alone.

Inside the house, the atmosphere was thick with unspoken tension. Everyone was going through the motions of preparing for bed, but the air crackled with unease. Tiffany bustled around, making sure everyone had a warm drink. Jennifer, usually bubbly and playful, was unusually subdued, her eyes darting nervously towards David.

Summer cornered David as he walked into the house. "David," she said, her voice tight. "What happened back there? Where's Kris?" David stopped, his back to her. He took a deep breath, steeling himself. "Kris won't be coming back, Summer," he said, his voice flat. Summer gasped. "What do you mean? What happened?"

David turned to face her, his eyes filled with a pain that made her heart ache. "The one that's been after us, the ambush? He was there," he said. "And Kris…Kris betrayed us, Summer. She was working with him." The words hung in the air, heavy and suffocating. Summer stared at him, her mind reeling. "No," she whispered. "That's not…Kris wouldn't…"

David reached out, gently cupping her face. "Summer," he said softly, his voice filled with affection and regret, "I know it's hard to believe. But it's true. I'll explain everything, but I need everyone together. Can you please get Tiffany, Little David, Aidan and Jennifer? Meet me in the living room. We need to talk." He gave her a reassuring kiss, then walked past her towards the living room.

Jessica and Lily were already waiting in the living room. Jessica, usually a whirlwind of sassy energy, was sitting quietly on the couch, her hand resting protectively on her small but growing belly. Her eyes, though, were sharp and observant, betraying her awareness that something significant had transpired. Lily sat beside her, her small face a mask of seriousness.

David stood before them, his expression grave. "Alright," he began, his voice low but steady. "As Summer may have mentioned, things…escalated tonight. We found the man responsible for the ambushes we've been dealing with. Tonight, he was using Lynn's parents as bait to lure us in." Tiffany gasped, her hand flying to her mouth. Aidan's jaw tightened. Jennifer whimpered softly, edging closer to David.

David continued, carefully choosing his words. "This man, Boyd, was a dangerous individual. He knew about our capabilities, our defenses. And it turns out, he's had his eye on us since before the blackout." Aidan raised his hand, a confused expression on his face. "Dad, how did this guy know about us anyway?" David sighed. "Apparently, he was a part of the crew that built the apartment bunker. His name was on the list that Brian made when the whole online thing happened."

"What about Kris?" Jessica asked, her voice barely a whisper. "What happened to her, Daddy?" David's gaze softened as he looked at Jessica. "Well, it turns out, you were right about her. She was too eager. Apparently, she was this guy's hail Mary," he said gently. "She was working with him. She betrayed us." The air in the room seemed to thicken, heavy with disbelief and shock. "No…" Jennifer breathed, shaking her head. "Kris? But she loved you, Master!"

David sighed. "I thought so too, Jennifer. And she might have. But she was also collecting information for Boyd. She was an unpredictable liability and apparently, had been at it long before we picked her up." "What did you do with Boyd, David?" Tiffany asked. "I killed him," he answered. "And Kris?" Summer asked, her voice trembling. "What happened to Kris?"

David took a deep breath. This was the hardest part. He looked at Lily, who was watching him with wide, unblinking eyes. He knew she had seen everything. "Kris…she made her choice," he said, his voice heavy with regret. "She chose to betray us, to put all of you in danger. I couldn't let that stand. I…" He hesitated, struggling to find the right words. "I took care of her too."

The silence that followed David's admission was deafening. Elena, ever the pragmatic one, frowned. "Took care of her? What does that mean, David? I didn't hear any shots, and I didn't see... well, anything. How did you 'take care' of them?" Her eyes narrowed, suspicion flickering in their depths.

David shifted uncomfortably, avoiding her gaze. He hated explaining this part. It felt…barbaric, even to him. But they deserved to know the truth, especially after everything they'd been through. He looked at Lily, a silent plea for understanding in his eyes. Lily, bless her heart, gave him a small, almost imperceptible nod.

He sighed. "It wasn't…pretty," he admitted, his voice strained. "There wasn't time for anything…clean. Boyd was a threat to Lynn's parents, Margaret, and Clarence. He was a threat to all of you. And Kris…well, Kris was actively aiding him. Waiting any longer would have had dire consequences. And the way I did it…it was…efficient."

He finally met Elena's gaze, his own filled with a weariness that belied his youthful appearance. "I crushed his neck with my bare hands. He died almost instantly. And Kris…I hugged her. Very, very hard."

The room erupted in a cacophony of reactions. Jennifer gasped, clutching her chest. Tiffany paled, her hand flying to her mouth again. Aidan stared at David, his expression a mixture of shock and awe. Summer simply closed her eyes, a single tear tracing a path down her cheek. Jessica, already emotional due to her pregnancy, began to sob softly.

Elena, however, remained stoic, although a muscle twitched in her jaw. "You…crushed them? With your bare hands? David, that's…that's…" Before Elena could finish, Tanya moved with a grace that belied the chaos of the moment. She knelt before David, her dark eyes locking with his. Her hands gently cupped his face. Then, she leaned in and kissed him. Not a chaste, comforting peck, but a deep, lingering kiss that spoke volumes of her understanding, her loyalty, and her unwavering love.

Her lips moved against his with a passionate intensity that chased away the shadows in his eyes, if only for a fleeting moment. She poured all her compassion into that kiss, a silent promise that she saw the burden he carried, the guilt that gnawed at him, and that she would help him bear it.

When she finally broke the kiss, David's breath hitched. His eyes, still haunted, were softened by the warmth of her affection. "Thank you," he murmured, his voice rough with emotion. Tanya rose, meeting each woman's gaze in turn, her expression calm and resolute. "You don't know what he thinks," she stated, her voice clear and steady. "He may be a killer. But I trust him. I trust his judgment. And more importantly," she paused, her eyes locking on Jessica's, "I trust his heart."

Jessica sniffled, wiping her eyes with the back of her hand. Tanya's words resonated deeply, cutting through the initial shock and horror. "But Kris…" Elena started, her voice tinged with disbelief. "She was…one of us." Tanya nodded, acknowledging the sting of betrayal. "Yes, she was. And that makes it all the more painful. But betrayal is a poison, and David acted to protect us all from its spread. He made a difficult choice, a terrible choice, but he made it for us."

Elena's stoicism cracked. "Protect us? By turning into… into the monster they all think he is? He always says he's not a hero!" Jennifer scoffed, stepping forward. "Oh, please, Elena. Spare me the theatrics. We all knew what we were signing up for when we chose David. Did you think he was going to solve our problems with therapy sessions and rainbows? He does what needs to be done. And yeah, sometimes that makes him the bad guy. But I'd rather have a bad guy protecting me than some bleeding heart getting us all killed."

Lily, who had been unusually quiet, piped up. "Daddy didn't want to. I saw. He looked sad." Aidan, ever the pragmatist, cleared his throat. "Alright, enough. We can dissect the morality of it all later. Right now, we need to focus on what comes next." He glanced at David, his expression serious. "We know Boyd had help. Kris confirmed that."

David spoke. His voice, usually a warm baritone, was flat, devoid of emotion. "Boyd didn't get the information from Kris about our plans. The leak started long before she moved in." He shifted his gaze, his eyes, usually so full of life, now held a chilling emptiness. He looked at Aidan. "Think back to when Jennifer discovered the map posted online. Remember the ambush on the medical supply run? What did those events have in common?" Aidan frowned, tapping his chin. "Both involved knowledge of our movements… of targets outside the ranch. The medical run… they knew the route, the timing…" He trailed off, realization dawning. "They knew details we hadn't shared with anyone outside this room, and a tight circle around us."

"Exactly," David confirmed, his voice regaining some of its familiar cadence. "Which means the source isn't likely someone who just joined our family. It's someone who's been around for a while, or someone with access to long-term information." Summer spoke up. "So, what, we're thinking a mole? Someone who's been playing us for fools this whole time?"

"Possibly," David conceded. "Or someone who had access to the ranch before the EMP." A muscle ticked in his jaw. "Boyd was a construction worker on my apartment bunker. He knew the details of the project. The schematics, the power grid, the shielded rooms…" Lily, who had been unusually quiet, perked up. "You're saying he could have planted something? Like... a listening device?" David nodded slowly. "An EMP-proof listening device. Something that could have been broadcasting our conversations, our plans, to someone else."

Chapter 29

A Protector's Burden

The air hung heavy with unspoken questions about Kris, the bubbly tattoo artist who had so abruptly disappeared. "Where did she go?" Nicole asked. "One minute she's here, offering back rubs, the next... gone." Taylor nervously adjusted her posture. "And David hasn't said a word. It's... unsettling." Kayla tried to offer a logical explanation. "Maybe she just left? This life isn't for everyone... maybe it spooked her."

Brian shook his head. "Kris seemed pretty adaptable. And honestly, anyone getting close to David is not a coward. She definitely had a mission. It doesn't make sense that she would just leave." Seo-Yeon nodded in agreement. "She was very persistent in her affections. It seemed unnatural, especially since I caught her snooping frequently. Where she should not have been"

Alissa frowned. "She was always asking questions. Subtle things, about the ranch security, David's routines...I just assumed she was curious. Maybe David noticed too but didn't say anything. He's been known to keep things close to the vest."

Meanwhile, the atmosphere in the dining room was thick enough to cut with a butter knife. Mark fidgeted beside his wife, Janet. David, usually a calming presence, was radiating an aura of controlled intensity. "Mark," David began, his voice neutral, almost clinical. "You knew Kris."

Mark swallowed hard. He knew this was coming. "Yeah. Janet and I worked with her uncle at a construction company in Austin. Real small operation, mostly road work. Good people." "And Kris?" David pressed. "She was... around," Janet interjected, her voice hesitant. "Usually after classes. She'd stay with us, because our house was closer." "So, you knew her well?" David's gaze pinned Mark, who shifted uncomfortably. "Not really, sir. Janet knew her better. She always seemed kind of... flirty, you know? With the older guys on the crew. Didn't want to get caught up in that."

David's eyes narrowed slightly, processing this information. "When was the last time you saw her before... well, before we found you?" Mark took a deep breath. "She showed up at our place almost a week before we left Austin. Said her uncle left town after the blackout, was looking for a safe place to go. We told her we planned on heading north. She asked if she could tag along... Janet and I didn't have the heart to say no, I guess... or to turn her back out into the streets by herself."

David steepled his fingers, his gaze unwavering. "Mark, if you were heading north, why did we find you south of Austin?" Mark paled, his Adam's apple bobbing nervously. "We... uh... we got turned around," he stammered, avoiding eye contact. "Roads were blocked, cars everywhere. We were trying to find a way around them." Janet placed a reassuring hand on his arm, her expression a mix of concern and suspicion.

"That doesn't quite add up, Mark," Summer spoke softly, her normally gentle voice laced with steel. "I reviewed the maps. Even with the blocked roads, a northerly route would have been more logical. You were heading directly away from your stated destination."

Sweat beaded on Mark's forehead. He glanced at Janet, who gave him a look that could curdle milk. "Okay, okay, fine!" he blurted out. "We... we heard rumors. Rumors about a safe place south of Austin. A ranch, run by some... some prepper guy. We thought it was worth checking out." "And Kris?" David inquired, his voice dangerously calm. "Was she also suddenly interested in this 'prepper guy's' ranch?"

Mark hesitated. "She... she might have mentioned something like that," he admitted. "Said she had a... a 'connection' down here. Someone she knew." A collective murmur rippled through the room. Jennifer, ever direct, spoke up. "Master, it sounds like they were intentionally trying to get here. That Kris was leading them, perhaps under Boyd's instructions."

David nodded slowly, processing the information. "Tanya, could you and Elena check Mark and Janet's apartment? Subtle search. Look for anything out of the ordinary. Kayla, I want you to keep an eye on Lori and Beth. Make sure they stay away from the work shed and the perimeter.

David turned to Aidan, his face softening slightly. "Aidan, son, I need a favor. A strange one." He handed Aidan a list scrawled on a notepad. "I want Little David to play these songs, each in a different apartment, on repeat. And I need you to find an analog receiver. After Little David has played the songs, I need you get on top of the work shed and try to pick up on any signal playing music from the apartment. See if you can determine the apartments that are re-broadcasting the signal."

Aidan raised an eyebrow, intrigued. "An analog receiver? Like an old ham radio?" "Exactly," David confirmed. "I have a hunch, and I need to confirm it. Also, can you ensure that Little David wears hearing protection when playing the songs?" Aidan grinned. "Consider it done, sir." He clapped Mark on the shoulder, a little too hard. "Come on, buddy, let's go find an analog receiver. You can tell me all about your camping trip."

Aidan found a dusty, but functional, analog receiver in the depths of the maintenance bunker. Mark watched him fiddle with the dials, his anxiety palpable. "So," Mark began, "what exactly are we looking for?" Aidan grinned, a mischievous glint in his eyes. "We're hunting ghosts, Mark. Musical ghosts. You wouldn't understand." He winked, leaving Mark thoroughly confused.

David needed a distraction, something to take his mind off Kris and Boyd, off the looming threats he couldn't quite define. He walked towards the barn, the familiar sounds and smells offering a small measure of comfort. The miniature cows, with their perpetually surprised expressions, were clustered around their feeding trough. He scratched one behind the ears, earning a soft, contented moo.

Summer was already in the barn, meticulously cleaning the automatic watering system. Her brow was furrowed in concentration, her movements precise and efficient. He loved her attention to detail, her unwavering dedication to the mundane tasks that kept their little society functioning. "Morning, David," she said, without looking up. "Everything alright?"

He leaned against a post, watching her work. "As alright as it can be, I suppose. Just trying to keep busy." Summer straightened up, wiping her hands on a rag. "Aidan and Mark looked like they were on a mission. Something interesting?"

Meanwhile, up on the roof of the work shed, Aidan meticulously adjusted the dials of the analog receiver. Mark, perched awkwardly beside him, looked increasingly bewildered. The sun beat down on them, reflecting off the metallic surface of the shed, making the air shimmer with heat. "So, we're listening for… what exactly?" Mark asked again, wiping sweat from his brow.

Aidan grinned. "Echoes, Mark. We're listening for echoes. Think of it like this: Little David is a bell, ringing in each apartment. If someone else is listening to that bell, and repeating the sound, we'll hear it here. Faintly, maybe distorted, but we'll hear it." Mark stared at him blankly. "You're saying someone is… re-broadcasting music they hear in the apartments?" "That's the theory," Aidan confirmed. "It's a long shot, but David's hunches are usually spot-on. Plus, Boyd did construction in David's apartment. It makes sense that the wiring we are listening to was done by him."

The silence stretched on, broken only by the hiss and crackle of the receiver. Aidan patiently scanned the frequencies, his brow furrowed in concentration. He knew David was counting on him, and he wasn't about to let him down. Suddenly, a faint, distorted melody cut through the static. Aidan's eyes widened. He swiftly adjusted the tuning, focusing on the faint signal. It was a recognizable tune, slightly off-key and overlaid with static, but undeniably there.

"I've got something!" Aidan exclaimed, his voice tight with excitement. "It's… 'Barbie Girl' by Aqua. It sounds like it's coming from… Apartment 1!" Mark blinked. "Apartment 1? That's… Parker and Jill's place. But why would they be broadcasting 'Barbie Girl'?" He scratched his head, thoroughly confused. "I thought they were more into, you know, classical music."

Aidan chuckled. "The music's not the point, Mark. It's just a signal. If it were Nirvana, it'd be Apartment 8. David used it as a locator. Now we know where to start looking for the repeater." He began packing up the receiver. "Come on, let's go tell David. He'll want to know."

They carefully climbed down the ladder from the roof of the work shed, Aidan holding the receiver securely. As they walked towards the main house, Mark was still trying to wrap his head around everything. "So, Parker and Jill… they're involved in this somehow?"

Aidan shrugged. "Maybe. Maybe not. They just live there. Someone could've planted the repeater in their apartment without them knowing. It could be under the floorboards, behind the walls, inside a teddy bear… anything. David will figure it out."

Suddenly, Aidan burst into the barn, his face flushed with excitement. Mark trailed behind him, looking slightly bewildered. "David! We found it!" Aidan exclaimed, his voice ringing through the barn. "The signal! It's coming from Apartment 1!"

David's head snapped up, his eyes locking onto Aidan's. "Apartment 1? Parker and Jill?" "Yeah," Aidan confirmed. "Playing 'Barbie Girl'." David nodded. "I know, I could hear it from your radio all the way in here." David stood up. "Tell Junior to turn off all the music! And meet us back at the main house. Now!" Aiden nodded before turning to leave.

As they all gathered in the living room of the main house, David explained the situation to everyone. "The individual apartments were built after the Apartment bunker was constructed, so Parker and Jill may not even know it's there. But someone, probably Boyd, planted that repeater, and we need to find out where it is."

David paced the living room, his brow furrowed. "Alright, new plan. Less Rambo, more…social work. Tiffany, Summer, Elena, with me. We're going to have a little chat with Parker and Jill. A friendly chat." He emphasized the 'friendly' with a look that could sterilize a hamster, just in case anyone thought he was losing his edge.

Tiffany raised an eyebrow. "Just walk in and tell them we think their apartment is bugged? That seems… direct." "Direct is good," David countered. "We gauge their reaction. If they're genuinely surprised and cooperative, they're probably not involved. If they start sweating and making excuses, we know Boyd found some useful idiots." He paused, a flicker of a smile playing on his lips. "Besides, I want to see their faces when I tell them we found it because Little David was blasting 'Barbie Girl'."

Summer nodded slowly. "It's a good test, David. And if they are innocent, we don't want to scare them unnecessarily." Elena added, "We can move them to Apartment Three, right? Get them away from the repeater." She winked at David. "Speaking of moving things… you still need to clean out Apartment Seven."

David grimaced. Apartment Seven. Kris's old apartment. But before the thought could fully take root, Kayla, Tanya and Taylor raised their hands. "David, my darling, we'll clean it for you," Tanya exclaimed, eager to lighten David's guilt.

David, followed by Tiffany, Summer, and Elena, approached Apartment One. He took a deep breath, trying to project an aura of casual neighborliness, which, considering his recent activities, felt like a particularly challenging acting role. He knocked on the door.

Parker, with his perpetually surprised eyebrows, answered the door, Jill peeked out from behind him. "David! Good to see you. What brings you by?" Parker asked, his voice genuinely welcoming. "We just wanted to have a quick chat," David said smoothly. "Mind if we come in for a moment?" Parker gestured them inside. The apartment was neat, if a bit spartan. Clearly, feng shui wasn't high on their list of priorities. "Sure, sure. What's up?"

David got straight to the point. "We've discovered something… unusual in the apartment bunker. It seems there's an analog repeater hidden somewhere in the vicinity of Apartment One." Jill frowned. "A repeater? What's that?" Parker explained briefly, keeping it simple. "It's a device that retransmits signals. In this case, it could be used to listen in on conversations."

He then turned to David. "You're saying someone's bugging us?" "Potentially," David replied. "We're still investigating. That's why we're here. We're hoping you haven't noticed anything strange. "Well," David continued, leaning back in his chair, "Aidan and Little David were playing music earlier to try and find the source of the signal." David explained, a smile playing on his lips.

Parker burst out laughing. "You're kidding! That's why that kid made us listen to that infernal song on repeat! I thought he just had a sick sense of humor." He clutched his stomach, tears welling in his eyes. "So, you're telling me, our apartment is potentially bugged, and we found out because of Aqua?" Jill couldn't help but giggle. "Oh, Parker, that's just too much."

David chuckled, enjoying their reaction. It was moments like these, absurd and darkly humorous, that made the apocalypse almost bearable. "Indeed. Barbie Girl, of all things, has led us to your doorstep. Now, here's the thing. We need to find this repeater. And frankly, your apartment is the most likely location."

Parker sobered up, though a faint smile still lingered. "Alright, so what do we do? Tear the place apart?" "Not quite," Tiffany said, stepping forward. "We have a plan. But it involves you two temporarily relocating." "Relocating?" Jill asked, raising an eyebrow.

David nodded. "We need to thoroughly search this apartment without you being here. We'd like to move you to Apartment Three, or any one of the other empty apartments."

David watched Parker's face morph from amusement to mild annoyance. He could practically see the gears turning in the man's head, calculating the effort involved. David knew Parker hadn't quite grasped the situation, or perhaps he was just too used to the pre-apocalypse inconveniences. "Relocating, huh?" Parker repeated, scratching his chin. "That sounds like a whole…thing. Packing up, moving all our stuff…" He trailed off, picturing boxes and heavy lifting in his mind.

Jill, ever the pragmatist, cut through his growing gloom. "Parker, honey, think about what he's saying. It's not like we're moving across town. It's right across the hall." She turned to David with a wry smile. "It's like trading in a used car for a new one, isn't it? Only thing we really need to move is our clothes and a few personal items." Parker threw his hands in the air. "Fine, let me go to the bathroom first."

David watched with a flicker of amusement as Parker disappeared into the bathroom, grumbling about the Herculean effort of moving a few belongings across the hall. He suppressed a smile. Bless Parker's heart; he was probably picturing a pre-apocalypse U-Haul situation, complete with bubble wrap and awkward ramps. Tanya, Kayla and Taylor, only a few doors down, poked their heads in.

"Alright, ladies," David said quietly, turning to his wives. "Let's make this happen. Tiffany, you handle Jill's closet. Summer, Elena, take the dressers and the smaller rooms. Taylor and Kayla, grab what you can from the common areas and the kitchen. Jill, you do direct placement and I'll wait for Parker." His instructions were calm, precise, and utterly unnecessary. He knew they'd already anticipated his every command before he opened his mouth.

Like a time-lapsed film of worker ants, the women sprang into action. David, meanwhile, maintained a watchful eye. The entire process transpired with a speed and efficiency that would have made a professional moving company jealous. Within two minutes, the apartment was stripped bare of any personal belongings. It was as if the Parkers had never even existed. It was impressive, and also slightly unsettling.

Just as the last item was being carried out, the bathroom door creaked open. Parker emerged, looking slightly sheepish. He glanced around the apartment, his jaw dropping. "Wow," Parker stammered, his eyes wide. "That was…fast. Did I…did I imagine unpacking?" David simply smiled enigmatically. "Time is of the essence, Parker. We have much to do." He clapped Parker on the shoulder, steering him towards the door. "Now, let's get you settled in."

As David ushered Parker out, he caught Tanya, Kayla, and Taylor returning to Apartment 7, dust cloths and cleaning supplies in hand. He gave them a nod of approval before turning his attention back to more pressing matters. "Alright," he said to Tiffany, Summer, and Elena, his voice low and serious. "Let's find this damn repeater."

"Right," David announced. "Aidan should be set up outside the work shed. Tiffany, you take the north-west corner, near the kitchenette. Summer, north-east, in the bedrooms. Elena, south-west, by the door, and I'll take south-east, in the master bedroom. Remember, keep talking, but keep it innocuous. We're just making noise."

As the women engaged in idle chit-chat about... whatever. Aidan listened intently, Static hissed in his ears, punctuated by snippets of conversation. He adjusted the frequency, fine-tuning the signal. "Okay, okay... I'm getting something. dad, your signal is a little weak. Mom, you're coming in okay, but not great." He paused, a flicker of excitement in his eyes. "Elena... Elena, you're crystal clear. Like you're standing right next to me."

David felt a surge of adrenaline. "Elena, stay put. Don't move an inch. Aidan, can you pinpoint the direction?" "Give me a sec," Aidan muttered, his brow furrowed in concentration. He manipulated the antennas, his eyes glued to the oscilloscope. "Okay... walk toward the kitchen... now back the other way. There! Wherever you are now, it has to be there!" David ran over, examining the wall. "Okay, that makes it simple. This is the closest concrete wall to the stairwell.

David grabbed a crowbar from the meticulously organized tool rack in the generator room above. He descended into the apartment bunker, a man possessed. The innocuous chatter of his wives faded into background noise, replaced by the pounding of his heart and the hum of purpose in his ears. Even his autism couldn't completely filter out the rising tide of anticipation, a strange cocktail of excitement and dread.

He found Elena standing exactly where he'd left her, a picture of poised curiosity. "Alright," he said, his voice clipped and professional. "Stand back. This might get messy." Elena, never one to shy away from a little chaos, simply raised an eyebrow and retreated a few steps. David wedged the crowbar between the drywall and the furring strips, grunting with effort. The drywall, surprisingly sturdy, resisted for a moment before finally cracking and peeling away in a jagged sheet. Dust billowed, coating the air with the musty scent of concrete.

Behind the drywall, as Aidan and Brian had predicted, was the concrete wall of the bunker. But something was off. A patch of lime plaster, noticeably different from the surrounding concrete, marred the otherwise smooth surface. It was as if someone had attempted to repair a blemish, but had instead only drawn attention to it. "Aidan," David spoke into the radio, "I've found it. A lime patch on the concrete, roughly in the center of the wall. About the size of a dinner plate." "That's it, Dad!" Aidan's voice crackled with excitement. "That's where Boyd must have hidden it. Be careful, we don't know what kind of booby traps he might have set."

David, ever cautious, paused. He ran his hand over the plaster, feeling for any irregularities, any hidden wires or pressure plates. Nothing. It felt solid, unyielding. He glanced at Elena, who gave him a small, encouraging nod. Taking a deep breath, David brought the crowbar down on the edge of the plaster. The plaster shattered with a dull thud, revealing a small, metal utility box embedded in the concrete. It was the kind of box used for electrical junctions or light fixtures, but this one was conspicuously devoid of any useful function.

"Bingo," David muttered, his fingers nimble as he pried open the box. Inside, nestled amongst a tangle of wires, was a tiny AC microphone and transmitter. It was cleverly designed to tap directly into the building's electrical wiring, using it as an antenna to broadcast everything said within the apartment. Vintage equipment, but effective.

"Aidan, we've got a microphone and transmitter," David reported. "Tapped into the building's wiring. Clever bastard." "Alright, Dad, destroy it," Aidan instructed. "Make sure it's completely fried. We don't want any surprises."

David, never one to do things by half-measures, pulled out his Leatherman multi-tool and began dismantling the device. He snipped wires with gusto, ripped out the microphone, and then, just for good measure, smashed the transmitter with the hammer end of the tool. The device was a mangled mess, completely useless. "Done," David announced. "The birdie has flown the coop."

A collective sigh of relief seemed to ripple through the apartment bunker. The women suddenly burst into genuine chatter, their voices lighter and more relaxed. "Okay, ladies," David clapped his hands, drawing their attention back to him. "Let's not get complacent. This just means Boyd was thorough, resourceful, and probably had help.

We still need to figure out how he knew what he knew." He paused, his gaze sweeping over his wives. "And we need to figure out if Parker was the only source." "I have an idea," Elena spoke up. "Let's talk to Parker. He's been working closely with you on the tactical stuff, right, David?" Elena had a point. Parker was privy to sensitive information. "Alright," David agreed. "Summer, can you get Parker? Tell him I need to see him urgently.

Within minutes, she returned with Parker in tow. Parker looked concerned, his brow furrowed with worry. "David, did you find it?" Parker asked, his gaze darting around the room. "Everything's fine, Parker," David reassured him, though his voice lacked its usual warmth. "Just need to ask you a few questions. Come over here." He gestured to a corner of the room, away from the others.

Parker followed David, his unease growing with each step. David held up the mangled remains of the transmitter. "This is what we found," David explained. "It's a transmitter, a sophisticated one. It was hidden in the wall. Someone was listening to everything that was being said in here." David replied. He paused, taking a deep breath. "Parker, you've been working closely with me on our security plans, our patrol routes, everything. You know things that very few other people know." "Yes, sir," Parker affirmed, his voice steady. "You trust me with that information, and I take that trust very seriously." "I know you do, Parker," David said, softening his tone. "But I have to ask. Have you ever discussed any of those plans, any of that information, with anyone else? With your wife, perhaps?"

Parker hesitated for a moment, his gaze flicking towards the floor. "Yes, sir," he admitted. "I have. Jill… she gets worried. About the patrols, about the risks we're taking. Sometimes, I tell her a little bit, just to reassure her that we're doing everything we can to stay safe."

David nodded slowly, his mind already processing the information. "Parker, you don't need to explain yourself. Jill is just as much a part of our community as you are. Her worries are valid, and it's natural you'd want to ease her mind." He clapped Parker on the shoulder, a gesture meant to be reassuring, but his eyes remained sharp and assessing.

"But," David continued, his voice losing some of its warmth, "it's crucial we understand the extent of the information that might have been compromised. I need you to be completely honest with me. When you talked to Jill, did you mention specifics? Patrol routes? Destinations? Movement times? Anything that could be used to anticipate our actions?"

David watched Parker's face morph through a series of emotions: initial relief, followed by dawning horror, and finally, a grim acceptance. The man was wrestling with his conscience, and David, despite the gravity of the situation, couldn't help but feel a flicker of sympathy. "Sir," Parker began, his voice strained, "it wasn't just Jill. I... I forgot. Eric and Scott. We had our team meetings in my apartment sometimes. We talked about the patrol routes, the potential threats... the whole nine yards." He ran a hand through his hair. "Damn it, I'm an idiot."

David exhaled slowly, a subtle release of tension that Parker likely missed. In truth, this was almost good news. Contained. Manageable. If the leak was only through Parker, Eric, and Scott, then David could work with that. It was far better than a systemic problem with wider implications.

He placed both hands on Parker's shoulders, his gaze locking with the younger man's. "Parker, look at me. This isn't ideal, but it's not the end of the world. You're not an idiot. You're a good man who cares about his family and his team. That's why you did what you did." He paused, letting the words sink in. "The important thing now is that we contain this. We limit the damage."

He lowered his voice, adopting a conspiratorial tone. "Think of it this way. We know where the crack is in the wall. Now we can patch it. We know who might have inadvertently shared information. That gives us control." Parker's shoulders slumped slightly, the tension easing from his face. "So… what do we do, sir?"

David smiled, a genuine, reassuring smile. "First, you're going to keep being the leader that you are. You're going to keep doing your job and doing it well. Don't let this shake your confidence. Your team needs you. Jill needs you. And frankly, I need you focused on the job."

He paused, his eyes hardening slightly. "Second, we need to adjust the patrol routes. We need to change the frequencies we use for communication. We need to assume that anything discussed in your apartment over the last few weeks is now public knowledge. We operate with that assumption, and we minimize the risk."

"Third," David continued, his voice dropping even lower, "we need to have a little chat with Eric and Scott. Not a confrontation, mind you. Just a friendly reminder about the importance of operational security. And maybe a little… incentive to keep things close to the vest from now on." He winked. Parker managed a weak smile. "Understood, sir." Before Parker left to go back, David stopped him. "Parker, next time you have a meeting, use the main house. The walls have an integrated faraday cage."

Back at the house, he gathered Nicole, Kayla, Taylor, Alissa, and Seo-Yeon in the living room. The atmosphere in the living room was heavy, a direct result of David's unsettling presence. "Kris," he began, his voice uncharacteristically flat, "She was complicit. With the people targeting our family."

Kayla gasped, "Complicit in what, David?" He proceeded to explain the events, carefully omitting the more brutal details. He revealed Kris's betrayal, Boyd's orchestration of the attacks on Lynn and Summer's convoy, and his connection to the construction of their apartment bunker.

Nicole gripped Taylor's hand, pale with shock. Alissa stared, wide-eyed. Seo-Yeon, ever the pragmatist, cut through the tension. "So, it was an infiltration. From the beginning." David confirmed, his gaze sweeping over each of them. "Seems that way. Boyd used Kris, who likely had her own motivations. They are not a threat anymore."

Silence descended, thick with the implications. David wasn't just protecting them; he was engaged in a dangerous game, and their lives were the pieces. Kayla, voice hesitant, finally broke the silence. "David, what about…how you handled it? Is that going to change you?" His blue eyes unwavering, David responded, "I do what I must to protect you all. This world demands certain actions. I don't relish them, but I won't hesitate."

Just then, Elena entered, her face a mixture of concern and apology. She'd overheard everything from the kitchen, where she'd been attempting to prepare brunch. "David," she began, her voice tight, "I wanted to apologize. I was so critical, I judged you. I was wrong. I didn't understand the full scope."

David softened, gently cupping her face. "Elena, I understand your concerns. I do things differently. But my intentions are always the same: to keep you safe. All of you.” He paused, searching her eyes. “I don’t need apologies. I need trust. And you need to understand that sometimes, the choices I make will be difficult, even unpleasant. But they will always be made with your best interests at heart.”

Elena met his gaze, a mix of relief and uncertainty swirling within her eyes. “I do trust you, David,” she said, her voice trembling. “It’s just…hard. Seeing this world…seeing what you have to do…”

David sighed, pulling her into a comforting hug. “I know,” he murmured, “It’s hard for me too.” A moment of silent understanding passed between them before he deepened the moment with a kiss that conveyed his love, dedication, and strength. “Better?” he asked softly, tracing her cheekbones. Elena nodded, a faint smile gracing her lips. “Much,” she admitted. “Thank you.”

Chapter 30

Placenta Citri Clavis et Sexus

Aidan lay sprawled across the queen-sized bed, the sheets tangled around his legs. He was still basking in the afterglow, the remnants of passion clinging to the air like the faint scent of ozone after a lightning strike. Alissa stood by the doorway, a goddess sculpted from moonlight and muscle. Water trickled down her chest from the glass in her hand, each drop a tiny mirror reflecting the light from the window.

"They're always watching, you know," Aidan murmured, his voice thick with contentment and a hint of worry. Alissa tilted her head, the water glinting in her dark eyes. "Who, babe? The squirrels? Because I swear I saw one giving me the side-eye this morning." Aidan chuckled. "No, silly. I mean outsiders. People on the road. We're a beacon, Alissa. Electricity, running water, enough food to last until the next ice age. They're going to be curious."

He propped himself up on his elbows, his gaze intense. "We need to be more vigilant. More observant. Who's lingering too long at the fence line? Who's asking too many questions at the checkpoint? We can't get complacent." Alissa took another swig of water, her eyes narrowing slightly. "You think David will ever trust outsiders again? After… Kris."

Aidan sighed, running a hand through his messy hair. "I don't know. He's still… David. Altruistic to a fault, but he's also seen the worst of humanity. He's got a different perspective than us, Alissa. I can't even imagine the… the baggage." "He carries it well," Alissa said softly, her gaze softening. "He's a good man, Aidan. A good husband, a good father. He just… he needs protecting too."

Aidan nodded in agreement. "He does. And that's our job. Our family's job." A mischievous look sparked in Alissa's eyes. "Speaking of family… you think he'll add any more to the harem?" Aidan groaned, falling back against the pillows. "Please, Alissa, don't even joke. Can you imagine? Another set of quirks, another set of dietary restrictions, another set of… well, you know."

He shuddered theatrically. "I love my father, I truly do, but the man has a type. And his type seems to be 'distressed damsel with hidden talents and a strong opinion about the proper way to fold a fitted sheet.'" Alissa chuckled, leaning over to playfully poke him in the ribs. "Hey, don't knock the fitted sheet folding. That's a valuable skill in the apocalypse, you know. Plus, you have to admit, the man has excellent taste. All those women are amazing in their own way."

"Amazing, yes. Manageable… debatable," Aidan countered, a glimmer of amusement in his eyes. "Imagine the logistics of a family vacation. It'd be like herding cats, each cat with a highly specialized set of skills and a penchant for arguing about the best route to the Grand Canyon." Alissa giggled. "Okay, okay, you have a point. But seriously, you don't think he'll stop? With Jessica pregnant, things are bound to get even more… interesting."

Aidan considered this for a moment. "I honestly think he wishes he could put a cap on it. He loves them all, I know he does. But even for a guy with his… organizational skills, it's a lot. Maybe Jessica being pregnant will be the turning point. Maybe he'll realize he's reached peak harem." He paused, then added with a wink, "Or maybe he'll just build another wing onto the house. Who knows with that guy?"

Alissa laughed again, the sound echoing softly in the room. "True. You never can tell with David. He's always full of surprises." She ran a hand down his chest, her touch lingering. "Speaking of surprises… are you rested enough for another round? I have a few ideas I'd like to test out."

Aidan's eyes widened, his exhaustion instantly forgotten. "Well, now that you mention it… I do feel surprisingly invigorated. And I'm always up for testing out your ideas, Alissa. Especially the ones that involve…" He leaned in close, whispering something in her ear that made her blush and giggle again. Alissa wasn't particularly creative or graceful, but she didn't need to be. She simply straddled Aidan and started riding him, like an oil rig, pumping him for resources with determined efficiency.

Upstairs, the atmosphere in the main house kitchen was a far cry from the bedroom shenanigans occurring below. It was a symphony of culinary pandemonium, a well-oiled machine fueled by caffeine and the collective responsibility of feeding a small army. The goal was 120 meals, a daunting task even with the division of labor they had perfected.

Tiffany stood at the butcher block island, cutting the meats into portions. Beef, pork and chicken, in varying shapes, cuts and flavors surrounded her in large pans, each one destined for a specific meal plan. Her brow was furrowed in concentration, but a small smile played on her lips as she occasionally glanced at the organized frenzy around her.

Jennifer, perched on a stool at the counter, cut through piles of fresh vegetables as Summer occasionally took from each bowl. "So why do we still keep food prepping? I thought the emergency rations did away with that?" Jennifer asked, scraping a pile of bell peppers into a bowl. "It's better for morale, plus, it's a sneaky way to slip some of these freeze dried foods into a meal," Summer answered. At the dining room table, Summer was assembling the meals into containers, taking portions of food from the rest as she put the finishing touches on the completed dishes.

Across the kitchen, Nicole was humming softly as she carefully measured flour and water, her hands moving with a rhythmic grace. Clouds of flour dusted the air around her as she kneaded the dough for a massive batch of pasta. Meanwhile, several steel pots rumbled as finished pasta boiled on the stove.

Next to the pasta, Kayla was stirring a simmering pot of sauce, her nose twitching as she adjusted the blend of herbs and spices. "When we slaughter the first cow, are we going to prep the entire thing?" she asked. Tiffany shrugged. "We'll probably cut most of it down, but David doesn't want us to waste anything. The dogs might even enjoy the bones."

As they worked, their conversation flowed easily, a comfortable mix of practicalities, inside jokes, and the occasional philosophical debate. They discussed everything from the alfalfa in the hydroponics to the best way to convince Grace that marrying Kyle was a terrible idea at her age.

Meanwhile, in the makeshift classroom set up in one of the guest rooms, a different kind of learning was underway. Janet, Lori, Beth, Mike, Bonnie, and Seth were gathered around a table, their faces a mix of concentration and amusement.

"Okay, everyone, repeat after me," Seth instructed, his voice surprisingly commanding for a boy of his age. " 'Omnes viae Romam ducunt.' " " " 'Omnes viae Romam ducunt,' " the others echoed, their pronunciation ranging from surprisingly accurate (in Janet's case) to utterly butchered (in Lori's, who was only repeating it phonetically). "Good!" Seth said, beaming. "What does it mean?" "All roads lead to Rome!" Bonnie chirped, her hand shooting up. "Correct!" Seth beamed. "Now, let's try another one..."

Suddenly, Lori, all of eight years old, raised her hand. "Seth?" "Yes, Lori?" "Why are we learning Latin? Are we going to, like, conquer Rome or something?" A ripple of laughter went through the room. Seth, however, looked thoughtful. "Well," he said, stroking his chin, "you never know. Latin is the root of a lot of languages, so it can help us learn other ones. Plus, it's good for your brain!" "And," Janet added, winking at Seth, "it shows a certain… sophistication, wouldn't you say?" "Sophistication is good," Mike agreed sagely, nodding his head.

Upstairs, the air in Taylor's room hung thick with the aftermath of vigorous lovemaking. Sunlight streamed through the French door, casting a delicate light across the room. David lay sprawled beside Taylor, one arm draped protectively across her petite frame. Taylor, flushed and radiant, snuggled closer, her fingers tracing patterns on his chest. "David," she murmured, her voice laced with contentment. "Stay with me?"

David smiled, a genuine, unguarded expression that softened his naturally stern features. "I promised you the day, didn't I? And I always keep my promises." Taylor giggled, a bright, bell-like sound. "Good. Because I have plans." "Oh?" David raised an eyebrow, intrigued. "And what kind of plans are those?" "Plans that involve you, me, and as little clothing as possible," she purred, nuzzling his neck.

David chuckled. "Sounds like a plan I can get behind." He leaned in and kissed her again, a slow, lingering kiss that promised more to come. "First," Taylor said, pulling back slightly, "breakfast in bed. I'm starving." David groaned playfully. "It's already after lunch. Besides, Tiffany and the others have taken over the kitchen with their prep cooking." You remember, the 120 meals? You were supposed to be helping."

Taylor's eyes widened, a flash of guilt crossing her face. "Oh, shoot! I completely forgot." She sat up, pulling the sheets around her. "They're probably furious." David reached out and stopped her, pulling her back down. "Relax. They understand. Besides," David continued, a mischievous glint in his eyes, "I think they'd rather you were here with me. Keeps me out of their hair."

Taylor laughed, relieved. "You silver-tongued devil. You always know what to say." She paused, then a thought struck her. "Wait a minute. 120 meals? What are we, running a restaurant?" David shook his head. "No, but with everyone doing different things, I figured we could use more options. Unless you like cooking for twenty people every day?"

Taylor hung her head. "No, it's hard, even when there's several of us in the kitchen. Can I get a snack instead?" she asked, looking up with her best puppy dog eyes. David grinned, a devilish spark igniting in his eyes. "A snack, you say? From the fridge? Now, that sounds suspiciously like a test of my…attributes." He winked, earning a giggle from Taylor. "Alright, challenge accepted. But be warned, my dear, I may cause a distraction in the kitchen. Tiffany might just chase me out with a spatula."

David threw back the covers, showcasing the impressive physique he maintained through rigorous training and a surprising amount of manual labor around the ranch. "Right then," he announced, striking a mock-heroic pose. "Operation Fridge Raid is a go! Wish me luck. I'm going in…" He paused for dramatic effect. "…commando." Taylor burst out laughing, burying her face in the pillows. "Oh, David! You are incorrigible."

David didn't bother with clothes. Why would he? He was comfortable in his own skin, and besides, he knew the reaction his impromptu appearance would elicit. He padded silently out of Taylor's room, a mischievous grin plastered on his face. He strode into the kitchen, a living, breathing, and decidedly naked exclamation point. The aroma of simmering spices and bubbling sauces hit him like a comforting wave, a stark contrast to the visual impact he knew he was making.

Jennifer was the first to react, as expected, though the extent of her reaction still managed to surprise him. Her eyes widened, a predatory gleam igniting within them. "Oh, Fuck yeah!" she exclaimed, her voice a sharp growl that cut through the kitchen chatter. With a speed that always seemed present at her convenience, she tugged down her leggings, a flash of bare skin preceding her as she bent over the counter, presenting herself with unapologetic enthusiasm.

Tiffany, however, nearly dropped the bowl of cut chicken she was holding. "David!" she sputtered, her cheeks flushing a delightful shade of pink. "What in the world do you think you're doing? There's food being prepared! And…and…decency!" Summer, meticulously labeling containers of pre-portioned chili, simply raised an eyebrow, a knowing smirk playing on her lips. "Well, isn't this…efficient," she commented dryly, never missing a beat with her task.

David chuckled, unfazed by the chaos he'd unleashed. "Just grabbing a snack for Taylor," he explained innocently, heading straight for the refrigerator. He knew exactly where the leftover key lime pie was, a weakness they both shared. Kayla, ever the pragmatist, stepped forward, wiping her hands on a dishtowel. "While you're at it, could you grab me a water?" she asked, using the endearment he'd begrudgingly accepted.

Nicole, usually shy, found her voice amidst the commotion. "And maybe a pickle for me, please? I'm craving something sour." She giggled, covering her mouth with her hand. David, already juggling a plate of pie and a water bottle, raised an eyebrow. "A pickle? Seriously? You ladies are going to be the death of me." Despite the teasing, he rummaged through the condiments, retrieving a large dill pickle.

Jennifer, still bent over the counter, let out a moan. "Master, you're teasing me. I need your… undivided attention." David sighed dramatically. "Jennifer, love, as tempting as that is, I promised Taylor pie." After delivering the water bottle and massive dill pickle, he punctuated his snack run with a resounding slap. The sound echoed through the kitchen, followed by Jennifer's delighted squeal. "There, there, love," David said, winking. "A little something to tide you over."

He then sauntered out of the kitchen, leaving behind a whirlwind of laughter, exasperation, and simmering desire. Tiffany shook her head, a fond smile gracing her lips. "Honestly, that man," she muttered, but there was no real disapproval in her voice. She knew this chaotic energy was part of what made their life, well, theirs. Summer chuckled, finally placing the last container of chili into a crate. "He's like a tornado of testosterone and key lime pie," she quipped, earning a chorus of giggles from Kayla and Nicole.

Jennifer, still flushed from the unexpected spank, turned to Tiffany with a playful pout. "He's going to pay for that later," she declared, her eyes gleaming with promise. "I'm going to make him earn that pie." Meanwhile, David navigated the hallway towards Taylor's room, a skip in his step. He knew his wives thrived on his attention, even in its most chaotic forms. It was a delicate balance, a carefully constructed dance of affection, dominance, and playful teasing.

He reached Taylor's door and gently pushed it open. She was sitting on the bed, reading a well-worn copy of "Pride and Prejudice." "Room service," David announced, presenting the plate of pie with a flourish. Taylor looked up, her face lighting up at the sight of him. "David! You remembered!" she exclaimed, setting her book aside. "You're the best."

He grinned, pleased with himself. "Only the best for my favorite Jane Austen enthusiast. Though," he added, lowering his voice conspiratorially, "I suspect Jennifer might disagree with that assessment right now." Taylor giggled, taking the plate from him. "She can wait her turn. Besides, I deserve a little spoiling."

David chuckled, the sound low and resonant in the small room. "Spoiling, huh? I can definitely get behind that." He set the half-eaten plate of key lime pie onto the nightstand, the sweet-tart aroma filling the air. Taylor, ever the picture of gentle affection, reached out and ran a hand through his fingers, pulling him closer. "Come here, you," she murmured, her voice a soft invitation.

David needed no further encouragement. He scrambled onto the bed, his movements surprisingly agile for a man his age. Taylor, already on her back, wrapped her legs around his waist, her small frame a perfect fit against his. The contrast between her delicate features and the intensity in her eyes was a potent combination.

He lowered his head, his lips finding hers in a slow, deliberate kiss. It wasn't the frantic, passionate kind he shared with Jennifer, nor the playful, teasing one he often enjoyed with Kayla. This was a gentle, comforting kiss, filled with a deep sense of connection and understanding.

Taylor responded in kind, her fingers digging lightly into his back. She was a creature of comfort, a woman who thrived on intimacy and affection. And David, in his own unique way, understood that need perfectly. As the kiss deepened, David's hands began to explore her body, tracing the delicate curve of her spine, the soft roundness of her hips. Taylor shuddered in his arms, her breath coming in shallow gasps.

David didn't wait for an invitation or permission, as he slowly slid his cock inside of her. Taylor gasped softly, but the sound was more of pleasure than surprise. She tilted her head back, closing her eyes, and let herself be fully immersed in the moment. David paused, allowing her to adjust, his own breath catching in his throat. The small room felt suddenly charged with a quiet energy, a shared understanding that transcended words.

He began to move, slowly at first, each thrust measured and deliberate. He watched Taylor's face, reading the subtle shifts in her expression, the way her lips parted slightly, the way her eyes fluttered behind her closed lids. He was acutely aware of her pleasure, her comfort, her needs. It was a form of communication he excelled at, a silent conversation of touch and sensation.

The pace gradually increased, becoming more insistent, more demanding. Taylor met him with equal intensity, her hips rising to meet his, her hands gripping his shoulders tightly. The sounds of their bodies moving together filled the small room, a rhythmic symphony of pleasure and desire.

Taylor's small frame trembled beneath David's touch as their passion escalated. She met his aggressive rhythm with a matching fervor, her nails digging into his shoulders, a silent language of need and surrender. David felt her body responding to his, a wave of heat radiating between them. He leaned down, whispering against her ear, his voice a low rumble, "Are you alright, Taylor? Am I being too rough?"

Taylor's eyes fluttered open, her gaze locking with his. There was a vulnerability there, a trust that both humbled and empowered him. "No, sir," she breathed. "Don't stop." He began to move slower now, more deliberate. He kissed her deeply, tasting the sweetness of her lips, the warmth of her breath. He wanted to savor this moment, to imprint it on his memory, to solidify the bond between them.

She locked her feet behind his waist, pulling him closer, her body molding against his. David continued to push, his movements fluid and graceful, each thrust a testament to his love and devotion. He watched Taylor's face, her eyes closed, her lips parted in a soft smile. He knew she was close, on the edge.

He whispered her name, his voice thick with emotion, "Taylor... my little pop tart..." And then, with a final surge of passion, Taylor reached her climax, a series of shudders that rippled through her body. She cried out softly, her voice a mixture of pleasure and release. David held her tightly, her body jerking aggressively.

As the aftershocks subsided, they lay entangled, their bodies slick with sweat, her breaths ragged. Silence descended upon the room, a comfortable silence filled with unspoken affection.

He lifted himself slightly, his forearms taking his weight, and gazed down at her. Her petite frame seemed even smaller beneath him. "Are you alright, little one?" he asked, his voice low and soothing. Taylor snuggled closer, burying her face in his neck. "Mm-hmm," she mumbled, her voice muffled. Then, she pulled back slightly, her eyes sparkling with mischief. "Now I'm really hungry."

She giggled, a light, airy sound that always warmed David's heart. Reaching for the key lime pie on the nightstand, she took a generous bite. Her eyes widened. "Oh my god, this is exactly what I needed." David chuckled. "I'm sure it is. Though I should warn you, it probably tastes like sex now," he said, raising an eyebrow. Taylor coughed, a blush creeping up her neck. "David!" she exclaimed, playfully slapping his chest. "You can't just say things like that!"

David watched as Taylor devoured the key lime pie, a small smile playing on his lips. Her uninhibited joy was infectious. "Alright, alright," he said, chuckling. "Before you eat the entire pie, how about we go for a swim? Burn off some of that... energy." Taylor's head popped up, her eyes shining. "Swimming? Yes! It's been ages." She hopped off the bed, her earlier languor replaced with a burst of energy. "But... shower first! I feel all... sticky," she said, wrinkling her nose playfully.

David chuckled, rising from the bed. "A shower sounds wonderful, darling. Lead the way." He followed her around the corner into the small but well-appointed bathroom. Taylor turned to him, a mischievous look in her eyes. "Together?" she asked, her voice a suggestive whisper. David's eyebrow quirked. "Is that an invitation?" Taylor grinned, stepping closer and wrapping her arms around his neck. "It most certainly is." She planted a soft kiss on his lips before turning on the shower.

The water cascaded down, quickly warming to the perfect temperature. They stepped into the tub, one after the other. Under the warm spray, their bodies met again, the earlier passion reigniting with a gentle heat. David lathered the soap, his large hands gliding over her petite frame, lingering on every curve. Taylor giggled as he tickled her ribs, then turned serious again as he massaged the tension from her shoulders.

The rhythmic drumming of the water against the shower wall filled the small space, punctuated by Taylor's occasional contented sighs. David meticulously washed her hair, his fingers working through the strands. Taylor leaned back against him, her eyes closed, completely relaxed. "David?" she murmured, her voice soft against his chest. "Hmm?" he replied, rinsing the shampoo from her hair. "Do you ever… miss it? You know, before?"

David paused, his hands still. The question hung in the steamy air, heavier than the water droplets. He'd thought about it, of course. Had analyzed it, dissected it, like he did everything else. But admitting it… that was different. "Miss what, specifically?" he asked, carefully. He hated vague questions. "Everything. The internet, movies, hot coffee whenever you want it, not having to worry about raiders every time you leave the house. Normal stuff."

He considered her words. "I miss the convenience, certainly," he conceded. "The predictability. The ability to research obscure historical trivia at 3 AM. But… no, I don't 'miss it' as a whole." Taylor tilted her head back, looking up at him with questioning eyes. "Really? Why not?" David turned off the water, the sudden silence amplified by the lingering echoes. He stepped out of the shower, grabbing a towel and handing one to Taylor.

David dried himself deliberately, his movements precise. He wrapped the towel around his waist, the gesture oddly formal in the humid bathroom. He turned back to Taylor, his gaze intense. "Before," he began, "I was… adrift. I was a set of skills and obsessions without a proper outlet. I was a square peg in a round world, constantly being hammered into a shape I wasn't meant to be." He paused, searching for the right words. "I was tolerated, not needed."

Taylor stepped out of the shower, wrapping the towel around herself. She waited patiently, knowing that David needed the space to articulate his thoughts. She understood, on some level, what he meant. Before, he'd been a high-functioning anomaly. Now, he was a leader. "I was always preparing for something," David continued, his voice softer now. "Especially after I regressed. I could see the cracks everywhere. I couldn't not see it."

"The apocalypse," he said, the word heavy on his tongue, "forced everyone to confront their true selves. The weak crumbled. The selfish preyed on others. And the capable… they stepped up. I finally found a place where my particular… skillset, is not only useful, but essential. I thrive here, Taylor. I lead."

He took a step closer, cupping her face in his hands. His touch was gentle, yet firm. "And more importantly," he said, his voice dropping to a whisper, "I have you. And Jessica, and the rest. I have my children. I have a family that I built. A family that needs me. That loves me." He paused, his gaze searching hers. "Before, I had none of that. I had… responsibilities. Obligations. But not a true, genuine connection. The world ended, Taylor, but I finally began."

Taylor leaned into his touch, her heart swelling with affection. "Taylor, are you worried? About the world… your safety… the future?" he asked, still holding her tight. Taylor looked into David's eyes, the crystal blue unwavering. "Honestly, David?" she said, her voice barely a whisper. "No. Not really."

He tilted his head slightly, a subtle gesture she'd learned meant he was processing something complex. "Explain." She took a deep breath. "Before… before all this," she gestured vaguely towards the world outside, "I was always… floating. Drifting. I had a job, sure. Friends. Family. But I never felt… anchored. Like I was truly contributing. Like I truly mattered." She paused, searching for the right words. "Everything felt so… disposable. So superficial. We worried about the latest trends, the newest gadgets, keeping up with the… Joneses. It was exhausting. And pointless."

David remained silent, his gaze unwavering, encouraging her to continue. "Now," she said, a small smile playing on her lips, "now everything has meaning. Every task we do, every decision we make, it matters. It affects our survival, our future. And I know, I know that I'm contributing. I'm helping to build something real, something lasting. I'm a part of this family, this community. And you… you make me feel safe. Protected. Like everything is going to be alright, even when it feels like the world is ending."

As they left the bathroom and walked back into Taylor's room, she dropped her towel, then asked. "So, where's Jessica?" a hint of playful curiosity in her voice. David considered the question, his mind cataloging the current activities of his household. "Jessica is downstairs in the recreational bunker," he replied, his voice calm and even. "She's doing water aerobics with Tanya, Seo-Yeon, and Elena."

Taylor's eyebrows rose in amusement. "Water aerobics? In the middle of the apocalypse?" "Maintaining physical fitness is crucial for overall well-being," David stated matter-of-factly. "And the pool provides a low-impact environment for pregnant women and those with joint issues." He paused, a flicker of a smile playing on his lips. "Besides, Jessica enjoys it. And a happy wife is a happy life, as the saying goes."

Down in the recreational bunker, Jessica was indeed enjoying the water aerobics, though she wasn't exactly thrilled about having to do them. The buoyant support of the water was a welcome relief to her increasingly burdened body, but the synchronized movements and Elena's relentless teasing were starting to grate on her nerves. "Come on, Jess," Elena called out, her voice dripping with playful sarcasm. "Keep up! You don't want the baby to get lazy, do you?"

Jessica glared at her, splashing a wave of water in her direction. "Shut up, Elena," she retorted, her voice laced with mock annoyance. "This baby isn't lazy. For all we know, it's going to be born with its concealed carry permit in hand, and a demolition technician certification."

Chapter 31

The Butcher's Benefit

The first meeting of May arrived with a surprising burst of heat, the temperature already climbing to a humid 80 degrees outside. Yet, the warmth of the spring air was not the only unusual element today. Compared to previous gatherings in David's spacious living room, this meeting had a distinctly different flavor, marked by a quiet undercurrent of unfamiliarity and apprehension. In addition to the usual array of community members – a varied group of men and women, young and old – Lynn's parents, Clarence and Margaret, were also present. They sat side-by-side on a large sofa, looking understandably bewildered, their faces a mixture of apprehension and profound curiosity.

Clarence, a man whose burly frame spoke of years spent in demanding physical labor, his hands weathered and strong like aged oak, kept his gaze sweeping nervously around the room. His brow was furrowed, a silent question etched onto his face as he took in the diverse group and the relaxed yet expectant atmosphere. Beside him, Margaret, a quiet and unassuming woman with kind eyes, sat straighter than usual, gripping her hands together in her lap, her eyes wide with uncertainty, absorbing every detail of the unfamiliar environment and the people within it. David, the clear anchor of the assembly, offered them a reassuring smile – a small gesture he instinctively knew they desperately needed in this overwhelming situation.

"Alright everyone," David began, his voice calm, steady, and possessing a natural authority that quieted the room instantly. "Let's get started. First, a few housekeeping items." He paused, his gaze briefly resting on various individuals before continuing. "As many of you know, we recently found a surveillance device in Apartment One. Parker and Jill, I want to express my sincere appreciation for your flexibility and willingness to move temporarily while we dealt with that. I'm happy to report that Parker, you'll be able to move back into your own apartment today. Aidan and his crew have finished putting everything back together and conducting a thorough sweep."

Parker, a man with a relaxed demeanor, nodded, a wave of relief washing over his face. Jill, seated closely beside him, squeezed his hand tightly, her smile echoing his sentiment. "Thanks, David," she said, her voice earnest. "We really appreciate it. I'm especially glad that whole mess is over with. And honestly," she added with a small, wry smile, "I definitely preferred being the closest to the exit anyway." A few chuckles rippled through the room.

David nodded in understanding, acknowledging her point before moving on. "Next, we're continuing our ongoing process of integrating our younger couples into the dedicated apartments. To that end, Josh and Lily, you two will be moving into Apartment Nine today." Murmurs of quiet agreement and pleasant acceptance moved through the group. Josh, ever stoic, simply gave a brief, almost imperceptible nod, while Lily, seated beside him, beamed, her arm tightening instinctively around his, a silent expression of their bond and excitement. David continued, "Brian and Seo-

Yeon will be taking Apartment Twelve." Brian flashed an enthusiastic thumbs-up from across the room, and Seo-Yeon, her face bright with happiness, leaned over to offer Tanya a quick, warm hug.

David then turned his attention directly to Aidan and Alissa. "You two will take Eleven," he stated, receiving confirming nods from the pair. Finally, David turned his gaze back to Clarence and Margaret, his expression softening slightly as he addressed them. "And finally," he said, his voice gentle, "Clarence, Margaret, we want to make you both as comfortable as possible during your stay. Given your age and the layout of the property, we've prepared a guest room for you in the main house. It's close to everything you'll need, the kitchen, the common areas, and we think you'll find it much more convenient than the apartments, which require a bit more climbing and walking across the property."

Clarence shifted in his seat, the furrow in his brow easing somewhat. He looked at David, then at Margaret, before speaking. "Well, I certainly appreciate that, David," he said, his voice a low rumble. "That's very thoughtful of you. This whole setup is... something else," he added, glancing around the room again, his bewilderment still evident despite the offered comfort. "It's certainly... more than Lynn told us." Margaret nodded vigorously by his side, her eyes still darting from face to face within the assembled community, trying to piece together the unspoken dynamics in the room. "It's very... organized," she offered, her tone one of cautious observation rather than simple compliment.

David smiled reassuringly at them both. "We try our best," he said simply. "Lynn can show you around properly later this afternoon and help you get settled. For now, let's move on to the more pressing matters." He turned his attention back to the group. "Tiffany?"

Tiffany cleared her throat, adjusting her posture before speaking. "Right," she said, her voice businesslike. "Following up on ranch duties. The three cows we picked up last month are in much better health. They've been gaining weight steadily, their coats are shiny, and they are, unfortunately," she paused, a brief shadow crossing her face, "ready for the abattoir." She paused again, her gaze sweeping over the assembled group, a clear question forming in the air. "Which," she concluded, her voice firm despite the unpleasant topic, "brings me to my next point: we need a volunteer butcher."

A palpable silence descended upon the room, heavy and immediate. The previous murmurs of domestic arrangement faded completely. David leaned forward slightly in his chair, his expression serious now. "Ideally," he stated, his voice low but clear, "we're looking for someone with experience cleaning game. Someone who understands the process and has a steady hand." He paused for a brief moment, then a subtle sparkle entered his eye, a hint of amusement playing around his lips as he added, "Or, I suppose, someone who has a... brooding proclivity for this kind of work."

The silence stretched, thick and uncomfortable, punctuated only by the persistent, annoying buzzing of a single fly that had somehow infiltrated David's otherwise meticulously clean living room. Eyes darted nervously around, no one willing to make direct eye contact with

Tiffany, let alone David. The idea of gutting and butchering a large animal like a cow, even a healthy, well-fed one, was not exactly the appealing task one envisioned for a warm Friday morning, especially given the diverse skills and preferences present in the room.

David finally broke the tension with a low chuckle, leaning back slightly. "Alright, alright," he said, his tone easing. "I understand. It's not exactly a glamorous job, is it? Nobody's lining up for the honor." He paused, then added, his voice turning more serious again, "But, it needs doing, and relatively quickly. And," he continued, his gaze briefly resting on Jessica, "I can't very well ask Jessica to do it in her condition, can I? He paused dramatically, milking the suspense for a moment, a slight smile playing on his lips. "So…"

His eyes swept across the room, fixing momentarily on several faces. "Here's the deal. Whoever volunteers to be our resident butcher, for the duration of their bovine-based duties, will be excused from all other community chores and responsibilities around here. All of them. Guard duty, patrols, hydroponics work, ranch duty, teaching the young ones… consider it a butcher's benefit." He held up a finger to clarify. "This, however, does not excuse you from your individual responsibilities as a parent to your own children, as a person maintaining your own living space, or as a spouse to your husband or wife. Those are personal."

A collective intake of breath swept through the room. Suddenly, the gruesome task of butchering a cow seemed a whole lot more appealing. The list of exemptions was extensive, encompassing the regular, necessary duties that took up significant time and effort in their communal life. "All community chores?" Janet asked, her voice betraying just a hint of cautious hope, confirming she had heard correctly. David nodded solemnly, his expression indicating the seriousness of the offer. "Every single community chore designated for the general group," he confirmed. "This kind of work, the focus, the physical toll, the... psychological aspect, takes a special constitution, and recovery time is important. You dedicate yourself to this, you get a reprieve from everything else."

Margaret leaned towards her husband, whispering, "See, Clarence? I told you this place was run differently. Lynn tried explaining bits, but..." Clarence, a man whose understanding of domestic duties peaked at changing a lightbulb and whose social circle had traditionally been limited to fellow construction workers, church members and family, merely grunted in response. He was still trying to process the sheer, bewildering number of women who seemed to consider David their husband, along with the complex web of responsibilities and the seemingly outlandish offer just made.

The buzz of the fly seemed to intensify in the renewed silence, amplified by the tension and calculation in the room. David's offer hung in the air, a succulent slab of meaty freedom that smelled, to some, sweeter than any perfume. Eyes, previously avoiding Tiffany's mournful gaze and the unspoken unpleasantness of the task, now sharpened with calculation, weighing the gore against the glorious respite from daily, demanding duties. The phrase "butcher's benefit" echoed in their minds, a siren song promising liberation from the endless cycle of ranch life.

Jennifer, never one to shy away from a challenge or an opportunity, spoke first, her voice a low purr that seemed to linger in the air. "Master," she said, using the term with a familiar ease that caused Clarence's eyebrows to shoot up, "I am at your service. I shall wield the cleaver with the same… enthusiasm… I dedicate to everything else." She shot a quick, sidelong glance at David, a wicked glint dancing in her eyes. David simply raised an eyebrow in return, a hint of amusement playing at the corner of his lips, but said nothing immediately.

Summer, ever practical and results-oriented, countered quickly, "While Jennifer's… exuberance is appreciated, Master, I believe a more methodical and experienced approach might be beneficial. I have experience with prepping meat for the jerky and sausage making; I understand the cuts. Let me handle it."

Elena, known for her organizational skills and sharp mind, interjected before anyone else could speak. "Both of you are missing the logistical nightmare of the situation," she stated, cutting through the rising tide of volunteers. "We need a system, a process for handling the animals efficiently and safely. I can organize the butchering schedule, allocate resources – tools, space, time, and ensure minimal waste. Think of it," she proposed, her gaze sweeping over the room, "as… optimized meat management."

Kayla frowned, her expression thoughtful. "Hold on, hold on," she said, injecting a note of communal spirit. "Why are we assuming this has to be a single person's responsibility for the whole duration? We're a community, aren't we? We can divide the labor, learn from each other. We can make it a collaborative effort, share the load, and share the benefits." She added with a quick, bright wink, "Plus, think of the bonding experience!"

Jessica, seated nearby, sniffed dramatically, drawing attention to herself. "Daddy," she pleaded, her voice laced with theatrical distress, "please don't make me watch! I can't even look at a hamburger right now without feeling nauseous, let alone a whole cow." Her hand rested protectively on her swollen belly, emphasizing her point.

David held up a hand, silencing the sudden cacophony of offers, counter-offers, and pleas. "Alright, alright, settle down, ladies," he said, a wry smile touching his lips. "I appreciate the… enthusiasm. It appears the butcher's benefits are even more enticing than I anticipated." He paused, a thoughtful expression coming over his face as he looked from one woman to another, taking in their various motivations: the eagerness, the practicality, the organizational drive, the desire for collaboration, the outright refusal.

David stood then, his calm demeanor shifting slightly, taking on a more decisive edge. He looked at each of his wives in turn, his gaze holding theirs for a moment before he spoke, his voice dropping some of its earlier amusement. "I would also like to say… you are all idiots," he stated flatly, though without true malice. The blunt assessment cut through the lingering tension and silenced any further arguments. He turned to Jennifer. "Jennifer," he said, his tone firm, "You run the hydroponics with Brian. That's a full-time job requiring constant attention. Plus, you're in charge of the filtration systems for the entire property. You have enough on your plate, regardless of your 'enthusiasm'."

He then turned his attention to Summer. "Summer," he continued, "You are excellent at preparing the meat after it's been processed. You make excellent jerky and sausages. But we aren't talking preparation here, are we? We're talking about death, dismemberment, and lots and lots of gore. That's a different skill set and a different stomach."

He nodded towards Elena, acknowledging her point about organization, then looked at Kayla. "And Kayla," he said, addressing the idea of collaboration directly. "While the thought of 'family bonding' over gutting a cow is… certainly unique, I think we should perhaps explore that particular dynamic another day." He paused, a different kind of spark entering his eyes, one of immediate, practical purpose. "Before we make this a family bonding experience, or optimize anything, or apply enthusiasm, how about everyone follow me outside for a field trip."

As they fell into step behind him, the barn's unusual design became increasingly apparent to Clarence and Margaret, who had likely not seen it up close before. It wasn't the rustic, weather-beaten structure one might envision on a traditional farm. Instead, it resembled a futuristic Quonset hut, its metallic skin gleaming in the morning sun, a stark contrast to the ravaged landscape beyond their secure valley. Clarence, a man with an eye for solid, functional architecture, squinted at it with a mix of curiosity and mild suspicion. "That's… quite the barn," he mumbled, an understatement that earned him a gentle, knowing nudge from Margaret. It wasn't just a shelter for animals; it looked engineered, optimized.

David reached the heavy barn door and pulled it open, revealing a surprisingly clean and organized interior. The anticipated pungent smell of livestock manure was absent, replaced by air that was notably fresh, carrying only the faint, pleasant scent of clean hay. The scene inside was a curious mix. Three large cows, standard dairy or beef breeds, maneuvered somewhat awkwardly among a herd of miniature cows, the latter looking almost comically small, like living stuffed animals. Their tiny size and often fluffy appearance lent an air of unreality to the space. Goats bleated cheerfully as they clambered and played on strategically placed bales of hay, while chickens clucked contentedly in their designated coop.

Clarence, his architectural interest piqued, surveyed the interior. He noticed the immense open space and, more strikingly, the walls stretching all the way across the one-hundred-foot ceiling looked like they were constructed entirely of round hay bales. It was an ingenious, if peculiar, use of materials. "David, how did you get the hay up there?" he asked, his eyes scanning for hoists, conveyors, or anything that could explain this gravity-defying fodder storage.

David smiled, that rare expression softening his usually stern features. "That's part of the automatic feeder," he explained. "Ten spools, twenty bales each. A simple gear system keeps the hay off the ground and feeds it down as needed. Kind of like one of those carpet roll dispensers, only on a much larger scale." It was another example of the sophisticated, low-tech solutions David implemented, blending simple materials with ingenious engineering.

"Alright, before we get lost with the inner workings of the barn," David said, bringing their focus back to the immediate task, "I want everyone to mingle with the animals. Remember how small these mini zebu's were when we first got them?" His tone was light, almost encouraging, a stark contrast to his initial address.

The group dispersed among the livestock. Tiffany, demonstrating a natural affinity for animals, naturally gravitated towards the largest of the standard-sized cows, scratching it behind the ears with a practiced, gentle hand. Jessica, despite her burgeoning belly, found herself utterly charmed by a particularly fluffy miniature cow, its soft fur inviting touch, and giggled as it nuzzled her hand, its trust immediate and unconditional.

Even Clarence, whose initial focus had been on the barn's structure and who remained somewhat skeptical of David's methods, found himself drawn to a stoic-looking miniature bull. Its brown eyes seemed to hold an ancient, quiet wisdom that transcended its diminutive size. Margaret, ever the cautious follower, stood beside him, her hand hovering nervously above the cow's back, hesitant to make full contact. Parker, Scott, and Eric, perhaps finding a moment of respite from other duties, seemed to relax a bit, each finding a bovine companion that appealed to their individual tastes, engaging in quiet interaction or simply observing the peaceful scene.

A few minutes passed, the sounds of gentle lowing, bleating, and clucking filling the air, punctuated by quiet murmurs and occasional soft laughter from the group. The initial tension from David's opening remarks had dissipated, replaced by a momentary sense of connection with the living creatures around them.

"Alright," David announced, his voice cutting through the gentle sounds of the barn, instantly recapturing everyone's attention. "Everyone got their favorite bovine buddy?" He paused, allowing the question to hang in the air, his gaze sweeping over the assembled group, reading their faces, their relaxed postures, their newfound ease around the animals. "Good. Now, tell me... how many of you are prepared to slaughter and butcher your new friend?"

The question landed like a lead weight in the sudden silence. A wave of uneasy quiet washed over the barn, replacing the earlier tranquility. Jessica's giggles died in her throat, replaced by a look of shock. Tiffany stopped scratching her cow, her brow furrowing in confusion and concern. Even Clarence, who had spent years in retirement raising cattle himself in a different lifetime, looked visibly uncomfortable. The abstract concept of meat on a plate had collided brutally with the reality of a living, breathing animal they had just connected with.

"Daddy? Are you serious?" Jessica asked, her voice small, laced with a hint of disbelief that David would propose such a task, especially after the "mingling" exercise. David nodded, his face serious now, the brief smile gone. "Perfectly serious, Baby. We were just discussing our need for a butcher. Well, these are the animals we're going to eat. Someone needs to kill them, skin them, cut them in half, then slice them up into little portions for everyone." He didn't flinch from the graphic details, presenting the harsh reality as a simple statement of fact.

David watched their faces, a small, almost imperceptible smile playing on his lips once more. He understood their hesitation, the visible discomfort. The disconnect between a cute cow and a steak on a plate was, for most, a wide one, especially for those who hadn't grown up in this life, this world where such tasks were unavoidable. He had intentionally manufactured this moment, the contrast between petting the animals and the brutal necessity of their fate. It was a harsh but necessary lesson, a reminder that survival wasn't always clean, pleasant, or easy.

"Alright," he said, breaking the prolonged silence, sensing the point had been made. "Seems some of you are having second thoughts about the 'butcher's benefit.'" He gestured towards the cows, which were now looking at the group with a mixture of bovine curiosity and mild concern, perhaps sensing the shift in atmosphere. "Let's be clear. This isn't a game. We need meat. We can't just wish it into existence. Someone has to do the unpleasant part."

He paused, allowing his words to settle, allowing the weight of the responsibility to sink in. He knew this group intimately, their strengths, their weaknesses, their hidden anxieties. He knew who wouldn't volunteer, who couldn't volunteer due to squeamishness or lack of required strength, and who might surprise him. He began to narrow the field, removing those whose current duties were non-negotiable. "Tiffany, Jennifer, Summer, Elena, Taylor, Tanya, Jessica, Aidan, Junior, Kyle, Janet, Brian and Andrea already have permanent assignments that are vital to our daily operations.

So, it can't be them, it has to be someone else. They are too important to what we already do." This eliminated the majority of the group, focusing the remaining pressure onto a smaller subset.

He waited, the silence stretching, punctuated only by the lowing of the cows, the bleating of goats, and the chirping of birds outside the barn doors. The tension was palpable, a silent negotiation unfolding until someone stepped forward.

It was Scott who finally broke the tension. Scott, the stoic construction worker, the man whose hands had helped build the very structure that would eventually be their final port of call. "I'll do it, David," Scott said, his voice steady and devoid of overt emotion, a quiet practicality underlying his offer. "I built the damn thing, might as well put it to use. Plus, Mike and I used to hunt back before… all this." He gestured vaguely towards the ravaged landscape beyond the valley, a brief acknowledgment of the world that had forced them into this new existence and the skills it demanded.

A collective sigh of relief, almost imperceptible but deeply felt, swept through the group. The tension that had gripped them dissipated like morning mist under the rising sun. David nodded, a hint of genuine gratitude softening his expression further. "Scott, I appreciate that. Thank you." He clapped his hands together, the sound sharp and decisive, signaling the conclusion of this particular ordeal and the start of a new assignment. "Alright then, Scott is our butcher. Consider it a skill enhancement program. He'll be taking on the responsibility of preparing the meat for everyone."

Jessica, her initial shock giving way to a more practical concern, tugged gently at David's arm. "Daddy, how much meat does a cow make?" David smiled, recognizing the shift back to logistics. His autism, as he sometimes perceived it, tingled with the comfort of quantifiable data and practical calculations.

He launched into a surprisingly detailed lecture on bovine anatomy and butchering yields, his previous bluntness replaced by an almost professorial expertise. "On average, a cow yields about 40% of its live weight as usable meat," he explained, outlining the conversion from a living animal to sustenance. "Our large cows weigh around 1,500 pounds, so we're looking at roughly 600 pounds of meat per animal. The miniature cows are closer to 500 pounds live weight, giving us around 200 pounds of meat. Goats… well, let's just say they're not winning any butchering contests. Maybe 40 pounds of meat, tops. Chickens, a measly two pounds each, if we're lucky."

He sighed, rubbing the back of his head, contemplating the numbers. "Truthfully, one of the big cows will last one or two months if we're modest. However, the miniature cattle, we'll have to slaughter at least once per month." Jessica's young brows furrowed with concern. "It doesn't sound like we'll have enough." David nodded, acknowledging the limitation. "Not if that was our only source of protein. Luckily," he added, offering a measure of reassurance, "we have plenty of freeze dried meat." This reserve provided a crucial buffer against lean times.

The informal discussion concluded, and the group began the procession back into the main house. The movement was a mix of murmurs and shuffling feet, a familiar rhythm of their shared existence. Adding to the amiable disarray were Homer, Judas, and Rahab, the resident dogs, weaving through the crowd with their stubby legs a blur, sensing the shift in atmosphere. Jessica, still holding David's arm, her earlier concern perhaps momentarily forgotten, returned to peppering him with questions about more palatable aspects of the process—meat cuts and the best ways to cook a goat.

Inside the living room, the heart of their communal space, routines quickly reasserted themselves. Tiffany, with practiced efficiency, directed everyone to their usual spots. Summer, another member of the group, took on the task of brewing a fresh pot of coffee – a precious commodity they still maintained a decent supply of, thankfully, a small luxury in their challenging world. Jennifer stretched out on the sofa, her posture relaxed, and beckoned David with a playful flick of her wrist. "Come, Master," she said, a hint of amusement in her voice, "tell us more about the magic of meat." Kayla, another woman present, echoed the sentiment. "Yeah," she interjected, "How long does it take to butcher a whole cow?"

David chuckled, a genuine sound that elicited smiles from several of the wives gathered. He settled beside Jennifer, ready to address the practical queries. "Ah, butchering," he began, directing his answer primarily to Kayla. "The time it takes depends on experience and equipment." He referenced the specific skills and tools available to them. "With Scott's efficiency and Aidan's motorized pulley system, a large cow takes us about six hours from start to finish. That includes skinning, gutting, quartering, and initial breakdown into manageable cuts." The smaller animals, as with yield, required less effort. "The mini cows are quicker, maybe three hours."

His eyes scanned the room, taking in the faces of those who relied on him. He noticed Lynn, Josh's mother, lingering near the doorway, her posture hesitant, looking unsure of where she fit or if she should even enter fully. He offered her a warm, inviting smile. "Lynn, please, come in and sit down. We're just discussing the… logistics of livestock." Lynn, still bearing the weight of recent events, perhaps the trauma related to Boyd and the earlier chaos mentioned implicitly, shuffled in cautiously and took a seat on the edge of an armchair, a picture of quiet apprehension. David understood that gaining her complete trust and easing her anxieties would be a gradual process.

Bringing the focus back to the immediate tasks at hand, David raised his hand slightly to command attention. "However," he stated, linking the discussion back to the workload, "that work only has to be done once or twice a month. So, you could say, it's a well paid job in this community." As murmurs rippled through the group, acknowledging the demanding but infrequent nature of the task, David steered the conversation towards the day's schedule. "Okay, Scott, I want you to start on one of the large cattle tonight. It's supposed to be hot this afternoon, and I don't want you working in that." He then turned his attention to Margaret and Clarence, newer additions to their group. "You two should be moved into your room by this afternoon. The boys will help as they move."

Addressing Mark, Scott, and Eric, key figures in managing the community's activities, David outlined the day's educational plan. "It's Friday, so no school in the classroom today. Today it's hand to hand combat training in the Rec bunker, so make sure the kids have exercise clothes on today." After receiving unified nods of understanding from the men, he turned back to Jennifer, clarifying her role in the training. "Seth and Grace will take this one, so you're in the clear." "Yes, Master," Jennifer purred in response, the title delivered with a familiar, almost teasing ease, earning a playful glare from David.

For Clarence, observing these interactions as an outsider, an internal monologue was reaching a fever pitch. "Master?" he thought, scratching his head beneath his worn baseball cap, the term jarring against the casual efficiency of David's instructions. He glanced at Margaret, who seemed largely oblivious, passively accepting the flow of events around her. He struggled to process what he was seeing, the dynamics of this seemingly self-sufficient community. Even the young girl, Jessica, who looked young enough to be his granddaughter, presented a puzzle; David seemed awfully solicitous of her. She was clearly pregnant, and Clarence was certain he'd caught David glancing at her with a certain… fondness. Was she David's daughter? Was this some weird, complex, apocalyptic commune they had stumbled into? The questions swirled, highlighting the layers of relationships, roles, and unspoken arrangements that formed the foundation of this rebuilding society.

Chapter 32

The Paradox of Training

Clarence and his wife Margaret found themselves in a reality starkly different from the ravaged world they had left behind. The external view of fortified walls and secure defenses gave way to an interior of surprising opulence. Bullet-resistant windows offered a view of a carefully maintained property, a stark contrast to the desolation outside. Yet, despite the apparent safety and comfort, a deep sense of unease settled upon Clarence almost immediately.

His observations sparked a cascade of bewildering questions. David, their host and apparent protector, was a figure of commanding presence, capable of swift, ruthless action, a fact Clarence had witnessed firsthand during their recent, violent encounter. Adding to the complexity was the array of women who seemed to form David's inner circle. There was Jessica, clearly pregnant, who looked young enough to be David's daughter, yet David treated her with a peculiar tenderness that suggested something deeper.

The other women were equally perplexing. Tiffany, possessing a formidable physique, Summer with an air of quiet intelligence, and Elena, whose knowing glances towards David further fueled Clarence's confusion. The atmosphere felt less like a typical survival group and more like a scene from a bizarre, perhaps unsettling, domestic drama playing out against the backdrop of the apocalypse. Clarence, shifting uncomfortably in a luxurious armchair, felt like an accidental audience member without any context or script.

David's voice, calm and genial, cut through Clarence's swirling thoughts. "Clarence?" he inquired, a gentle smile on his face. "Is everything alright? You look a little… lost in thought. Margaret's settling in, I hope?"

Clarence blinked, pulled back to the present moment. He stammered a reply, gesturing vaguely. "Uh, yeah, yeah. She's… admiring the, uh… the décor." He added weakly, "It's…something," an understatement that barely scratched the surface of his astonishment at the lavish surroundings. Deciding to confront his most immediate puzzle, he took a breath. "David, I appreciate everything you've done, truly. But… that girl, Jessica? Is she… your daughter?"

A warm, genuine chuckle escaped David, momentarily easing some of Clarence's tension. "Jessica? No, Clarence. She's my wife." Clarence's reaction was visceral. His jaw dropped, and his mouth worked silently for a moment before he managed a choked, "Your… wife?" His voice cracked with disbelief. "But… she looks young enough to be your daughter!"

David smiled, a hint of amusement in his eyes. "Jessica is my wife. And yes, you're right, she might be old enough to be my daughter, if I were an irresponsible teenager, but that's not the case." Standing up, David added, "So is Tiffany, Summer, Jennifer, Kayla, Elena, Taylor, Tanya and Nicole." The color drained from Clarence's face. He looked utterly stunned, stammering, "W-wives? All of them?" He glanced around the spacious room as if searching for an explanation that defied modern understanding.

Taking a visible deep breath, David attempted to clarify the complex situation. "If you must know," he began, "I am only legally married to Jessica. Technically speaking, Tiffany, Jennifer, Summer, and Nicole are my ex-wives, and Elena, Taylor, Tanya and Kayla are more like concubines. However!" He emphasized with a pointed finger, "We are a team. A loving and supportive team." Clarence, still beet-red, sputtered, the words catching in his throat like gravel. "Concubines? Ex-wives? What kind of a… a… harem is this?" The accusation hung in the air, heavy with judgment and disbelief.

Just as the awkward silence threatened to solidify, Jennifer, never one to miss an opportunity for playful teasing, sashayed back into the room. Her entrance was a deliberate interruption, a splash of vibrant energy against the strained atmosphere. Her eyes twinkled with mischief as she moved, and with a graceful, almost provocative movement, she leaned against David, draping an arm casually around his shoulders. "A very efficient one, Clarence," she purred, a smile playing on her lips. "And David's a very… attentive Master." She punctuated the statement with a wink towards Clarence, earning a playful swat on the rear from David, a gesture that spoke volumes about their comfortable, easy rapport, and simultaneously widened Clarence's eyes even further.

"Jennifer!" David groaned, a sound that was half exasperation and half fond amusement. Summer, ever the diplomat, stepped forward. "We all love David, and he loves us. We're a unit. And we're very good at what we do." Her gaze was steady and reassuring, a beacon of stability in a confusing situation, sincerely hoping to diffuse the tension that clung stubbornly to Clarence.

David took a deep breath, striving for a calm he didn't quite feel. He needed to address the elephant in the room: the nature of his relationships. "Clarence," David began again, adjusting his stance, shifting from defense to a more deliberate, almost educational posture, "I know you're a man of faith. A believer in the Bible?"

Clarence nodded slowly, his brow still furrowed, wary but compelled to answer. "Then you know about the Old Testament," David continued, watching Clarence's reaction closely. "You know about the patriarchs. Abraham, Jacob, Solomon, even David himself. They had… large families. Many wives?"

Clarence blinked, the cogs in his mind visibly turning. The historical context was undeniable, a part of the scripture he revered. "Well, yeah," he conceded, the hesitation clear in his voice, "but... that was different. That was... a long time ago. And they were, you know... patriarchs. Chosen men." The implication was obvious: David, in Clarence's eyes, was no Abraham.

David nodded, a faint smile playing on his lips. He saw the opening, the thread of shared understanding within their differing perspectives. "And what makes you think," he asked, his voice softening slightly but laced with a hint of playful arrogance, "that I'm not chosen?" He paused for effect, letting the question hang in the air, challenging Clarence's pre-conceived notions. "Clarence, I am a faithful follower of God. I believe in His word, His commandments, and His promise to bless those who serve Him. I strive to live by His principles, to protect the innocent, and to provide for those in my care."

He gestured towards the sprawling ranch visible through a reinforced window – the sturdy fortifications, the meticulously organized defenses, the signs of life and growth under the harsh, post-apocalyptic sun. "Look around you, Clarence. In this broken world, what did I do? Did I plunder and pillage? Did I hoard resources for myself? No. I built a sanctuary. A place of safety and abundance. And I built it with the help of these women." His gesture encompassed not just Jennifer and Summer standing nearby, but the entire community of men, women and children who thrived under his protection.

David sat down. "I didn't compromise my principles for them," he stated clearly, addressing potential accusations head-on. "I didn't kill or steal these women from their husbands. I didn't lie to any of them, and I did follow the law. I never married more than one at a time, and they all have a share in the family we built."

It was true. David had built something extraordinary out of the ashes, a functional community where life had meaning and people were safe. But... multiple wives? A family structure that defied everything he had been taught? It was a concept that still felt alien, almost offensive, to his deeply ingrained moral code rooted in a very specific, modern interpretation of scripture. "But... but it's... wrong," Clarence stammered again, shaking his head, unable to reconcile what he saw with what he believed. "The Bible says... one man, one woman. It's... adultery!"

David sighed, the sound barely audible. He knew this conversation was inevitable, a hurdle any newcomer from the 'old world' would trip over. He was prepared, or as prepared as one could be for challenging deeply held beliefs. He just hoped Clarence was open-minded enough, or perhaps desperate enough given the state of the world, to truly hear him out.

"Clarence, you're right," David conceded gently, acknowledging the validity of Clarence's traditional understanding. "The traditional interpretation, the one most people are taught, is one man, one woman. But let's delve a little deeper, shall we? Let's consider the context, the spirit of the law, rather than just the literal wording." He steepled his fingers, leaning forward slightly. "Adultery, at its core, isn't about numbers, Clarence. It's about betrayal. It's about breaking a sacred vow, about deceiving and neglecting, about placing personal desires above the well-being of your partner. It's about not valuing the gift God gave you."

He leaned further forward, his voice earnest. "Tell me, Clarence, look at these women. Look at their faces. Do you see any of them deceived? Neglected? Cast aside? Do you see them unhappy? Do you see me breaking any vows? I vow to love, cherish, and protect each of them…and I do. Each of them knows the situation, willingly chose it, and thrives within it. They are loved, respected, and secure. They contribute to this family, this community, and they are valued beyond measure." He paused, letting the truth of his words settle, letting Clarence see the evidence for himself.

Before the conversation could spiral further, before they got pulled into another exhausting debate about morals, ethics, and the letter of the law versus the spirit in a world where survival demanded new codes, David decided it was time to provide that promised "more comfortable" accommodation. He gave a subtle nod to Aidan, who had remained patiently nearby. Aidan stepped forward, and Clarence and Margaret, still looking utterly bewildered but perhaps slightly less antagonistic, were politely but firmly escorted downstairs to their room.

David watched Clarence and Margaret disappear down the stairwell, a wave of weariness washing over him. Debating scripture and morality with a man who saw the world in rigid black and white, whose framework for life had survived the apocalypse intact but was utterly ill-equipped for its aftermath, felt like an exercise in futility. He needed a break, a genuine distraction, a shot of pure, uncomplicated joy that didn't involve navigating the emotional minefield of his new guests.

The recreational bunker, buried deep beneath the surface, sounded like just the antidote. It was a space designated for leisure, a place where the usual anxieties of their world could, theoretically, be suspended. He made his way down, each level a step further away from the surface-level worries, the crushing weight of responsibility and uncertainty momentarily lifting with each descending foot.

Finally, he reached the open space, the air slightly cooler, the lighting softer. And there they were. Grace and Seth, his two youngest, held court in the center of the room. Their small bodies were radiating an unusual intensity, a quiet focus that immediately piqued his interest. And with them, gathered in a rough circle, was a truly motley crew of the younger generation, and perhaps a few unexpected adults.

David couldn't help but be impressed. He'd started teaching Grace and Seth self-defense techniques almost as soon as they could walk. It wasn't just about survival in their world; it was about discipline, awareness, and building confidence. But to see them now, passing on that knowledge, translating complex maneuvers and principles into something even the youngest, most easily distracted minds could grasp? It was a testament to their unique abilities, a quiet display of the remarkable individuals they were becoming.

Then there was Kyle, standing at the edge of the group with a perpetually bewildered expression plastered across his face. David wasn't entirely sure what was funnier: the image of this physically imposing figure earnestly, if clumsily, attempting to mimic Grace's incredibly graceful, almost ethereal movements, or the fact that Grace seemed completely unfazed by his presence, her focus entirely on patiently guiding the younger children through the intricacies of silent takedowns. It was absurdly charming.

Mike, Lori, and Beth, despite their size, were surprisingly adept. Their small bodies seemed to instinctively understand the mechanics, mimicking the movements with an eagerness that, while heartwarming, bordered on the slightly alarming given the subject matter. And then there was Bonnie, a sweet girl who was currently tripping over her own feet but whose eyes were absolutely locked on Seth, a blush creeping up her cheeks every time he so much as glanced in her direction. Poor kid was probably absorbing zero self-defense, but getting an excellent lesson in puberty.

Janet was also in the mix, a brave sight trying to maintain some semblance of dignity while contorting herself into various pretzel-like positions that bore little resemblance to the fluid blocks Grace was demonstrating. "Alright, my little ninjas," Grace announced, clapping her hands together, her voice clear and commanding despite her age. "Let's review the pressure points. Kyle, honey, you paying attention?"

Kyle, startled by the sudden direct address, nearly face-planted mid-mimic. "Uh, yeah, Grace. Paying attention," he stammered, straightening up quickly and puffing out his chest, making a rather transparent attempt to look like he knew exactly what pressure points were and where they might be located on a human body or, more likely, where Grace might be pointing. Grace sighed dramatically, rolling her eyes in a way that was eerily reminiscent of her mother, a gesture David had seen countless times. "Okay," she said, clearly unfooled by Kyle's posturing. "Pretend Beth here is an attacker. She's trying to steal our precious… Legos."

Beth, a tiny menace with formidable twin braids, immediately transformed, baring her teeth and hunching her shoulders in a surprisingly convincing assailant impression for a seven-year-old. Kyle hesitated, sweat beading on his forehead. Attacking Beth, even pretending, seemed like a terrible idea. Seeing his struggle, David decided to offer a lifeline. "Grace, sweetheart," he interjected smoothly. "Perhaps you could demonstrate for Kyle? Show him how it's done."

Grace beamed at David, her earlier exasperation melting away, replaced by delight at her dad's participation.

She then turned back to Kyle, her eyes gleaming with mischievous intent. "Alright, darling. Watch closely." In a flash, she moved towards Beth, demonstrating the pressure point technique, a light, precise touch, on her arm. Beth immediately giggled, collapsing into a heap of mirthful laughter on the floor, the 'attack' thwarted not by pain, but by ticklish persuasion.

"See, Kyle, baby?" Grace instructed, standing over the giggling Beth. "Like that. Not too hard, just enough to… persuade them to reconsider their life choices." Kyle gulped, nodding furiously. "Right. Persuasion." He looked relieved that the demonstration hadn't involved actual force against a giggling child.

David chuckled, a deep rumble that vibrated pleasantly in the recreational bunker, cutting through the squeals of laughter. "Persuasion, indeed," he agreed, walking forward. This was better than he'd imagined. The innocence of the 'Lego attacker' scenario, combined with the underlying seriousness of the skills, was exactly the kind of uncomplicated joy he needed. "Alright, Grace, sweetheart," he said, his voice settling into a calm, authoritative tone. "Let's give this class a real demonstration. Bring out the, uh, slightly bigger attacker. I'll be your opponent. You show everyone how it's done against someone who actually wants your Legos… and maybe your lunch money."

A ripple of excited murmurs spread through the little group. The prospect of seeing Grace go against David, the man they knew as a protector and leader (and maybe a little bit legendary), was clearly thrilling. Even Janet seemed to perk up, abandoning her awkward pretzel pose for a better view.

Only Seth and Bonnie remained largely unfazed; Seth's focus was unwavering, entirely on the task at hand and observing the techniques, while Bonnie's focus remained unwavering, entirely on Seth.

Grace's eyes sparkled with pure, unadulterated excitement. "Oh, Daddy, you're the best!" she exclaimed, bouncing lightly on the balls of her feet. "Okay, Kyle, watch very carefully. Everyone watch! This is how a ninja… flies." She winked at David then back at the class, a flash of pure, delightful mischief dancing in her eyes. The air in the recreational bunker, moments ago filled with giggles and awkward shuffling, now crackled with anticipation.

David, all of six feet of honed muscle and ingrained lethal skills, stood opposite his daughter, Grace. He was dressed casually in trousers and a t-shirt, looking every bit the approachable dad, but the glint in his eyes was anything but. It was the look of a professional assessing a challenge, mixed with a deep pride for the person standing before him.

"Remember, everyone," David said. "This is never about brute strength against a larger opponent. It's about leverage, precision, timing, and knowing your opponent." He glanced at Kyle, who looked paler than usual, perhaps imagining himself in David's place. David offered him a reassuring nod. "And most importantly," he added, the tone becoming slightly more serious, reminding them all of the stakes in their world, "it's about staying alive."

Grace, barely reaching his chest, stood poised, radiating confidence. She didn't look at all intimidated by the imposing figure before her. "Ready when you are, Daddy!" She grinned again, a picture of youthful exuberance, a stark and fascinating contrast to the deadly serious lesson about to unfold.

David walked over to a rack displaying various weapons. He pulled a ninjato, a straight, single-edged sword, from its hooks, then adjusted his grip, the cool steel a familiar, balanced weight in his hand. "Alright, sweetheart," he said, turning back to Grace, the "Lego attacker" scenario replaced by a palpable seriousness. "No holding back. Show us what you've learned." He adopted a neutral stance, betraying nothing of his intentions, his muscles relaxed but ready.

Then, with terrifying speed, he moved. It wasn't reckless; it was controlled, precise. The ninjato flashed in the artificial light, a silver blur aimed not at Grace's midsection exactly, but at the space she occupied, a target designed to test her reaction time.

Grace reacted instantly, her training kicking in. Instead of trying to meet the blade head-on with a block, a futile effort against his strength and speed, she sidestepped, her movements fluid and silent, like water flowing around a rock. She used David's momentum against him, subtly guiding his strike past her with a precise, almost imperceptible pressure of her small hand on his wrist. The ninjato whistled harmlessly through the air where she had been a fraction of a second before.

"Good," David grunted, already recovering, his body instinctively coiling for his next attack. He feinted high, drawing her attention upwards for a split second, then went low, a classic maneuver designed to exploit a defender's anticipation and sweep them off balance. The ninjato arced towards Grace's legs, aiming to trip her fundamentally.

Again, Grace refused to engage directly with the force of the attack. She didn't try to block the blade with her own strength. Instead, she executed a perfect backward roll, a blur of motion. The ninjato passed inches above her as she tucked and rolled gracefully. As she came out of the roll, she wasn't further away as might be expected; she was closer to David, minimizing the weapon's effective range, her eyes locked on his, completely focused.

"Remember," David said, his voice low, a teaching point delivered even in the heat of the simulated combat. "Distance is your friend against a longer weapon. But closing the gap at the right moment is how you control the fight, negate their advantage."

He pressed his attack, increasing the speed and complexity. It was a flurry of jabs and slashes, each strike designed to probe her defenses, to find a weakness, any crack in her poise. The speed was relentless, a terrifying display of David's combat prowess for anyone watching, especially those who knew him only as the quiet leader. He moved with the practiced precision of a seasoned warrior, his every movement calculated, economical, utterly lethal.

Grace, however, remained completely unfazed by the onslaught. She was a whirlwind of controlled motion, a dance of evasion and redirection. She blocked some strikes with the reinforced parts of her forearms, deflecting and redirecting the force away from vital areas. Others she simply avoided, slipping past the blurring blade with deft footwork and subtle shifts of her weight and center of gravity. She was like a ghost, a shadow, always just out of reach, frustratingly difficult to pin down.

Seth watched with a critical eye, noting the subtle adjustments she made, the tiny shifts that allowed her to anticipate David's movements a fraction of a second before he fully committed. Bonnie, her face creased with concentration, was no longer focused just on Seth; she was mimicking the blocks and dodges in her mind, the crush momentarily forgotten in the face of the spectacle. Mike and the younger children watched with wide, silent eyes, mesmerized by the display of skill and the underlying tension. Janet, surprisingly, was entirely on her feet now, leaning forward, her earlier contortions forgotten, utterly captivated.

David changed tactics again. He abandoned the direct assault and began to circle Grace, forcing her to constantly adjust her position, to keep him in her line of sight, to prevent him from gaining an advantageous angle. The ninjato weaved a complex pattern in the air, a constant, moving threat that Grace had to track and anticipate. "This is about more than just blocking and dodging," David said, his voice a steady growl as he moved. "It's about controlling space, about dictating the terms of engagement. You can't just react. You have to anticipate, to control the flow."

Grace, never one for unnecessary words when action sufficed, responded with movement. As David continued his circling maneuver, subtly probing for weaknesses, she shifted her weight, adjusted her stance, not just to defend, but to steer him. It was a subtle manipulation, guiding him almost imperceptibly towards a specific area near the weight racks. It was a trap, laid not with ropes or nets, but with positioning and anticipation.

David, with the heightened awareness, recognized it instantly. A smile, sharp and predatory, curved his lips. "Ah, setting a trap, are we?" he acknowledged, a hint of genuine pleasure in his voice. He didn't hesitate. Recognizing the challenge, he pressed his attack, feinting once more to test her reaction, then launching a brutal overhead strike. The ninjato came down with terrifying speed, a silver blur aimed directly at Grace's head.

This was the moment of truth. This time, Grace didn't try to evade, didn't step back to block the full force of the blow. Instead, with timing born of intense practice and a deep understanding of momentum, she stepped inside David's guard. Moving so close that the ninjato couldn't complete its deadly arc, she used his own forward motion against him. In the same fluid movement, she grabbed his wrist with both hands and twisted.

David, caught off balance by the unexpected closeness and the sudden application of force, grunted in surprise. He allowed the pressure to continue, a split-second decision knowing that resisting completely would likely dislocate his wrist. Grace was strong, deceptively so, a testament to the rigorous and unconventional training she had embraced. With a final, seamless motion, she used the momentum of the twist and his off-balance stance to throw David over her shoulder. It was executed with such precision and efficiency that he landed surprisingly softly on the padded floor, the air whooshing dramatically from his lungs.

A moment of quiet hung in the air, broken only by Grace's slightly heavy breathing. Then, David chuckled, the sound rumbling from his chest as he pushed himself up from the mat. He clapped slowly, a genuine smile now replacing the predatory one. "Excellent, Grace. Absolutely excellent." His voice was laced with pride. "You baited me, used my attack against me, and executed the throw flawlessly. You've been paying attention." Grace, catching her breath and with a triumphant gleam in her eyes, offered a small, respectful bow. "Thank you, Daddy. I've been practicing."

Seth, always observant and enthusiastic, piped up, his voice cracking slightly with excitement. "That was awesome, Grace! You totally flipped him!" He turned to Bonnie, who was gazing at Grace with wide-eyed admiration. "See, Bonnie? That's what I was talking about. Silent martial arts is about using your opponent's strength against them. Grace is gonna be a ninja!" Bonnie, her eyes still wide, nodded enthusiastically. "You're so cool, Grace!"

The shift from intense combat to proud father and admiring onlookers was swift, but the lesson lingered. Janet, who had been watching with a mixture of fascination and apprehension, stepped forward. She carefully picked up the ninjato David had dropped, examining the blade with a nervous frown. The cold steel felt alien and heavy in her hands. "This is… real? This is incredibly sharp. Are you all… are you actually fighting with this?"

"Yes, Janet, it's real," David said, his voice calm and reassuring, drawing her attention away from the intimidating edge of the blade. He met Kyle's gaze then, a flicker of intense understanding passing between them. Kyle recognized the fine line David had walked. He hadn't been playing it safe. He'd allowed Grace to push him, to genuinely test her skills against a real, albeit controlled, threat, forcing her to expose herself to risk. It was a calculated risk, the kind only a supremely confident and capable fighter would take, trusting both his own ability to pull back and Grace's skill to execute.

David took the ninjato from Janet, his movement fluid and graceful even after being thrown. He held it out, hilt first, to Beth, the youngest of the group. "Beth, hold this." Beth, initially hesitant, reached out and took the sword. It was far too large for her small hands, the weight surprising, but she held it with surprising steadiness, her brow furrowed in concentration. "It's… heavy," she said, stating the obvious but also acknowledging the tangible reality of the weapon.

"It is," David agreed, his voice gentle. "Now, the most important thing to remember is to respect it. This isn't a toy. It's a tool, like a hammer or a saw. And like any tool, it can be used for good or for bad. We're learning to use it for good." He smiled gently at Beth, taking the sword back and placing it carefully back on the rack.

He turned to the group, his expression becoming more serious, encompassing everyone present. "It doesn't matter the weapon or the number of attackers out there," David stated, his voice filling the large space. He gestured towards Grace. "Grace knew that I could have killed her during that exercise. That's why she took it seriously."

"Grace's skill," David continued, his gaze sweeping across their faces, "gives her confidence. Because she is confident, she can focus on the attacks without paralyzing fear or crippling worry. Fear is a luxury we can't afford in a fight. It clouds judgment, slows reactions, and turns a potentially winnable situation into a disaster. It gets you killed faster than a dull blade."

"So," David went on, the intensity in his eyes holding their attention, "what is the purpose of all this? Why are we spending our mornings learning to fight hand-to-hand? Learning to shoot accurately? Learning to use our environment as a weapon, like Grace just did with the weight racks?" He paused, letting the question hang in the air, inviting them to consider it deeply. "Is it just to become proficient killers? Is that all we are building here?" He shook his head slowly. "No. Absolutely not. It's about control. Control over yourselves, control over your environment, control over your fear."

He gestured around the opulent bunker, a symbol of their resilience and foresight. "We have built this. We have the resources, the skills, the community to not just survive the world out there, but to live in it, to build something new. But that life, that sanctuary, that hope, can be snatched away in an instant if we aren't prepared to defend it." His voice hardened slightly, reflecting the harsh reality beyond their reinforced doors.

"The world out there is a constant threat. Marauders looking to take what isn't theirs, desperation driving people to terrible acts, sickness that can fell us quickly... they're all waiting to prey on the weak. But we are not weak. We are strong. We are protectors. And we are more than capable of facing whatever comes our way because we are prepared." Janet, normally reserved and hesitant, a voice of caution, raised her hand again. "But... isn't all this focus on fighting... doesn't it make us afraid? Constantly thinking about the danger that's out there?"

David smiled, a genuine, reassuring smile that reached his eyes, dispelling some of the tension in the room. "That's the paradox, Janet," he said gently. "It's the exact opposite. We don't fear the world because we are trained. We fear the world when we feel helpless, when we face the unknown with no tools or skills. Fear comes from feeling vulnerable. When you know you can defend yourself, when you know you have the skills to react effectively, the fear fades away." He paused, letting the truth sink in. "It's replaced by a quiet confidence, a deep-seated sense of preparedness."

He leaned forward slightly, his voice dropping, drawing the group closer metaphorically. "Think about it. Before the blackout, before the chaos, how many of you truly enjoyed life? How many of you felt empowered to pursue your passions, to take risks, to live without constant worry about things you couldn't control?" A few hesitant hands went up, a quiet acknowledgment of a different, perhaps less fulfilling, past.

"Now," David continued, his voice returning to its normal volume, "we face challenges every single day. Scavenging for supplies in dangerous territories, defending our perimeter from threats, navigating complex negotiations with other groups just trying to survive. These are, potentially, life-or-death situations, every single time. But because we're trained, because we're prepared, because we've built confidence through facing simulated danger, we can face these challenges with courage, with ingenuity, and even... dare I say... with a certain level of enjoyment."

Chapter 33

A New Life and a Tunnel

Alissa's stomach churned, a familiar wave of nausea washing over her, this time tangled with a frantic knot of anticipation. She leaned against the cool, patterned tile of the bathroom wall, the faint scent of lavender soap doing little to calm the frantic beating of her heart. Any minute now, the small plastic stick clutched in her hand would deliver its verdict, and her whole world, the future she and Aidan had whispered about in the dark, would pivot on its axis.

The seconds stretched into an eternity. She squeezed her eyes shut, picturing Aidan's face, the way his eyes crinkled when he laughed, the comforting strength of his arms around her. Would his laughter crinkle around tears of joy? Or would there be a different kind of comfort needed?

Finally, the suspense was unbearable. She couldn't wait another second. With a shaky breath, Alissa steeled herself and forced her eyes open, looking down at the tiny window on the test. Two pink lines stared back. Alissa's breath hitched in her throat. Two lines. Bright, undeniable pink lines. Pregnant. She was pregnant.

A watery giggle escaped her lips, bubbling up from somewhere deep inside her chest, a pure, irrepressible joy she hadn't known she could contain. She covered her mouth with her hand, her eyes welling up with tears that weren't from nausea or anxiety, but from overwhelming happiness. She was going to be a mother. Aidan was going to be a father.

Their quiet dreams, shared in hushed tones and hopeful glances, were suddenly, wonderfully real.

She glanced back towards the bedroom, where Aidan's form was a peaceful lump under the duvet, his face serene in sleep. How was she going to tell him? Her mind raced. Should she wake him up right now, in the quiet intimacy of their bedroom? Or plan some grand, special reveal, something he'd remember forever? Alissa shook her head, a wide, unstoppable grin spreading across her face. Plan something special? Impossible. She couldn't wait. Not even a minute longer. She wanted to share this explosive joy, this incredible, life-altering news with him immediately, watch his face light up, feel his arms around her as they absorbed the shock and wonder together.

Carefully, as if the small plastic stick held all the magic in the world, she set the pregnancy test on the bathroom counter. Then, padding softly across the floor, she went back into the bedroom. She knelt beside Aidan, her heart pounding a joyful rhythm against her ribs, and gently stroked his hair, the strands soft between her fingers. "Aidan," she whispered, her voice thick with emotion, barely louder than a breath. "Honey, wake up."

He stirred, groaning softly, the picture of sleepy reluctance, burrowing deeper into the pillow as if trying to escape the morning. "Five more minutes," he mumbled sleepily, tugging the blanket higher. Alissa chuckled, the sound a little choked with unshed tears and boundless excitement. "No, you have to wake up," she insisted gently, leaning closer. "I have something to tell you. Something important." Aidan slowly blinked his eyes open, a confused, slightly worried expression clouding his features. "What's wrong?" he mumbled, pushing himself slightly up on an elbow. "Is everything okay?"

She brushed a stray strand of hair from his forehead, her hand trembling slightly. "Everything," she said, her voice trembling with the sheer force of the news about to burst from her, "is more than okay. It's... it's amazing." She took a deep breath, the words tumbling out in a rush. "I'm pregnant." Aidan's sleepy haze vanished instantly. His eyes widened, his pupils dilating in disbelief. He sat up abruptly, his movement jerky as he reached out and grabbed her hands, his grip firm. "Pregnant?" he asked, his voice hushed, almost reverent. "Really? Are you sure, Liss?"

Alissa nodded, tears finally spilling over and streaming down her face as she pulled him into a tight hug, burying her face in the familiar comfort of his shoulder. "Two pink lines," she whispered against his skin. "I'm sure. We're sure." He held her just as tightly, burying his face in her hair, inhaling the scent of her as if trying to anchor himself in the reality of her words. "Oh, Alissa," he whispered, his voice thick with emotion, raw and full of wonder. "This is... this is incredible. This is everything."

They stayed like that for a long moment, wrapped in each other's arms, the world outside their bedroom fading away. They were lost in the silent, shared joy of their biggest dream finally coming true. The air crackled with excitement, love, and the sudden, overwhelming weight of the future stretching out before them, bright and full of possibility.

Finally, Aidan pulled back, his hands cupping her face, his thumbs gently wiping away her tears. His eyes, usually sparkling with mischief, were now shining with a deep, profound happiness. "I'm going to be a dad," he said, the words ringing with disbelief and wonder. A wide, uncontainable grin spread across his face, mirroring hers. "I'm actually going to be a dad!"

His energy was infectious. He jumped out of bed, grabbing Alissa's hand and pulling her up with him, bouncing slightly on the balls of his feet. "Okay! Okay! We have to tell everyone! We have to tell Dad! And Summer! And Jessica! And Lily and Josh... everyone!" Alissa laughed, wiping the last of the tears from her eyes, her body still buzzing with adrenaline and pure joy. "Okay, okay," she agreed, trying to sound calmer than she felt. "Slow down, future dadzilla. Let's at least get dressed first."

But getting dressed proved to be a challenge with the sheer, palpable amount of excitement buzzing between them. Aidan, ever the playful one, the one who could turn any mundane task into a moment of shared laughter, couldn't resist peppering Alissa with kisses as she tried to pull on her jeans. He nuzzled her neck, his breath warm against her skin, making her giggle and squirm. "Aidan," she laughed, swatting playfully at his chest, pretending exasperation she didn't feel. "Stop it! I'm trying to get ready. We have big news to share!"

He just grinned, that mischievous glint back in his eyes. "But you're so much more fun than getting ready," he murmured, trailing kisses down her shoulder, earning a delightful shiver from Alissa that had nothing to do with the morning chill. "We really should tell everyone," she said again, her voice slightly breathless as his hands gently found their way beneath her t-shirt, resting warmly against her back.

"Especially Dad. He's going to be so thrilled. And mom too, she'll scream." "He will be," Aidan agreed, his voice low, his touch sending pleasant shivers through her. "Everyone will be over the moon." He paused, his eyes holding hers, sparkling with a different kind of mischief now. "But maybe... just maybe... before the big announcement... we could take a little celebratory detour?"

Alissa rolled her eyes, but a smile played on her lips. She knew that look. She knew exactly what kind of "detour" he meant. "Aidan!" she said, trying to sound stern, though her tone betrayed only amusement. "We don't have time for any 'detours'! Breakfast will be ready soon." "Just a quickie," he pleaded, his voice a low rumble against her ear, his thumbs tracing lazy circles on her skin. "For the baby? To celebrate its future existence?" "Don't you dare use the baby as an excuse," she retorted, though she was already weakening. He knew exactly how to get to her, the little rascal. His particular blend of playful charm and genuine affection was her kryptonite.

Before she could protest further, Aidan had scooped her into his arms with surprising strength, carrying her back towards the rumpled bed as if she weighed nothing. Alissa let out a surprised squeal that quickly turned into a laugh, wrapping her arms around his neck, pressing her face into his shoulder. "Aidan, seriously, we are going to miss breakfast," she said, though the words lacked any real conviction. The truth was, the rush of hormones, emotion, and pure happiness had ignited a different kind of spark inside her, one that only Aidan could extinguish. "Breakfast can wait," he murmured, his gaze intense and full of love as he gently placed her back onto the soft mattress. "This," he said, leaning down to kiss her deeply, "can't."

Alissa wasn't in the mood to argue. The new information, the sheer, exhilarating shock of it, had ignited a fire inside her, a craving for connection and intimacy that felt utterly necessary in this moment of profound change. She needed the reassuring weight of his body, the familiar rhythm of their closeness, to ground herself in this new reality. Aidan reached out, his movements unhurried but purposeful, grabbing the hem around the ankles of her pants, slipping them off in a single pull. When Aidan wanted something, wanted her, there was certainly nothing Alissa could do, or wanted to do, to stop him.

Meanwhile, in the sprawling main, the bustle of morning was in full swing. Jessica, noticeably pregnant, sat at the large dining room table, stirring a bowl of oddly reconstituted freeze-dried fruit with a wooden spoon, the aroma of coffee and cooking food filling the air. Across the kitchen, Summer, ever the steady anchor, finished scrambling a large batch of eggs.

Lily and Josh were already in the kitchen, helping Summer set the table and sneak bits of breakfast. They'd moved into one of the apartments a little while back, but the gravitational pull of main-house breakfast was apparently too strong to resist. "Why is it that even after you get your own apartment, you guys insist on coming over for breakfast almost every morning?" David asked, a fond exasperation in his voice as he pulled a golden pan of waffles from the oven.

Lily smiled, grabbing one of the waffles like a large cookie, her eyes sparkling. "I just like being around everyone," she answered simply, taking a bite out of the still-warm waffle. The truth was, the main house was more than just a place; it was where the energy was, where the whole family collided and connected each morning. David shook his head, a small smile playing on his lips despite his feigned grumbling. "Okay, but at least leave us the weekends," he muttered good-naturedly, plating the growing stack of waffles. "This isn't a community club house."

Lily leaned over, kissing David on the cheek. "Love you, Daddy." "Love you too, kiddo," he responded, his tone softening instantly as it always did when one of his kids showed him affection. He sat down in his regular spot, settling his own plate. "Master, what was the new project you got Junior working on?" Jennifer, quiet but observant, asked from her seat. As everyone filled their plates, navigating around each other in the busy kitchen, the conversation naturally turned to David's latest venture. "Ah, yes," David said, spearing a piece of sausage. "I have the boys, Junior, and whoever else I can rope in, digging a tunnel to the apartment bunker. But they have two feet of reinforced concrete to break through on each side, and that's a lot of drilling. And dust."

Josh piped up, mouth full of waffle. "I thought the service tunnels connected everything already?" David nodded as he swallowed his food. "They do, they do, but they're narrow. I want something more… useful. Man-sized. Something you can walk through comfortably, maybe even drive a small cart through." He sighed. "Though, it will be really difficult building it from the inside out, starting from the bunker side. We might have to work from both ends."

"How are you going to do it then?" Tiffany, always practical, inquired.

"Well," David mused, thinking aloud as he looked at his plate, "I think after the holes are cut through the bunker walls, and the tunnel is dug out, probably using that small excavator and then a lot of shoveling by hand, we can just line the walls and ceiling with rebar and wire mesh, then spray the concrete in like stucco, or lap it on like plaster. Should be solid." "Daddy, can we leave it rough cut inside?" Jessica suddenly asked, a cheerful smile on her face. "So, it looks like the ice tunnels on Hoth?"

David paused, a slow grin spreading across his face. He chuckled, reaching out to wrap an arm around her shoulder. "I love you, Baby girl," he said, his voice full of warmth and amusement. Leave it to Jessica to bring a sci-fi reference into building a concrete tunnel. "We'll see. It'd definitely be quicker that way..."

"Now I just have to figure out what to do with 115 cubic yards of dirt," David said, staring at his breakfast as if the answer might be hidden somewhere in the scrambled eggs. Digging the tunnel was one thing; getting rid of the displaced earth was another logistical challenge. "Let's just fill sandbags," Seth suggested quietly from his end of the table, offering a practical solution. "We can stack them somewhere out of the way and figure out what to do with them later. They might even be useful for future projects."

David's face brightened. He scooped an extra, generous serving of freeze-dried fruit onto Seth's plate. "That's a very good idea, son," David commented, a proud gleam in his eyes. "A very good idea indeed. I'm sure the boys can find a good use for several thousand sandbags."

David, fueled by scrambled eggs and Seth's ingenious sandbag solution, was mapping out tunnel logistics in his head when Alissa, finally freed from Aidan's amorous ambush, burst into the kitchen of the main house. Her cheeks were flushed, her hair was a little disheveled, and her words came out in a rush. "David! Everyone!" she exclaimed, her words tumbling out in a rush, vibrating with an energy that crackled through the room. "I have news!"

A silence, quick and absolute, fell over the table. Forks paused mid-air, mugs were set down carefully. All eyes were on Alissa. Tiffany, spoke first, her voice laced with gentle concern. "Are you alright, sweetie? You look like… like you walked backward through a hedge." Alissa dissolved into a fit of giggles, a nervous, excited energy bubbling up and spilling over. "I'm more than alright!" she managed between laughs. "I'm… well, I'm pregnant!"

The stunned silence that followed lasted only a beat, a collective intake of breath, before the room erupted. A wave of noise, shouts of congratulations, and gasps of delight washed over Alissa. Tiffany was the first to reach her, enveloping her in a warm embrace, tears of happiness already welling in her eyes. Jennifer, never one for subtlety, let out a loud whoop of her own and delivered a hearty clap on Alissa's back that nearly sent her off balance.

Elena, leaning back in her chair, offered a knowing smirk and raised a single eyebrow toward Aidan, who had just sheepishly entered the kitchen, trailing slightly behind Alissa. David, who was dissecting his breakfast, paused. He met

Aidan's eyes across the room and subtly, almost imperceptibly, offered a thumbs-up. It was a silent, yet perfectly clear, acknowledgment from David. A mission, it seemed, had been well and truly executed.

Jennifer, her eyes sparkling with pure mischief, sauntered over to Aidan, her movements fluid and confident. She playfully nudged him with her elbow, a smile on her face. "Well, well, well, Aidan," she purred, her voice low enough for just him to hear, though her expression broadcast her amusement widely. "Looks like someone's been a busy little bee, hasn't he? Alissa practically glows! I bet that news wasn't delivered gently, was it?" She punctuated her teasing with a rich chuckle, her voice thick with playful innuendo. "Am I sensing a little pre-announcement celebration went down?" Aidan sputtered, visibly uncomfortable under Jennifer's direct assault. "Jennifer! That's… that's private." He darted a glance at Alissa, who was happily wrapped up in conversation with Tiffany, oblivious to Jennifer's wicked teasing.

Jennifer just leaned closer, completely ignoring Aidan's discomfort. Her voice dropped to a low whisper, edged with something surprisingly serious beneath the jesting. "Embarrassed? Honey, you shouldn't be embarrassed. You're a man, acting like a man in a world that needs men to act. Own it! I'm proud of you, Aidan, really." Her expression softened slightly, though the mischief remained in her eyes. She straightened up, giving him another hearty clap on the shoulder. "Now, go join your glowing wife. You've earned it."

Aidan, still slightly flustered but managing to regain some composure, forced a weak smile. "Thanks, Jennifer. I think." He then made his way across the suddenly boisterous kitchen, slipping an arm around Alissa's waist and pulling her close. Tiffany and Alissa had already moved onto the next crucial topic: baby names. "So," Tiffany began, her maternal instincts, always simmering just beneath the surface, now kicking into serious high gear. "We need a name. Something strong, something timeless. For a girl, I was thinking maybe...Elizabeth?" she offered, her voice laced with a hint of hopeful tradition.

Alissa wrinkled her nose playfully. "It's pretty, definitely, but it's also... overused. I was hoping for something a little more unique. Maybe something nature-inspired?" She mused, her eyes drifting thoughtfully upwards. "Like Willow, or River?" Aidan, still slightly red-faced from his encounter with Jennifer, chimed in. "Darling, if you name our baby River, Willow, Rain, Sequoia or anything like that, then you can move into the barn. Because that's where names like that belong."

David, who had been quietly but attentively listening while continuing his meticulous dissection of his breakfast, cleared his throat. "Tyler." Everyone at the table turned to look at him. The suggestion seemed to appear out of nowhere, dropped into the conversation with characteristic David-like precision. "Tyler?" Tiffany repeated, her brow furrowed slightly in surprise. It wasn't quite the traditional or nature-inspired options they'd been tossing around.

David blinked, unfazed. "It's a strong, simple name," he stated plainly, finishing his bite. "Gender neutral. Not too similar to any of our names. And it sounds like a first-born name." His reasoning was, as always, rooted in logic and practicality. Jessica, who had been picking at her breakfast and observing the scene with quiet amusement, giggled. "Leave it to Daddy to choose a name based on efficiency," she commented with a grin that held no malice, only affection. "It does sound nice, though. Tyler. I like it."

Alissa tilted her head, considering the name. She hadn't thought of anything like it. "I don't know..." she murmured, trying the name out in her head. "I hadn't really considered it. But it does have a certain... ring to it. Tyler." She repeated the name, letting it settle. "It's easy to say, easy to remember." Aidan shrugged, looking between Alissa, Tiffany, and David. "I'm okay with it," he said. "It's better than some of the other names I've heard floating around," he added, glancing pointedly at Tiffany, who now wore a slight look of disappointment that her traditional suggestion hadn't landed. "Okay. Okay," Tiffany conceded with a dramatic flourish, throwing her hands up in mock surrender. "Tyler it is. At least for now. We still have plenty of time to change our minds," she added.

Tiffany, ever observant, noticed David's gaze seemed to have drifted again, his focus pulling back towards the unseen, strategic problems beyond the kitchen walls. "David," she said softly, drawing his attention back to the more immediate, domestic concerns. "Have you even thought about names for Jessica's baby? Or are we just throwing random, gender-neutral names into the hat based on... efficiency?"

Jessica, who had been quietly finishing her toast while listening to the name discussion, chuckled, a warm, melodic sound. "Oh, we have names, don't we, Daddy?" she purred, her hand resting protectively, almost subconsciously, on the gentle curve of her swollen belly. David turned his gaze towards Jessica, and the transformation was immediate. The sharp, strategic focus softened, replaced by a noticeable tenderness. "We do, Baby," he confirmed. "Jessica and I discussed potential names rather early on." He paused, a flicker of something akin to amusement, or perhaps deep contentment, in his eyes. "In fact," he added, "I believe we finalized them the first time."

Summer's head snapped towards David, her eyes wide. "That long?" she breathed, the implication hitting her. "Back when she was Samantha?" David nodded, a quiet affirmation, as Jessica chuckled again, clearly enjoying the reveal. "And?" Tiffany pressed, leaning forward, eager to hear the choices that predated everything. "Don't keep us in suspense. Boy or girl names?" Jessica smiled, her eyes sparkling. "We had both," she said. "For a girl... well, we had two favorites. Poppy or Lily."

A hush fell over the group again, different from the stunned silence after Alissa's announcement, this one filled with a gentle anticipation. All eyes turned, almost in unison, to Lily, who had been quietly listening, her head tilted slightly to the side. Her expression was a mixture of pure surprise and shy, blossoming delight. "Lily?" she squeaked, her voice an octave higher than normal. David nodded, his gaze softening even further as he looked at her. "Yes," he said gently. "We thought it was a beautiful name, but it's yours now."

Jessica reached out a hand across the table and gently ruffled Lily's hair, her smile warm and genuine. "It suits you, sweetie," she said softly. "In fact, I always imagined Lily would look just like you, so it's perfect." Lily blushed, her cheeks turning a deep, rosy shade of pink, genuinely touched by the unexpected revelation and the sentiment behind it. "I... I didn't realize it was so significant," she mumbled, her eyes fixed on the ground, a small, private smile playing on her lips.

"And if it's a boy?" Elena prompted, her voice returning some playful energy to the conversation after the tender moment. "Matthew," David replied without the slightest hesitation. The name was spoken with a quiet certainty. Tiffany tilted her head. "Matthew," she repeated thoughtfully. "Wasn't that... wasn't that your youngest son's name?" David nodded, his expression becoming slightly more distant again, though the softness lingered. "It was," he confirmed. "And an appropriate name, I might add."

The brief, intimate interlude about names seemed to draw to a close, and the practical realities of their situation began to creep back into the forefront. Aidan looked around the table, sensing the underlying tension or strategy that had been present before he and Alissa had arrived. "What were y'all talking about before we interrupted?" he asked, pulling out a chair and settling in, a determined look in his eyes. "Dirt," David explained succinctly, the strategic side of his mind reasserting itself. "We're digging a tunnel, and there's going to be a lot of dirt."

Aidan leaned forward, interest piqued. "Tell me about it," he said, ready to contribute. David elaborated on his plans for the tunnel, outlining the scale of the project and the significant logistical challenge the excavated earth would present. He even brought up Seth's ingenious idea for turning the dirt into sandbags.

Aidan pondered the idea for a moment, picturing the sheer volume of earth David was describing. "I don't think we'd have enough sandbags for that," he concluded, shaking his head. The tunnel was a massive undertaking. "But," he continued, "we can make Hesco barriers around the property. Use the dirt for that. It's going to be a slow project either way," he admitted. "Might as well plan for the long haul."

David nodded slowly, considering Aidan's suggestion. "Indeed," he agreed. "Get with Junior and come up with a plan for Hesco barriers and sandbags. Coordinate the excavation spoil with the construction. And," he added, his gaze becoming sharp and focused once more, the immediate next step clear in his mind, "I'd like to start drilling the concrete out as soon as possible. And it's going to take the strongest of you to break it."

Aidan scratched his stubbled chin, still mulling over the tunnel project. "We've got a hammer drill, right?" he asked. David confirmed, "In the work shed. Industrial grade. Should make short work of the concrete, relatively speaking. Now, I want you, Junior, and Brian to start drilling the concrete first. Should be at least three feet wide and seven feet tall." David turned his attention to Alissa, his tone softening, "see Andrea whenever you get a chance. She's a nurse, and it's important to keep you and the baby healthy."

Alissa nodded, a nervous smile gracing her face. "I will, David. Thank you." Jessica, trying to wrap her head around the project, looked at David with a confused expression. "Daddy, why are they drilling holes if they're just going to smash through it?" David smiled slightly as he grabbed a waffle, poking holes in the middle with his fork.

"Because Baby, Drilling the holes creates a clean break line, so the hammering doesn't vibrate through the rest of the bunker." As he explained, he held up his waffle, and with the flick of his finger, popped out a heart shaped hole from the middle.

Jessica reached out and grabbed the heart-shaped piece from his plate and put it in her mouth. "Is it going to be hard digging through the dirt?" she added. "No Darling, everything around the bunkers was backfilled, so it's all pretty consistent, down to thirty-five feet." "Dad!" Seth interjected. "Can we make carts for the mine?" David's eyebrows shot up at the suggestion. "Like Minecraft?"

Seth, emboldened by David's interest, launched into a detailed explanation. "Yeah! We could use the laser level to make sure the tracks are straight, and maybe even hook up a little generator to make them powered!" David stroked his chin, his mind already racing. Automated minecarts might be a bit…ambitious, given the circumstances. But the core idea had merit. "Powered carts might be a bit much, Bud, but we can definitely build some robust four-wheeled tubs for hauling the dirt. Easier to maneuver in a tight space, too." He paused, a mischievous glint in his eyes. "And…well, we do have those miniature cows gathering dust in the barn. Think they'd be up for a little pulling duty?"

A wave of laughter erupted from the table. Jessica, her pregnancy making her especially prone to giggling, choked on her orange juice. "Oh, Daddy, that's ridiculous! Imagine those tiny cows pulling carts full of dirt!" Josh, transfixed by the thought, muttered, "It's finally happening," eyes glazed over with a nostalgic fervor. Lily, ever the devoted wife, squeezed his hand and giggled, picturing her stoic Josh consumed by the possibility of real-life Minecraft.

Summer sighed dramatically, though a smile played on her lips. "Of course, you would think of using miniature cows as draft animals. Honestly, David, sometimes I wonder if you're deliberately trying to turn this place into a petting zoo." But she knew he wasn't. It was David's particular brand of practicality, tinged with a healthy dose of whimsical madness, that she found so endearing.

"Josh, I want you to get Parker and the boys to make us at least eight carts with a simple rope harness. Then you can start planning the corral to guide them from the back of the bunker to the lift. I don't want them stopping by the hydroponics for a snack." Josh nodded, writing the information down. "Aidan, start drilling in the maintenance bunker first. Once the opening is made, we'll all take turns digging."

"Jennifer, start making treats for the cows, I want their hard work rewarded. Something with alfalfa and dried fruit." Jennifer nodded, already conferring with Tiffany. "There's only one way in or out. Walking the dirt out the garage is much easier than carrying it up and out of the work shed," David said, finalizing the excavation plan. "It should take us two to three months to finish, once the concrete is removed."

Chapter 34

The Laundry Rebellion

Deep in the maintenance bunker, little David was already three meters into the massive dirt tunnel, cut through the concrete wall. Seth shoveled loose dirt into carts as Josh, with the help of Mike, Bonnie and the girls, led the miniature cattle in an endless rotation of guided paths and cable lift rides, topside.

The dirt was surprisingly easy to cut through, even without Junior's surprising strength. After breaking through the bunker wall, the broken concrete was removed and the rebar cut. Little David, with surprising ease, simply bent the cut rebar outward, into the excavated tunnel, planning to tie them into the tunnel's reinforced walls.

Josh, who seemed to be enjoying this project more than most, handled his responsibility with a sense of ownership and satisfaction. Josh led his favorite miniature steer, Sir Loin, as Bonnie and Mike followed his lead, guiding the cattle train along the trail through the maintenance bunker. At first, the cows were skeptical of the cable lift, but with a little encouragement and Jennifer's alfalfa biscuits, the cattle train seemed to move on it's own.

Meanwhile, at the bottom of the Apartment bunker's stairwell, Aidan was hard at work. Drilling the pilot holes into the exterior bunker wall from the opposite side. Parker and Eric worked hard to keep the debris and dust clear, carrying buckets of broken concrete up the stairs and dumping them into the nearby Hesco barriers.

Aidan stopped to take a break as Alissa approached with a glass of water. "Darling, are you ready for some lunch?" Aidan took the water and kissed Alissa on the cheek. "Yes ma'am, I believe I am. Just grab something quick from the emergency rations. No need to fix up something," he said, setting down the hammer drill.

As Parker and Eric returned with empty buckets, they offered Alissa a kind nod. "Good afternoon Alissa, hope you're feeling well," Parker said, setting his bucket down. Alissa nodded. "Good morning boys, can I bring you something too?" she asked, turning to go back inside. Eric looked at Parker, before settling back on Alissa. "Sure, anything's good," he replied.

Back at the main house, Jessica looked at the thermostat. "How could it already be 95 degrees, it's barely June?" David, who was folding laundry with Kayla in the living room, simply shrugged. "It's going to get hotter, Baby girl. That's why I want that tunnel dug out." "Can you imagine how miserable it would be without electricity? Or without this remarkably insulated house?" Kayla added.

Jessica furrowed her eyebrows, as she realized something. "Daddy, I've been meaning to ask. How come I haven't heard the air conditioning running since we've been here?" she asked, pointing at the vents. David stopped, mid-fold, as if listening to the house for an answer. "Probably because it hasn't gotten hot enough yet." Jessica shot him a sharp look. "Daddy, it's almost a hundred degrees outside!"

David shrugged. "Well, the hydrothermal pumps keep the house pretty well regulated, and that water is stored in the lowest bunker. Which, even now, is just below sixty degrees." Jessica's eyes widened. "Oh, that's why we went to see that guy in the Emirates?" "Yes Baby, that's exactly why," he answered. "Plus, the air conditioning system is just another level of redundancy. Believe me, if I wanted to make this house as cold as Greenland or as hot as Kuwait, it wouldn't be difficult."

Jessica plopped back down on the couch, watching David and Kayla as they continued to fold the laundry. David grabbed a basket of folded clothes and walked toward the front hallway, toward Seth and Grace's bedrooms, putting their clothes away before crossing the hallway into Nicole and Taylor's room.

Nicole, watching David carrying in the basket, closed her book, placing it gently on the nightstand. The soft 'thud' was the only sound in the room besides the rustle of clothes as David methodically distributed the laundry. She watched him, a subtle smile playing on her lips, the sweet, trusting gaze she always reserved for him intensified. "David," she said, her voice low and melodic, a gentle drawl that hinted at something unspoken. David paused, a neatly folded stack of Taylor's jeans in his hands. He turned to Nicole, his expression instantly softening. "Yes, Love?" he asked.

He knelt beside her chair, a position that always made Nicole feel cherished, placing him literally at her level, focusing entirely on her. He took her hand in his, his large hand enveloping hers. "I... I was enjoying my book," she began, her eyes meeting his. In their shared gaze, a silent conversation passed, a skip over pleasantries to the heart of her thought. "But I think I'd enjoy something else... much more." She squeezed his hand gently, her meaning perfectly clear, a simple confession wrapped in soft words that held the weight of desire.

David's lips curved into a slow, knowing smile. It wasn't a sudden, wide grin, but a gradual unfolding of warmth and understanding that reached his eyes. "Is that so?" he teased, his thumb tracing lazy, warm circles on the back of her hand, a gesture that sent a pleasant shiver up her arm. The air in the room, which had been comfortable and still, suddenly felt several degrees hotter, thicker with unspoken possibility.

David leaned in, his gaze locking with Nicole's, intensifying the connection between them. He brought her hand to his lips, kissing each knuckle with a tenderness that perhaps belied his outwardly dominant nature. This was the core of David, powerful when needed, but infinitely gentle and devoted to the women he loved. "Then," he said, his voice a deep whisper pitched just for her, "it would be my pleasure to ensure you enjoy yourself thoroughly." The promise hung in the air, heavy with mutual anticipation.

He leaned in closer, his lips meeting hers in a slow, deliberate kiss. It wasn't a sudden, passionate, demanding kiss designed to overwhelm, but a deeply affectionate one, a careful exploration that deepened with each passing second. Nicole responded instantly, her body relaxing into his touch, all the small anxieties and uncertainties of the day seemingly melted away under the warmth of his focused attention.

The kiss deepened, growing in intensity, and Nicole's hand, almost instinctively, moved to the buttons of her blouse. Her fingers, usually so graceful and sure, fumbled slightly with the small closures, a testament to her eagerness, her body reacting before her mind could fully process. David gently took over, his nimble fingers making quick work of the buttons, his efficiency now turned towards revealing the soft skin beneath.

As Nicole shed her blouse, letting it fall forgotten beside her chair, Taylor gracefully rose from her own seat. Her movement was fluid and elegant, drawing the eye without demanding it. Her gaze met David's with a silent invitation, a silent acknowledgement of her place in the unfolding scene. She approached him with a quiet confidence that was uniquely hers. Her fingers danced over his waist, teasing the hem of his simple t-shirt, a light, playful touch. She stretched slightly, her body a picture of lithe strength, to lift his shirt over his head, exposing his chest and abdomen to the soft light and the warm air. Her hands lingered for a moment, tracing back down his body, her touch feather-light yet sending shivers down his spine, a different kind of shiver than Nicole's, one of deep, familiar connection.

Taylor's hands lingered on his skin for a moment more, tracing the lines of his abdomen, the planes of his muscles, before moving lower to the buckle of his belt. Her touch was light, affectionate, a silent acknowledgment of the powerful, unspoken bond they shared, a language of touch that had developed over years of shared intimacy. David watched her, his eyes filled with a quiet admiration that shone clearly. He loved the way she moved, the inherent kindness that radiated from her, the gentle strength in her touch.

He reached out, his hand finding hers as it rested on his hip, and brought it to his lips. He kissed her palm, a tender, reverent gesture, his deep eyes locking with hers. "Thank you, Love," he murmured, the words barely audible in the quiet room, yet filled with a genuine affection that resonated between them. His voice, usually so measured and controlled in the world, held a warmth, a vulnerability, a depth of feeling that only his wives truly understood, only they were privy to.

Taylor smiled, a soft, radiant smile that lit up her entire face, transforming her serene expression into something breathtakingly beautiful. It was a smile reserved only for him, a secret language spoken entirely with her eyes, a silent echo of his shared sentiment. She stepped back then, completing her role in the prelude, allowing David to finish undressing himself, her gaze never leaving his, a quiet, loving presence.

Nicole, now completely undressed and reclined on the soft cushions of her chair, watched the interaction between David and Taylor with a contented sigh. There was no jealousy, no reservation, only a deep sense of rightness. The intimacy between David and Taylor felt natural, a comfortable rhythm they had established over the years alongside the rhythm he shared with her. David's love wasn't a finite resource to be divided; it flowed freely, a boundless current encompassing all of them, nurturing their individual bonds and the collective one they shared.

He finished undressing, standing before them for a brief moment. Nicole extended her hand, reaching out to his, an invitation for him to join her fully. David leaned down, accepting her invitation without hesitation, and laid Nicole between the sheets of her bed. The soft cotton felt cool against his skin, a stark contrast to the heat radiating from Nicole's body as he settled beside her.

He kissed her deeply, his tongue teasing the seam of her lips, seeking entry, seeking connection. Nicole moaned softly, a low, throaty sound of pleasure as his fingers tangled in her hair, holding her head gently as the kiss deepened. He explored the depths of her mouth, tasting her, savoring her sweetness, the unique flavor that was purely Nicole. His hands, large and strong yet so gentle, moved down her body, tracing the curve of her breasts, the soft plane of her stomach, the subtle flare of her hips. He rediscovered her shape, the familiar geography of her skin, making each touch a form of praise.

He began to kiss a path down her neck, leaving a trail of warmth, across her collarbone, and onto her chest, pausing to lavish attention on her nipples, teasing them with his tongue and teeth. Nicole gasped, a sharp intake of air, arching her back into him, offering herself more fully. Her hands gripped his shoulders tightly, her nails digging slightly into his skin in her building urgency, a welcome pressure he met with increased focus. "David," she managed to gasp out, her voice ragged with desire. He loved hearing his name on her lips like that, a sound that always ignited something deep within him, a testament to the powerful connection they shared in these moments.

He continued his exploration, moving lower and lower, planting kisses and tracing patterns of touch until he reached the apex of her thighs. With a gentle touch, he parted her legs, opening her to him, and began to devour her with his mouth, dedicating himself entirely to her pleasure. Nicole's body tensed, and she gasped again, louder this time. She tried, instinctively, to quiet herself, covering her mouth with her hand, but her moans and whimpers still escaped, muffled vibrations against her palm, sounds that told him everything he needed to know.

His mouth closed around her, focusing his efforts, and she began to shake uncontrollably, overwhelmed by the intensity. She whispered his name over and over again between gasps, her legs locking around his head, pulling him closer, urging him deeper into the swirling vortex of her pleasure. The intense, shaking experience lasted only a few minutes before her body relaxed, the fierce tension draining away, her muscles no longer clenched, leaving her breathless and vibrating.

Nicole looked down at him, her gaze fixed and intense. He rose slightly, meeting her eyes. "I… I need you, David. I need you now." Her voice was thick with emotion, a raw confession of lingering need. She didn't wait for a response, shifting her position, straddling him on the bed, kissing him with renewed fervor, deep and demanding this time. He pulled her close, his hands cupping her breasts, his thumbs teasing her nipples, already sensitive from his earlier attention. She moved against him, a slow, sensual dance of friction and heat that ignited their coupled lust.

He guided her hips with his hands as she began to ride him, setting a rhythm, her movements graceful and fluid in their shared space. He held her close, continuing to pleasure her upper body, bending to lick her nipples, kissing her breasts, his hands caressing her back and her hips, urging her on. He could feel her heat building again, quicker this time, her muscles clenching around him in anticipation. "You feel so good, David," she whispered, her voice hoarse with desire, breath catching in her throat.

He didn't need to say anything in return. He responded with his body, with his touch, with the deep, guttural sounds that rumbled from his chest, sounds of his own building pleasure and release. He matched her rhythm, driving deeper into her with each thrust, pushing her closer and closer to the precipice of sensation once more.

Finally, with a cry of pure release that echoed the earlier sounds, she came again, her body shaking with the force of it, collapsing onto him. He held her tight, letting her ride out the wave, his own pleasure building rapidly to a crescendo as her body softened around him. He continued to hold her as he thrust his cock deep inside her, now using her quivering, sated body for his own sexual release. As he came inside of her, his body clenched, and he pulled her impossibly tighter against him, holding her fast, the intense, almost painful pressure of their joined bodies in that moment forcing him deep within her as his cum spilled out into her.

They collapsed against each other, their bodies slick with sweat, their hearts pounding in unison against each damp skin. The intensity slowly subsided, leaving behind a shared sense of peace and completion. After a few moments,

David gently rolled them over, settling back against the pillows and cradling Nicole in his arms, pulling the sheets up around them. "Thank you," she murmured into his chest, snuggling closer, burrowing into his familiar warmth. "I needed that. You always know how to make me feel... whole."

David kissed her forehead, the gesture light and tender. He didn't need words to explain the depth of his feelings for her. Their connection ran deep, forged over years of shared life, laughter, and challenges. "Anytime, my love. Anytime." David laid back against the pillows, his chest rising and falling slowly, the remnants of exertion fading into a pleasant languor. Nicole, sated and content, was nestled in his arms, her fingers tracing lazy patterns on his chest, a soft, faraway look in her eyes. They were a picture of quiet post-coital bliss.

But bliss in their household was rarely a solitary or contained event. Taylor, who witnessed their lovemaking from her own bed across the room, shifted nervously. She thought she could remain indifferent, but the sounds, the movements, the sheer palpable energy had drawn her in, holding her captive in a swirl of complex emotions; admiration, longing, a knot of her own desire tighter than she could stand.

The air in the room was thick with the scent of sex and something else, a tension that only David could truly perceive. He knew Taylor hadn't just been passively observing. He could feel her desire, raw and exposed, her unspoken plea radiating across the room like heat waves on a summer day. It wasn't a demand, but a quiet ache that resonated with a part of him always ready to comfort, to provide, to connect. He met her gaze across the softly lit space, and a flicker of understanding, of acknowledgment, passed between them. "Taylor," he said, his voice soft, drawing Nicole slightly closer as he spoke, not wanting to exclude her. "Are you alright?"

Nicole stirred slightly, her eyes fluttering open. She followed David's gaze across the room and a soft smile spread across her face. Taylor blushed slightly, her eyes darting back and forth between David and Nicole, caught in the sudden spotlight. "I… I'm fine," she stammered, but the lie hung heavy in the air, thick with the unspoken wants she usually kept carefully hidden.

David gently disentangled himself from Nicole, careful not to disturb her contentment entirely, but shifting his weight to properly address Taylor. He sat up, his broad shoulders casting a shadow over the bed. "No, you're not," he said, his voice gentle but firm, stripping away her pretense with quiet authority. "And that's perfectly alright. There's nothing wrong with needing. Especially here." He held out his hand to her across the space separating their beds. "Come here, Love."

Taylor hesitated for only a moment. The invitation, the tacit permission to embrace her desires, was too tempting to resist. It was a lifeline thrown when she felt herself quietly drowning in longing. With a deep breath that seemed to gather all her courage, she stood up, immediately pulling off the simple t-shirt and shorts she wore. Her small frame, usually hidden under modest apparel, was now exposed in the warm afternoon light filtering through the curtains, revealing the delicate curves that David found so endearing, so vulnerable and appealing. She stood before them, naked and vulnerable, her gaze fixed on David.

Nicole shifted slightly to give Taylor more room on the bed, leaning back against the pillows with a comfortable sigh. A wry smile growing as she lazily propped herself up on an elbow, watching the exchange with interest and affection. "Well, don't just stand there, Taylor," she purred, her voice laced with playful teasing, breaking some of the tension that held Taylor rigid. "He's not getting any younger... or harder, for that matter."

Taylor's blush deepened at Nicole's words, feeling completely exposed in every sense, but a small smile tugged at the corner of her lips. Nicole's acceptance, her active inclusion, made it easier. She moved with confidence, a grace born of sudden determination, stepping between David's legs where he sat on the edge of the bed and carefully straddled him. The contact was instantly quenching, a rush of sensation that chased away the last vestiges of her hesitation. His thick cock, the intense pressure of being completely filled in a way she specifically craved, and the profound, unexpected shamelessness of getting to have him so freely, so openly, set her on fire from the inside out.

She paused for a moment, her hands resting lightly on his chest, feeling the steady beat of his heart beneath her palms, her eyes searching his for something she couldn't quite name. "Master?" she whispered, the title slipping out naturally. "I know you're probably tired... or spent. I... I just need to cum. I need you to do it for me." The words tumbled out in a rush, bordering on a plea. "Tired?" David chuckled.

"Taylor, love, you wound me. Spent is a… relative term. I have all the energy I need for you."

He reached up, cupping her face in his hands, his thumbs gently stroking her cheekbones, meeting her searching gaze with warmth and understanding. "You don't need to ask, Taylor," he said softly, his gaze locking with hers, conveying a depth of care that went beyond the physical. "You deserve to feel good. To be selfish, even just for a little while. To put your own needs first. I want you to be selfish right now. And I want to be the one who gets to make that happen for you." He held her eyes for another moment, letting the truth of his words sink in.

He nodded slightly, acknowledging Nicole's playful teasing and the truth behind it. He knew she enjoyed this, the openness and freedom of their relationship, the way they navigate their desires together. He watched them both, naked and unashamed before him, and a wave of profound contentment washed over him. "And Nicole is right, my love," he added, a playful glint in his eyes, bringing the shared humor back into the moment. "I am not getting any younger and I am not getting any harder. You should take advantage of what I have to offer before it all goes to hell."

Meanwhile, in the living room, with Kayla still folding laundry, Jessica rolled her eyes. She knew David would get distracted. She had heard the soft murmurs, the shift in sounds from the bedroom. It was a familiar pattern. One or more of them would slip away with David, and the rest of the household would carry on.

"Men," she muttered under her breath, but a smile played on her lips despite her exasperation. Luci rubbed against her massively swollen belly, purring loudly, feeling the warmth and the gentle vibrations. "Don't worry, Luci," Jessica murmured, stroking the cat's head. "Daddy will be back to rub your mommy's feet later. He always is. Though maybe not as soon as I'd like right now."

Back in the bedroom, Taylor leaned forward and kissed David, a deep, lingering kiss that spoke volumes, of gratitude for his understanding. She began to move her hips, slowly at first, finding her rhythm, the initial awkwardness giving way to instinct. Nicole sat back on the bed, watching them with a knowing smile, a silent cheerleader in their interconnected dance. "That's it, Taylor," Nicole purred, her voice laced with encouragement. "Ride him good. Make him work for it. He's got plenty to give." She wiggled her eyebrows suggestively in David's direction. "And more than enough for both of us, don't you think, babe? Save some more for me!"

David smirked, glancing at Nicole. "Don't get any ideas, Nicole. I'm trying to focus here. Taylor needs my undivided attention right now." He winked at Taylor, who was now breathing heavily, her cheeks flushed with rising passion, her focus entirely on the sensations building within her. He shifted his grip, moving his hands from her face to her hips, guiding her movements, deepening the connection between their bodies. He could feel her tightening around him, her pleasure building rapidly, a wave about to crest. "Just... like... that... Master," Taylor gasped, her eyes fluttering closed, surrendering to the relentless climb towards climax.

Taylor vibrated fiercely, her orgasm a powerful wave that washed over David, pulling him further into the moment, sharing in her release. Her cries were sharp and satisfying, a sound of pure, unadulterated pleasure filling the room. He held her close, ensuring she felt safe and secure as the aftershocks subsided, her body trembling against his. Now that Taylor had been serviced, brought to her release with such care and focus, Nicole rolled her eyes at David with mock impatience as she playfully pushed Taylor aside. "Alright, Alright, move over, sis! It's my turn again! You had your moment."

In the next room, Jessica sighed again, louder this time, the sound a little more dramatic than necessary. The sound of Taylor's orgasm, distinct and carried on the air that drifted from the slightly ajar bedroom door, had a… particular effect on her. It was a heady mix of envy, arousal, and the overwhelming, gnawing pangs of pregnancy hormones that made everything feel amplified. She was folding tiny baby clothes, each one a soft, miniature reminder of the life growing inside her, David's child, their child. The sight was supposed to make her feel… fulfilled, nesting, content. Instead, at this precise moment, hearing the sounds of pleasure from the other room, it was making her feel incredibly… left out.

"Oh, for crying out loud," she muttered, the sound barely audible. Here she was, five and a half months pregnant, feeling like a hormonal volcano, stuck with a mountain of laundry while they were having all the fun. The audacious thought popped into her head: "Maybe I should just march in there and demand my share of the attention!"

And with that, the laundry basket might as well have been a declaration of war. Jessica stood up with a snap, the neatly folded onesie landing on the pile with a defiant thump. She marched towards the doorway, her usually petite frame radiating a surprising force. The sound of her footsteps grew louder, a prelude to the storm about to break. Without knocking, she threw open the door, her voice ringing out with a mixture of exasperation and playful anger.

"Alright, you two! That's enough!" she declared, hands planted firmly on her hips. "Get off of him!" She gestured emphatically, adding, "I'm carrying his child, for God's sake! I deserve some attention too! And frankly, I'm tired of folding laundry while you two are having all the fun. It's simply unfair!" The scene she interrupted was definitely… a scene. Nicole, caught mid-ride, froze, her eyes wide with surprise. Taylor, still flushed and slightly dazed, looked up from her sprawled position next to David, a sheepish grin spreading across her face.

David, ever the diplomat, chuckled, a warm, rumbling sound that managed to be both amused and apologetic. He gently disentangled himself and sat up. "Jessica, sweetheart," he said calmly, his voice laced with affection. "I understand. You're right, it's not fair of us to leave you out. But, I was in the middle of putting away the laundry." He gestured towards the pile, a pathetic attempt to justify the situation. "I didn't mean to neglect you."

Jessica narrowed her eyes, her foot tapping impatiently against the hardwood floor. "Oh, is that putting away laundry, David?" she challenged, her voice dripping with playful sarcasm. "Because if that's how you do it, I've definitely been doing it wrong all these years. Maybe I should start folding shirts with my thighs or something." Nicole giggled, quickly stifled by a sharp elbow from Taylor, who was trying (and failing) to maintain a serious expression. "Hush, you," Taylor whispered.

"Maybe you should," David said, a wicked glint entering his eyes. He leaned forward, his voice dropping to a low, suggestive murmur that only Jessica could hear. "I bet you'd be incredibly good at it, Baby girl." "David!" she gasped, though a smile tugged at her lips. "Don't you start with me. I'm supposed to be mad at you, remember?" But the fire in her eyes betrayed her true feelings.

Nicole and Taylor exchanged knowing glances. The tension in the room shifted, morphing from awkward interruption to playful banter. "Mad?" David feigned innocence, his eyebrows raised in mock surprise. "But why, sweetheart? I thought you were just... observing our advanced laundry folding techniques." He winked, and Jessica's resolve crumbled a little further. "Oh, you are impossible," she sighed, the fight draining from her voice. "You know exactly what you're doing."

David stood up, a mischievous grin plastered across his face. He moved towards Jessica, his movements deliberate and sensual. "And what, precisely, is it that I'm doing, baby?" His hands slowly circled her waist, his face inches from hers. Nicole, leaning back against the dresser, seemed content to watch the show, while Taylor started gathering their discarded clothes. "Seducing me," Jessica breathed, her voice barely a whisper. "And it's working."

"Good," David whispered back, his lips brushing against her ear. "Because you know I'll always make time for you." With a burst of strength, David scooped up Jessica, her protests of mock indignation muffled against his shoulder. Still naked, unashamed, and radiating an aura of playful dominance, he began to carry her out of the room.

"But the laundry," Taylor interjected, a hint of amusement in her voice. "What about the laundry, oh mighty laundry folder?" David paused at the doorway, a devilish glint in his eyes. "Consider it… a load too hot to handle. You two can finish it." He blew them a kiss and disappeared around the corner, the sound of Jessica's laughter echoing behind him. It seemed that sometimes, a little bit of chaos was exactly what the doctor ordered. And the laundry? Well, it could wait.

Chapter 35

Radiation and the Tunnel Rat

Jessica, visibly pregnant and radiating a heat that seemed to amplify her discomfort, draped herself across the arm of David's favorite armchair. She fanned herself with a magazine featuring a disturbingly cheerful woman from the Before Times, a relic of pre-EMP advertising for wrinkle cream. "Ugh, it's still hot," she groaned, her voice laden with theatrical suffering. Perched on the armrest, Lucipurr blinked languidly, offering no sympathy, merely observing Jessica's plight with the detached air of feline royalty, seemingly unimpressed by human suffering.

Across the room, David was sprawled on the adjacent couch, enjoying a moment of pampered relaxation. Summer meticulously cleaning his fingernails with a small, specialized tool. David raised an eyebrow. "Jessica, darling," he said, his voice smooth and reassuring, "we're inside. It's practically arctic compared to outside." Jessica shifted, pulling Lucipurr closer. The cat, for her part, settled possessively onto Jessica's growing lap. "I know, Daddy," Jessica whined. "But I can feel it. It's like…radiating through the walls. It's probably bad for the baby."

Summer paused her task, her brow furrowing slightly as she considered Jessica's statement. "That's not really how radiation works, Jess," she began gently, as David chuckled, cutting her off before she could launch into a detailed explanation. "Jessica, my sweet, dramatic Jessica," he said.

"You're worrying about phantom heat waves through these walls? You're going to give Lucipurr here an existential crisis with that kind of fantastical thinking." He gestured towards the cat, who responded by yawning, a wide, pink display revealing a surprisingly concerning number of sharp teeth.

He continued, his voice softening further. "Look, the walls are thick. Very thick. Reinforced. Water-cooled. Triple insulated. They could probably withstand an inferno raging right outside. Not to mention, it's more than thirty degrees hotter outside. That's a huge difference." He paused, leaning forward slightly. "Plus, if you're still melting, you're more than welcome to crank the AC in your room. Each part of the house has its own unit, just for you and your… delicate constitution."

Summer leaned close to David. "Have I told you that I loved you today?" she asked, her voice low and sultry. David smiled back, kissing her with warmth that went deeper than mere affection. "You probably did," he responded, "but I can never hear it enough." Jessica, despite her theatrical pouting, couldn't entirely suppress the small smile that tugged at the corner of her lips. She knew David was teasing. "Fine, Daddy," she conceded, now cradling Lucipurr like a furry, opinionated hot water bottle. "But if the baby comes out pre-cooked, I'm blaming you."

Summer, eyes still sparkling with the moment shared with David, quipped, resuming her manicure with a mischievous glint. "Pre-cooked? Now there's a headline for the apocalypse news. 'Local Daddy's Delightful Daughter Delivered Deliciously Done…' I'm stopping there," she said, dissolving into giggles.

Just then, Jennifer strolled into the living area, wiping grease from her hands with a rag, and wearing a pair of Aidan's old overalls and a comfortable tank top. "What's all the commotion?" she asked, looking around with a curious expression. "And why does it smell faintly of impending doom and burnt toast in here?" "Jessica thinks the baby is being microwaved," David deadpanned, his expression perfectly serious, which only made Summer giggle harder.

Jennifer burst out laughing, a hearty sound that filled the room. "Only you, Jess," she said, shaking her head fondly. "Only you could weaponize existential dread before dinner." She sauntered over to Jessica, who was now attempting to look offended, and playfully ruffled her hair. "Relax, sweetheart. You're tougher than you think. Besides," she added, "Master wouldn't let anything happen to you."

The conversation was interrupted again as Elena entered from the kitchen, her long, dark hair pulled back in a sleek, practical ponytail, carrying a stack of books that looked suspiciously like textbooks. "Someone mentioned impending doom?" she asked, raising an eyebrow, a playful smirk playing on her lips. "I was beginning to think all the excitement had passed me by. Are we talking bandits, rogue government agents, or just Jessica's hormones?" "Hormones with a side of geothermal radiation," Summer clarified dryly. "Ah, the usual Wednesday afternoon then," Elena responded, placing the books on the counter with a solid thud. "I'll get the lead aprons."

Jessica huffed, pushing herself up from the low couch with a dramatic groan. "Fine, laugh it up, you vultures," she muttered, waddling towards the hallway. "But when this kid comes out glowing in the dark, don't come crying to me," she called back over her shoulder. "And I am turning the thermostat down to sixty. You can all wear sweaters."

David watched her go, the fond smile lingering at the corner of his lips. He turned back to the others. "Alright, enough teasing," he said, his voice losing its playful edge. "Jess is sensitive right now, and she's got a point, even if it's… exaggerated." His gaze swept over Summer, Jennifer, and Elena, and then to Tiffany, who had quietly entered and plopped onto the couch, having just returned from somewhere downstairs. "Tiffany, what's the progress on the tunnel?" David asked, cutting straight to one of the most pressing matters.

Tiffany adjusted herself on the cushions, her eyes focused on David. "Halfway there, give or take," she reported, her voice tired but steady. "The kids are working like little badgers, especially Seth and Grace. They seem to think it's a game to see who can remove the most dirt." Summer nodded, sipping her iced tea. "Josh is streamlining the removal process," she added. "He's rigged up a pulley system with buckets. It's not any faster than using the cattle they trained for hauling, but it's a lot less work involved for the people doing the digging." David exhaled slowly. "Good. Keep me updated. We need that tunnel functional as soon as possible."

Elena, who had opened one of her imposing textbooks, spoke up. "Speaking of secure, I've been reviewing the geological surveys of this area. There's a minor fault line a few miles west of here. Nothing major, historically, but the recent… unusual seismic activity, combined with Jessica's 'geothermal radiation,' has me a bit concerned. I want to run some independent tests on the well water and the soil."

David leaned back in his chair, his posture relaxed. "Elena, you're right to be cautious," he said, his gaze sweeping over his wives. "The extreme weather is almost certainly due to ozone layer damage from the CME. The geological anomalies might just be thermal expansion and the water table dropping from the heat, but we need to be sure. Run your tests. Let's get soil samples from different depths and locations, focusing on areas near the fault line and the well." Elena nodded, already making mental notes.

Jennifer chimed in, ever practical despite her playful demeanor. "Master, should Brian and Seo-Yeon help? He's getting pretty good at analyzing soil nutrients for the garden." David smirked. "Yes, Jennifer. Put Brian to work. He likes getting his hands dirty." He paused, "But don't let him work Seo-Yeon too hard."

From the dining room, where she had been quietly observing, Taylor spoke softly, her voice gentle but carrying a quiet weight. "David, do you think we should reinforce the walls of the house and bunkers? If there is seismic activity, even minor, wouldn't it be better to be prepared?"

David's expression softened as he looked at Taylor. "Come here darling," he gestured, pulling her close to his side. "When I designed this house, I knew what was coming. I didn't just build a house; I built a sanctuary, a fortress against anything the world could throw at us." Tiffany and Jennifer sat on the opposite couch, listening as he continued, his voice filled with quiet pride and deep reassurance. "Think of it as… overkill insurance."

He launched into a detailed explanation. "This house isn't just built; it's engineered for survival. You could drop our entire ranch from the stratosphere, and it would remain intact. The foundation goes down fifty feet into solid bedrock, anchored with enough reinforced steel and concrete to build a decent-sized bridge. It's tornado proof, hurricane proof, earthquake proof to a magnitude most of the planet will never experience, radiation proof, flood proof, fire proof, and yes, bullet proof against pretty much anything short of specialized ordnance."

He paused, letting the catalogue of defenses sink in. "And as for the water you mentioned, Elena, don't worry too much. We're tapped directly into two aquifers, 800 feet and 2000 feet deep. They're entirely independent of surface water tables and are fed by ancient, deep reserves. The water table can drop to the center of the earth; we'd still have enough water to open a water park." Tiffany snorted with laughter. "A water park, David? Really?"

David nodded, a genuine smile returning. "Well, maybe not with slides initially, but you get the idea. Point is, water isn't our worry. And the structural integrity? It's not always the shifting or the wind that destroys a house during a storm. Sometimes it's the debris being hurled at it. Tornadoes are a lot more destructive when they're throwing cars and trees at you, or when earthquakes bring down buildings onto others. We can withstand direct impact."

Jennifer, ever the one to push the boundaries with playful questions, interjected, her eyes sparkling. "So, Master, you're saying we could have a meteor shower and still be sipping iced tea in the living room?" David chuckled. "Pretty much, Jennifer," he confirmed. "The photochromatic glass in the windows isn't just bullet-resistant, as you know; it's designed to filter out harmful radiation, intense light, and even some EMP effects. And the entire structure is sealed, with a sophisticated, multi-stage air filtration system that can handle chemical, biological, or radiological contaminants. Radiation? Chemical attacks? Massively destructive weather? Seismic shocks? We're covered."

He paused again, his gaze finding Elena's. "Elena, you want to run those water and soil tests? By all means, go ahead. Don't hesitate. Knowledge is power, even if I'm 99.999% certain everything's fine." He knew the value of independent verification, of addressing every potential threat. "I'll have Little David get you the testing kit and meter. If you need help, ask Alissa, she likes science too. It's good for them to learn how to monitor our environment." Elena smiled, a flash of white teeth against her olive skin. "Thank you, David. I appreciate it. Just a little peace of mind."

But the conversation had, perhaps inadvertently, stirred something beneath the surface of their calm. Taylor, small and usually vibrant, shifted, her brow furrowed. "David," she began, her voice laced with a fragile emotion, "you've taken such good care of us, I almost forgot how bad it is out there." She gestured vaguely towards the distant hills. "I mean, we can't even see the devastation from the valley. It's like we're living in a bubble here. It's... almost unsettling, how normal things are."

A ripple of agreement passed through the room. It wasn't ingratitude; it was a shared feeling of cognitive dissonance. How could life feel so ordinary, the sun warming their faces, the plants growing, the simple rhythm of their days, when unimaginable horror had engulfed the rest of the world? Even Tiffany, typically the picture of unflappable calm, chewed on her lip, her gaze distant. The "normalcy" felt precarious, almost wrong.

David met Taylor's gaze, his expression gentle. "Taylor, don't feel guilty for our security. We worked for this. We prepared." He paused, his hand reaching out to place a reassuring touch on her knee. "And we're not hoarding our resources. We've offered shelter to others, brought Mark and his family here, and are providing support to Lynn and her parents. Besides, our safety is essential for helping others in the long run. We can't do any good if we're vulnerable." It was a pragmatic truth, hard but undeniable.

Taylor hung her head slightly, her voice low. "I'm not ungrateful. I just don't want to lose my grip on reality here." Summer shifted in her seat, her brow furrowed with a different kind of concern, one focused on the macro scale of the tragedy. "David, do you have any projections on the death toll? I hate to ask, but I need to know."

David sighed. "The estimates are… grim, and our scouting missions only seem to confirm it." He spoke the numbers flatly, devoid of hyperbole, which only made them more chilling. "We're probably looking at around 1.8 billion, give or take a few hundred million." He explained the horrific sequence of events that had led to such a number. "The initial wave was the EMP, followed by the grid collapsing, and then the breakdown of society, starvation, and disease. It's a cascading effect."

A wave of stunned silence washed over the room, broken only by the quiet sound of indrawn breaths, small gasps of disbelief and horror. "That's... that's almost a quarter of the world's population," Nicole whispered, her eyes wide, her voice barely audible, "and it's only been four months." The speed of the collapse was as terrifying as the scale. "Yes," David confirmed, his voice regaining its steady, if somber, tone. "And that's just the beginning. The next few years will be critical."

As the devastating number settled over them, the quiet was pierced by the sound of sniffles. Tiffany, despite her usual composure, closed her eyes as a single tear streamed down her cheek, a silent acknowledgment of the unimaginable loss. Jennifer, usually quick with a joke or a light comment, broke down immediately, her face crumpling as she lunged at David, seeking physical comfort from his solid presence. Even Elena couldn't maintain her composure, tears welling in her eyes. "That's an absolute nightmare."

"It's too much," Taylor choked out, her voice muffled against Summer's soft cotton shirt, where she had sought refuge. "How... how will anyone cope with that much death? That much loss?" Her mind reeled, trying to grasp the scale of individual tragedies within that number. "They'll be broken," she whispered, her voice barely audible, articulating the fear that echoed in many hearts. "Everyone will be broken."

Summer gently pulled Taylor back from the embrace, her hands cupping Taylor's face. "David survived this, remember? Alone, for seven years. He was broken too, but he rebuilt himself." It was a simple, powerful truth. David sitting before them was living proof that survival, even after profound loss and trauma, was possible.

Then, Taylor moved, a blur of motion fueled by a sudden, overwhelming surge of raw emotion. She launched herself at David, burying her face in his chest, her small frame trembling against his, her sobs a raw and ragged sound that filled the room more effectively than any scream could have. "How did you do it?" she sobbed, her voice thick with tears and pain. "How did you survive all that, all alone?"

He wrapped his arms around her, his large hand gently stroking her hair, feeling the subtle tremors that wracked her body. "I didn't," David said finally, his voice low, rough around the edges, a confession rather than a boast. "Not entirely." He pulled her back just enough to look into her tear-filled eyes, his expression open and honest. "I had to become someone else, someone… different. I had to shut things down, build walls." He didn't romanticize it. "It wasn't pretty, Taylor." He acknowledged the cost to his own humanity during those long, solitary years.

He could feel Summer's hand on his back, a silent offering of support, a reminder that he wasn't alone now. "But I learned," he continued, his gaze holding hers, intense with purpose. "I learned what mattered. I learned how to survive. And that's what I'm doing now, Taylor. I'm using everything I learned, everything I went through, to make sure you don't have to go through what I went through."

Taylor looked up at David, her eyes glistening with unshed tears, the raw emotion still etched on her face. "I love you," she whispered, the words catching in her throat. "I love you so much, David." David's chest tightened at her words.

He wasn't used to that kind of effusive emotional expression directed at him. He was better with action, with ensuring her needs were met, with building the walls that kept her safe. But Taylor needed more than that right now.

"I love you too, Taylor," he managed, his voice rough around the edges, the words feeling clumsy and inadequate even to his own ears. He pulled her close again, holding her, nuzzling her hair. "More than you know, more than you know." He repeated it, trying to pour the depth of his feeling into the simple phrase. He wasn't built for flowery declarations of love, not yet. But he was learning. For Taylor, and for the others, he would learn.

Suddenly, jarringly, Taylor pulled away from him, her face pale. "Oh God," she gasped, clapping a hand over her mouth. Without another word, she bolted for the bathroom, leaving David sitting there, a knot of immediate anxiety twisting in his gut. The sudden shift was alarming.

Jennifer was already on her heels. "Taylor, honey, what's wrong?" Her voice was a blend of concern and mild exasperation. Jennifer wasn't one for unnecessary drama, and sudden dashes to the porcelain throne tended to fall squarely into that category, though in this world, even mundane events could signal something serious. The unmistakable sounds of retching echoed from the bathroom, followed quickly by Jennifer's soothing reassurances. Summer's hand on David's arm was a welcome, grounding force, her touch steady amidst the sudden uncertainty.

"Give them a minute, David. It's probably just the heat," Summer said, her voice calm, trying to offer the simplest, most benign explanation. But he knew she was also considering other possibilities. Was it just heatstroke from being outside earlier? Simple food poisoning from something overlooked? Or something far more sinister, something related to this sudden increase of radiation that they had been monitoring recently? The last possibility sent a jolt of adrenaline through him.

He stood abruptly, his movement a study in controlled energy, his mind already shifting into crisis management mode. "Elena, go downstairs and get Andrea," he ordered, his voice clipped and efficient, cutting through the lingering emotional tension. "And Summer, find Kayla. I want to know how many iodine tablets we have on hand."

Elena, ever responsive and quick to follow orders, was already moving towards the doorway before he even finished speaking. "Right away, David." He watched her disappear, his gaze already shifting to Summer, his trusted second-in-command. She was a rock in his chaotic world, capable and calm under pressure. "Already on it," Summer replied, her brow furrowed with her own concern, but her voice steady. "I'll check the inventory."

Just as David had anticipated, efficiency was the order of the day. Elena, moving with practiced speed, reappeared almost immediately, bringing Andrea with her. Her black bag, worn and familiar, was already in hand. Andrea escorted Taylor, accompanied by Jennifer downstairs towards the infirmary.

The sudden flurry of activity, the hushed but urgent voices, didn't go unnoticed. In the hallway, a figure emerged from a doorway, wrapped protectively in a blanket. It was Jessica, disturbed from whatever semblance of rest she'd managed to find. "What in the actual hell is going on?" she demanded, clutching the blanket tighter around her. "I finally got the bedroom down to arctic levels, and now everyone's freaking out. What happened?"

David turned towards her, his expression shifting slightly from the steely leader to the worried husband. "Taylor's sick," he explained, keeping it concise. "We don't know if it's the heat or radiation or worse. We're taking precautions." The word "radiation" landed like a small, cold stone. Jessica's sleep-deprived irritation, her sarcasm about the temperature, it all evaporated in an instant, replaced by a very distinct, sharp worry. "Radiation? Seriously? What the heck happened now?" Her voice was suddenly higher, thinner. "Did someone find a reactor core? I swear, if Junior is messing with plutonium in the garage…" Her voice trailed off, the thought too unsettling to finish.

"There is no fucking plutonium here," a voice cut in, firm and slightly exasperated. It was Little David, emerging from the depths of the bunker access, his face streaked with dirt. He wiped a hand across his forehead, leaving a dark smear of grime in its wake. "I'm digging the tunnel, remember?" he reminded them. "And besides, we have rad counters on the roof, Dad. They haven't budged. UV radiation might have been elevated, but not enough to make someone sick."

His gaze then shifted to Jessica. "Hey, Jess," he said, a hint of a smirk playing on his lips, "aren't you always complaining about the heat? Why the blanket? Did the weather suddenly turn into a blizzard in the last five minutes?" Jessica huffed, pulling the blanket even tighter around her, as if daring him to question her sartorial choices. "I turned my room into my own private arctic retreat," she defended, her voice laced with annoyance. "It's the only place I can get some damn relief from this infernal Texas summer. Plus, Luci was starting to pant like a dog. I can't have her overheating."

Little David raised an eyebrow, thoroughly unimpressed by her logic, or perhaps just enjoying the opportunity to poke the bear. "It's less than 70 degrees in the house, Jess," he pointed out dryly. "And if you're going to wrap up in a blanket, why even bother turning on the AC? Seems a little… counterproductive, don't you think?" The smirk returned, wider this time.

Jessica's patience, already frayed by being woken up and the underlying worry, snapped a little. "Look, tunnel rat," she snorted, "I'm pregnant, okay? My body temperature is all over the place." "It's Doctor Tunnel Rat to you," Little David corrected instantly, unfazed, not missing a beat. The grin on his face widened. "The doctorate in Applied Excavation is still pending, but the title is technically accurate." He then pivoted smoothly, already heading towards the kitchen, the immediate argument over, leaving the scientific debate for another time. "I'm grabbing some water before I go back down to the mole kingdom."

Jessica rolled her eyes, the fight draining out of her as quickly as it had flared up. She muttered something under her breath about men and their incessant need to be right. She adjusted the blanket again, the slight chill of the main house now feeling more pronounced to her pregnancy-heightened sensitivity. The desire for her personal, polar climate zone was strong. She turned back towards her room, intent on retreating back into her blissful, self-made winter.

A few minutes later, just as she was settling back into the quiet coolness of her room, a soft knock echoed through the arctic air. Wrapped up like a burrito, she padded over to the door, pulling it open cautiously. "Dirt goblin, what do you want?" she asked, expecting another teasing remark, another scientific counterpoint. Little David didn't say a word this time. He simply stood there, a mug held out towards her. Jessica leaned forward, the scent unmistakable, warm and comforting. Hot chocolate.

She reached out, surprised, taking the mug from his hands. It was a small gesture, unexpected, a peace offering perhaps, or just a simple act of kindness from someone who understood her better than he often let on. "Thanks," she murmured, genuinely touched, before gently closing the door. Leaning against the door, the heavy blanket a comforting cocoon, a genuine smile finally graced Jessica's lips. The warmth of the mug seeped through the blanket, a perfect, soothing contrast to the deliberate coolness of her room. "Okay, tunnel rat," she whispered to herself. "You're alright."

She settled back onto the bed, sighing softly. Luci, her fluffy companion, was already purring contentedly on a pillow nearby. The hot chocolate was perfect, thick, rich, and not too sweet. Just the way she liked it. As she sipped, the brief irritation faded, replaced by a quiet reflection. Her thoughts drifted back to the commotion, to Taylor. David, even in his calm, capable demeanor, had seemed genuinely worried. And Little David, despite his jokes and his practicality, wasn't dismissive either. He'd focused on the radiation aspect, the big scary thing, but he hadn't said "she's fine" about Taylor. She knew her husband and stepson well enough to recognize their subtle cues, the unspoken weight they carried.

A few minutes later, another knock echoed through the chilled air of her room. This time, it was different. More deliberate. It was David. He entered without waiting for an invitation, his presence filling the space with a sense of reassurance, of grounded strength. He closed the door gently behind him, his eyes scanning the room, taking in the cocooned figure on the bed, the mug in her hand. "How are you feeling, Baby?" he asked, his voice dropping to a soft, intimate tone, laced with unmistakable concern. He saw the mug. "Did Junior bring you that?"

Jessica nodded, sipping the warm drink. "Mmhmm," she confirmed, a small smile touching her lips. "He's like his dad." A compliment, simple and true, acknowledging not just the act of kindness but the thoughtful nature they shared. David smiled softly, moving closer, sitting on the edge of the bed beside her. "You're right, he is. He's got a good heart." He chuckled softly. "And how are you really feeling? The heat getting to you?"

Jessica sighed, leaning into his touch. "Honestly? The house is fine, David. You know that. You keep it perfect, as always." She took another slow sip of the hot chocolate, the warmth spreading through her. "It's just... hormones, I guess. One minute I'm boiling, the next I'm freezing. And I get... unreasonable. I snap at Junior, I demand arctic temperatures in my bedroom... I'm a peach." She made a face, a self-deprecating grimace.

David's hand moved from her hair to cup her cheek, his thumb gently stroking her skin, a gesture of deep affection and understanding. "Hey," he said softly, his eyes holding hers. "You're allowed to be hormonal and unreasonable sometimes, we all are." He paused, his smile returning. "And honestly, you're handling apocalyptic pregnancy like a champ. A very sassy, blanket-wrapped champ, but a champ nonetheless." He leaned down and kissed her forehead, a tender, reassuring gesture that spoke volumes. "Besides, Junior can handle a little sass. He gives as good as he gets."

She smiled then, a genuine smile that reached her eyes, chasing away the last wisps of self-recrimination. "He does, doesn't he?" she agreed. "But you're right. He's a good kid. They all are." Her voice turned softer, more reflective. "It's… comforting, knowing they'll be okay, no matter what happens." She gestured around the room. "And thank you," she said, her voice thick with emotion, "for this. For everything."

Just then, the door swung open, nearly scaring Jessica to death. "David! It's Taylor." David stood quickly. "How is she, is she alright?" he asked, his tone serious. "She's not sick." Jennifer stated flatly, her eyes meeting David's. David's breath caught in his throat. "What? What do you mean, she's not sick?" Jennifer took a deep breath, a hint of a smile playing on her lips. "She's pregnant."

Chapter 36

The Well Pump Saga

"You sure about this, Aunt Elena?" Junior asked, his eyes, so like Jennifer's, scanned the perimeter. "Dad said the radiation readings were negligible. Maybe we should just trust the filtration system." Elena sighed. "Trust, but verify, Junior. That's your father's motto, isn't it? Besides," she added with a sly grin, "it's good to get out. I'm starting to feel like a kept woman in the house." Junior chuckled, a rare sound that always warmed Elena's heart. "Okay, okay. Just promise me you won't start lecturing me while we're digging around in the dirt." "No promises." Elena winked. "But I might give you some tips on picking up girls. You know, the ones who aren't your mother."

Junior's face turned a shade of pink. They continued their trek toward the northeast corner of the property, the crunch of their boots on the dry grass the only sound besides the incessant chirping of insects in the dark. Elena, despite her initial joking, was genuinely concerned. The cracks appearing in the earth were multiplying, and though David assured her it was just the drought, a niggling fear persisted. Radiation, even in small doses, was a long-term threat.

They reached the sight of the well, a massive boulder parking the location. Elena eyed it with a mixture of apprehension and determination. "Alright, kiddo. Time to earn your keep. This bad boy needs to move." Junior grinned, cracking his knuckles. "Piece of cake." He positioned himself behind the boulder, bracing his feet. "Ready when you are, Aunt Elena." "Alright, hotshot," Elena said, adjusting her flashlight, "Just remember what your dad always says: 'lift with your legs, not your back.' We don't need you throwing out something before we can even check the water." She rolled her eyes at the half boulder.

Junior grunted with effort, his muscles straining against the weight of the stone. He moved the boulder with surprising ease, pivoting it to the side with a slow, controlled motion, exposing the manhole lid. She gestured towards the opening. "Careful with that thing. Don't want to drop it down there, we'll never get it out," Elena cautioned.

Junior heaved the lid, exposing a dark, gaping tunnel. A wave of cool, earthy air rushed out, carrying with it the scent of damp concrete and something else... something vaguely metallic and unsettling. Elena's worry spiked. The heavy air felt ominous. "Well, that's... inviting," Junior commented, his tone laced with sarcasm. He was clearly picking up on her apprehension. "Ladies first?"

Elena took a deep breath, trying to steady her nerves. "After you, Mr. Muscles. You're the one who's going to be hauling out samples if need be. Just... be careful. And yell if you see anything weird." Junior grinned, grabbing his own flashlight from his belt. "Weird is my middle name, Aunt Elena." He said as he swung himself down into the hole, disappearing into the darkness.

Elena waited, her senses on high alert. The chirping of crickets seemed to amplify the silence. She pulled her pistol from its holster, checking the magazine reflexively. It was unlikely anything dangerous was lurking down there, but

David had drilled them all to be prepared for anything. "Clear!" Junior's voice echoed from the darkness. "Ladder's secure. Feels… damp down here."

"Damp is an understatement, I see," Elena said as she reached the bottom of the ladder, her boots landing with a soft thud on the dirt floor. The air in the underground wellhouse was thick and heavy, clinging to her skin like a humid blanket. The beam of her flashlight danced across the cramped space, illuminating the well pump cap, expansion tank, and the old-fashioned hand pump bolted to the wall. Droplets of condensation glistened on every surface, turning the rough concrete into a shimmering mosaic.

"Smells like a mushroom farm down here," Junior commented, wrinkling his nose. "And… is that rust?" He aimed his flashlight towards the base of the well pump, revealing streaks of orange staining the concrete. "Not good. Rust means oxidation, oxidation means… well, bad things for water quality, I'm guessing."

Junior reached up and flicked off the breaker to the well pump. The low hum that had reverberated through the small space ceased, leaving an even heavier silence in its wake. "Alright," he said, dusting off his hands. "Time to see what's going on inside that metal beast." He grabbed a wrench from his tool belt. "Hopefully, it's something simple. I don't want to have to explain another 'unexpected surprise' to Daddy." He winked. "He's got enough on his plate with Taylor's… condition."

Elena rolled her eyes, though she couldn't help but chuckle. "Don't let him hear you call him 'Daddy' when Jessica isn't around. You know how she gets." She pointed her flashlight at the well cap. "Alright, let's get this thing off. See if Armageddon has decided to take up residence in our water supply."

Junior began working on the bolts that secured the well cap. They were rusty and stubborn, but with a grunt and a final wrench, he managed to loosen them. With both hands, he carefully lifted the heavy metal cap off, revealing the dark, mysterious depths of the well. He peered inside, shining his flashlight down the shaft. "Huh. Looks clean. Surprisingly clean, actually. No mutant alligators, no glowing green sludge… just darkness. And the pump housing looks… fine."

Elena moved closer, her own flashlight joining his. "Really? No rust? No… anything?" She squinted. "Well, I'll be… It does look clean. So, what's causing the rust stains on the outside?" She gestured toward the orange streaks on the concrete. "Maybe it's not coming from the well." Junior shrugged, scratching his head. "Could be rain runoff from… I don't know, the metal casing of the well itself? Maybe the metal is rusting outside the well." He leaned closer, sniffing the air cautiously. "Smells like… well, water. And a faint whiff of disappointment that there aren't any radioactive super-fish down there."

Elena snorted. "Speak for yourself. I was kind of hoping for a three-eyed carp. At least it would give us something interesting to talk about at dinner, besides Taylor's… condition. Okay, so the water looks fine. But looks can be deceiving. We need to know what's going on down below the surface." She tapped her chin thoughtfully. "What if we pull the pump? See if there's anything… clinging to it?"

Junior blinked. "Pull the pump? Elena, that's a submersible pump. It's hundreds of feet down. We'd need some serious equipment, and a whole afternoon, to get that bad boy out. Not to mention, what if we break it? Then we really have a water problem." He imagined the conversation with David. "Hey, Dad, I accidentally broke the well pump while looking for radioactive carp." Yeah, that wasn't going to go well, even without Jessica breathing down his neck.

"But what if it's important, Junior?" Elena persisted, her voice laced with a theatrical urgency. She fluttered her eyelashes, a weapon she knew was devastatingly effective, especially on her younger "nephew." "Think of the children! Think of Jessica's baby! What if this is the key to saving everyone from…from…radioactive mole people!"

Junior groaned, rubbing his temples. "Radioactive mole people are not a thing, Elena. And even if they were, wouldn't a geiger counter be a better defense than a broken water pump?" "Details, details!" Elena waved a dismissive hand. "The point is, we can't just stand here and assume everything is fine. David wouldn't want us to be complacent. He'd want us to investigate! To proactively seek out and neutralize any and all potential…glowing threats!" She struck a heroic pose, nearly tripping over a loose rock.

Junior sighed, defeated. "Alright, alright. But if we unleash a horde of subterranean, bioluminescent rodents on the ranch, I'm blaming you entirely." He knew, deep down, that Elena was right, at least about David. His father would want them to be thorough. Hell, he'd probably be down there with them if he wasn't busy… being David. "That's my boy!" Elena beamed, clapping him on the shoulder. "Now, let's find some rope and some brute force. Luckily, we have plenty of both around here thanks to our… unique family dynamic." She winked, and Junior just shook his head, already regretting this.

A few minutes later, Junior emerged from the work shed dragging a heavy-duty pulley system. "Found this old thing. Probably hasn't been used since before the, you know…" he gestured vaguely at the world outside. "But it should do the trick. And check it out." He pulled a grappling hook from his pocket, a wicked-looking thing forged in the work shed's depths. "I whipped this up last week between digging. Figured it might be useful for… retrieving things." Elena raised an eyebrow. "Retrieving things, huh? Like…evidence of a subterranean conspiracy?"

"Sure, let's go with that," Junior deadpanned. After they returned to the well, he secured the grappling hook on the edge of the service hatch, allowing its rope to hang freely into the wellhouse. After he and Elena returned to the pump, little David tied the pulley system to the rope. With a strained pull, little David managed to pull the t-handle far enough out to get it around the pulley.

"Alright, Elena, stand back. This thing might fight us," Junior said with a smirk, wrapping his hands around the rope. "Remember to bundle that electrical cable as I pull. Don't need any sparks down here." He took a deep breath and started to pull. At first, it felt like pulling a stuck SUV out of mud. But with a steady, rhythmic heave, the pump slowly began to rise. Grunting with exertion, Junior continued, beads of sweat forming on his forehead despite the relative coolness of the well house.

"Looking good, Junior! Just a little more!" Elena coached, carefully gathering the thick black cable, forming a neat coil. "Think of the refreshing water we'll have once this is fixed. Ice-cold showers for everyone!" Junior grunted, the muscles in his arms screaming. The pulley system creaked ominously with each pull. "Ice-cold showers, huh?" he wheezed, pausing to wipe his brow with the back of his hand. "Right now, I'd settle for just...not sweating like a yeti in a sauna."

Nearly an hour in, Elena chuckled, her eyes sparkling in the dim light of the well house. "Almost there! You're doing great. Just think, you're providing hydration for the entire… family. That's like, what, thirty-odd people and three furry freeloaders, not to mention a clowder?" "Cat," Junior corrected automatically, then groaned. "Don't remind me. Luci's been giving me the evil eye lately. Probably knows I'm about to disturb her underground lair." He pulled again, and another section of pipe emerged from the hatch, gleaming wetly. He paused again and tied off the rope, allowing the strain on the pulley to diminish. "Electrical cable, please."

With a practiced hand, Elena bundled another section of electrical cable as Junior struggled to break free the pipe. "You know, for someone who spends so much time shooting things, you're remarkably good at this low-tech stuff." Junior smirked, leaning against the well wall for a moment. "Comes with the territory. Dad always said knowing how to fix things with your bare hands is just as important as knowing how to protect someone. He's a fountain of folksy wisdom like that." He leveraged the pipe off the pump, and vaulted it through the hatch above, deposited it outside with a loud clang.

"Alright, last bit of cable tied off. I only have two questions." Elena quipped. "Number one: Are you alright? And number two: How the hell far down was That!?" Junior chuckled, "I'm alright! I think I'm a full inch taller now than when we started. I can tell you it was down pretty far, because my back is saying things that would make a sailor blush." He paused, peering into the casing. The pump was finally within reach. "Alright...let's see..." He reached down and grabbed the end of the pump, pulling it free.

Junior, sweat plastering his hair to his forehead, finally hauled the last bit of the six-foot pump out of the casing. He leaned it against the wall with a sigh of relief that was almost a groan. "Behold!" he announced, gesturing dramatically at the pump. "The stainless steel savior! Or, as I like to call it, the reason my spine feels like it's been through a meat grinder."

Elena circled the pump, her brow furrowed. "Well, it looks fine." She tapped it thoughtfully with a manicured nail. "You know, if you squint, it kind of looks like a giant stainless steel tampon. Just...industrial strength." Junior snorted, then winced. "Please, Elena. I'm trying to forget my back pain, not compound it with… that image." He wiped his brow with the back of his hand. "Let's get it examined before we start making jokes about its resemblance to feminine hygiene products."

Elena carefully filled a sterile vial with water draining from the pump, labeling it meticulously. "Alright, water sample one secured. Now, for the other water sample." She gestured towards the archaic hand pump next to them with a sigh. "Gotta compare apples to...slightly rusty apples, I guess."

Junior grabbed his own vial and filled a secondary sample from the hand pump. He grunted as the old pump complained with each stroke. "You know," He huffed out, "For all the tech we have around here, sometimes you just need a good ol'fashioned arm workout to get the job done."

He handed her the vial, his face flushed. "Alright, water sample number two: Armageddon edition. So," he cracked his knuckles, "now what? I'm starting to think that getting the pump back down there is going to be worse than getting it up." Elena chewed on her lip, her mind already racing through potential issues. "Well, we can't just leave it sitting here. Let's get both samples back to the lab for analysis. Then… hmmm. You know, this whole thing got me thinking. David is a fan girl for redundancy, right?"

She glanced at Junior, who was already nodding. "Of course. He plans for everything. Even stuff that seems like a complete waste of time." "Exactly! So… spare well pumps? Does Daddy Dearest have any tucked away in his magical fort?" Elena asked, her eyes gleaming with a mixture of hope and amusement. Junior held up four fingers, not saying a word.

Elena scoffed, rolling her eyes but a grin playing on her lips. "Figures. Four spares, of course." She shook her head. "Okay, new plan. Instead of wrestling this thing back into the earth's digestive system, let's grab one of those spares. A fresh pump will, at the very least, give us a baseline for future water quality, right? And," she added with a conspiratorial wink, "it'll give us a chance to inspect this one properly back in the lab. Who knows what horrors lie within?"

Junior straightened up, relief evident in his posture. "Are you sure that's the right call? I mean, won't David want us to… I don't know… appreciate the original pump's… character? He can be a little sentimental about that kind of stuff, you know." Elena snorted, the sound echoing slightly in the confined space of the well house. "Sentimental about a well pump, Junior? Really? Has David started having pillow talk with the generator belts too? I mean, I love the man, but sometimes his… fixations… are a little out there."

She paused, tapping a finger against her chin. "No, David will appreciate the initiative. That's the key phrase here, sport. He's all about proactivity, about anticipating problems before they become… problems. And," she added, lowering her voice, "between you, me, and the rusty ladder, I'd rather face a hoard of feral dogs than tell him we broke the well pump because we weren't careful enough getting it out."

The thought of David's gentle, yet intensely focused, gaze analyzing a broken piece of crucial infrastructure sent a shiver down her spine. He wouldn't be angry, not exactly. More… disappointed. And for Elena, a woman who thrived on David's approval, disappointment was far worse than any yelling. "Think of it this way," she continued, her voice regaining its usual playful tone. "We're simply optimizing preventative maintenance. It's like… rotating a full sized spare. Now, disconnect the power leads, before we all end up looking like rejected science fair projects."

Junior, already halfway through removing the power leads, chuckled. "You always know how to put things, Elena. Okay, leads are off. Now what? I am really feeling this in my lower back, by the way." He winced, stretching his back. "Teenage mutant ninja well pump removal is not good for my spine." "It's a very good thing we have a team of expert massage therapists on call then," Elena replied, a mischievous glint in her eye as she playfully bumped Junior's shoulder. "Tanya will have you feeling like a million bucks… after she's done scolding you about your posture, of course."

With the pump clumsily resting between them, they started the short trek towards the garage. "How heavy is that thing anyway?" Elena asked, looking at the pump resting on his shoulder. Little David considered a moment before answering. "Probably ninety or a hundred pounds," he answered. Elena furrowed her eyebrows. "That should be nothing to you, why was it so hard?

"Ninety pounds is nothing," Junior retorted, puffing out his chest a little. "But you forgot the fun part! First, imagine holding that weight above your head while balancing on one leg because the well housing is smaller than my shoe size. Then, try disconnecting all of those discharge pipes, that adds a lot of weight too. And then, picture the unrelenting suction of the water trying to pull it back down. It's like fighting a liquid gremlin that really, really wants to keep its pump!"

Elena stopped in her tracks, her hand flying to her forehead with a dramatic flourish. "Oh, Junior, you absolute champion! You're right, I completely forgot about the tunnel.

That explains… everything." She gave him a sympathetic, if slightly amused, look. "You have been working non-stop."

She fell into step beside him again, her voice softening. "Look, you should have said something. You know we wouldn't have asked you to do this if we knew you were already pushing yourself to the limit." She paused, thinking for a moment. "Actually… scratch that. David probably would have still made you do it. He's got this… efficiency-driven, benevolent dictator thing going on. But I wouldn't have made you do it, understood?"

She reached out and gently squeezed his bicep. "Alright, hero of the hour, let's get this pump back to the garage, and then you are officially off duty for the rest of the day. Tanya gets you first, then Seo-Yeon. I will personally ensure you get a full body massage and a nap the length of the Lord of the Rings trilogy. Sound good?"

As they approached the garage, Elena spotted David near the entrance. Her stomach did a little flutter of anxiety. She composed herself, trying to project an air of nonchalant competence as they drew closer.

"David, darling," she called out, her voice light and breezy. "We've retrieved the pump! Junior here was a total beast, hauling it out of the well like it was a wet noodle. Though, he might need some TLC from our resident massage experts afterward. Tunnel digging and heavy lifting don't exactly mix, apparently."

David turned, his gaze, as always, intense and all-encompassing. He scanned Elena, then Junior, and finally, the pump itself. Elena could practically feel his mind cataloging every detail, every possible issue, every potential solution. "Why did you remove the pump, did it malfunction?"

Elena plastered a smile on her face, hoping to preempt any of David's characteristic deep dives into the minutiae of well pump mechanics. "Well, darling," she began, her voice laced with a playful tone, "it wasn't exactly 'broken,' per se. More like... undergoing a preemptive spa day. I just wanted to take a peek, make sure everything's shipshape down there. You know, future-proofing and all that." She fluttered her eyelashes for emphasis. "Plus, I thought it was a good idea to get a sample from the source."

Little David, still nursing the twinge in his back, chimed in with a weary sigh. "She wanted to see the impeller. And the stator. And the, uh... all the other bits and bobs." He punctuated his statement with a roll of his eyes that only Elena could see.

David's expression remained unreadable for a moment, before a hint of amusement flickered across his face. "I see," he said slowly, his voice calm and even. "So, no actual malfunction. Just a... preventative investigation. Excellent. I appreciate the initiative, Elena." He reached out, brushing a stray strand of hair from her face. The casual affection was a subtle way of reassuring her, of letting her know he wasn't displeased.

He then turned his attention to Junior, his expression softening slightly. "Son, put that pump on the corner of the platform there. And be careful." After Junior complied, wincing slightly as he straightened, David said, "Alright, your back is bothering you. Go inside. Tanya and Seo-Yeon are waiting for you in your room. Consider yourself officially off-duty for the day."

Junior didn't argue. He knew arguing with David about his health was a fruitless endeavor. "Yes, sir. Thanks, Dad," he mumbled, already heading back towards the main house. He knew exactly what Tanya and Seo-Yeon had planned for him, and honestly, a massage from them sounded pretty good right now.

As Junior disappeared into the house, David pulled out his radio. "Aidan, come in. Aidan, this is David." A crackle of static followed before Aidan's voice, clear and concise, filled the airwaves. "Aidan here, Dad. What's up?" "I need you to grab one of the smaller well pumps from the storage bunker. One of the 30-gallon pumps should do. Bring it to the northeast well. Elena and I need to get it installed." There was a momentary pause. "Understood. ETA fifteen minutes."

David clipped the radio back onto his belt and turned to Elena, his blue eyes, sharp and observant, meeting her own. The late afternoon sun cast long shadows, turning the already red Texas earth a deeper crimson. The air hung heavy and still. Elena, ever the curious one, didn't waste a second. "David," she began, her brow furrowed slightly, "why do we even have so many spare well pumps? It seems… excessive, even for you." She gestured at the pump Junior had set aside, its metal casing gleaming dully in the fading light. "I mean, this one looks practically brand new."

David tilted his head, his gaze drifting momentarily towards the horizon. "Elena," he began, his voice calm and measured, "you need to think of this… not just in terms of now, but in terms of forever. This well," he gestured towards the giant half boulder, still sitting near the access hatch, "taps into an aquifer. It will likely be here long after we are all gone."

He turned back to her, his autistic mind already racing to calculate the odds and possibilities. "Pumps, inherently, wear out. They're mechanical devices subjected to constant use. Without maintenance, they fail. With maintenance, they still fail, eventually. So, let's quantify this, shall we?" He paused, his eyes twinkling with a hint of amusement.

"The average lifespan of a well pump, with reasonable maintenance, is roughly 25 to 30 years. However, that lifespan decreases dramatically if something goes wrong; a power surge, debris clogging the intake, a sudden drop in water level. We have one pump in place. We have four spare pumps. That means, hypothetically, we can maintain a reliable water source from this specific well for another hundred and forty years. Assuming, of course, we don't encounter unforeseen disasters."

He stepped closer, lowering his voice slightly. "But let's be even more conservative. Let's say we only get twenty years out of each pump, due to unforeseen circumstances. That's still a century. A century of fresh, clean water. In a world where access to potable water will likely become a very valuable commodity, that's not just 'excessive,' Elena. That's foresight."

He closed the distance between them, his large hand gently cupping hers. The air, thick with the scent of dry grass and dust, seemed to still around them. He watched her, his gaze intense, taking in the elegant curve of her jaw, the slight furrow in her brow, the way her dark eyes reflected the setting sun.

"Doesn't my provocative beauty enjoy her hot showers?" he asked, his voice a soft murmur only she could hear. "The feel of clean, cool water cascading over her skin, in the luxury of her own pool?" He continued, as he pulled her body gently toward his. "Don't you want me to take care of you forever?" His breath tickling her ear. "I'm not modest, my darling. I'm excessive. And even though I've never gotten you a bouquet of roses, is this not better?" He was right. This, the stability, the security, the unwavering dedication, was far more valuable than any fleeting romance. It was a promise, a commitment that resonated deep within her soul. And, yes, she did love long, hot showers.

As Elena's lips touched David's, a familiar sound cut through the quiet. Aidan cleared his throat. They broke apart, Elena flushing slightly, though it was more from the intensity of David's gaze than embarrassment at being caught. Aidan stood a few feet away, the porch lights forming a halo around his figure. He held a brand new pump over his shoulder, the metal gleaming. "Got the replacement, Dad," he said, handing it over. "Where do you want this one?" he asked, pointing at the used pump.

David took the new pump, the weight seeming insignificant to him. "Take it into the garage, Aidan. Disassemble it, check the impeller, the wiring, everything. I want it cleaned and like new for reinstallation. Document everything you find." Aidan nodded, hoisting the old pump back onto his shoulder. "Will do. Let me know if you need anything else." He turned and headed back towards the main house.

David watched him go for a moment, then turned back to Elena. "Let's get this installed. I promise, a long, hot shower awaits you." He winked, a hint of mischief in his eyes. They approached the service hatch, the metallic tang of the well water already in the air. David surveyed the scene, the haphazard pile of stainless steel discharge pipes mocking his meticulous nature. "Junior's enthusiasm often outpaces his...organization," he murmured to Elena, a wry smile tugging at his lips. "A trait I seem to have passed down, alas."

Elena chuckled, a melodic sound that always managed to soothe him. "He was trying to be efficient, David. Just...a different definition of efficient than yours, perhaps." She lightly touched his arm. "He did get the job done. And he collected excellent water samples." David turned his full attention to Elena, his gaze intense. "And what were you doing while my Herculean son was wrestling with that pump, my love? Admiring his physique?" He raised an eyebrow, a playful smirk dancing on his lips. Elena laughed, swatting playfully at his arm. "Don't be ridiculous. I was coiling the electrical cable, making sure it was neatly out of the way."

David chuckled, a rich sound that echoed slightly in the confined space of the well house. "Coiling the electrical cable, you say? A noble pursuit, indeed. But I trust you were also ensuring young Junior didn't strain himself too much, my dear?" He gently cupped her cheek, his thumb tracing a soft line along her jaw. "Though I wouldn't mind a little of that benevolence directed my way later."

Elena leaned into his touch, her eyes sparkling with affection. "You always get your share, David. You know that." She glanced at the pump, a frown creasing her brow. "We're going to need to get those pipes reconnected as we lower the pump. It's not something we can easily manage with just the two of us." "You're right. A third pair of hands would be beneficial. Someone to feed us the pipe sections. Less chance of dropping anything into the abyss." He reached for his radio, clipping it to his belt. "Safety first. Always."

He keyed the microphone. "Brian, this is David. Are you available?" A crackle of static, then Brian's voice, clear and cheerful. "Go for Brian." "I need your assistance at the northeast well. Elena and I are about to install a new pump, and we need a third person to hand down the discharge pipes as we lower it. Can you spare some time?" "Sure thing, Dad. Give me five minutes. Anything else I should bring?" "Just yourself and a pair of work gloves. We have everything else we need here, and tell Seo-Yeon I said hello. Brian chuckled. "Will do, Dad. See you in a few."

Chapter 37

The Goodfellow Encounter

"Alright," David began, his voice calm and measured, "Elena, you've got the floor. Report on the water and soil samples." Elena consulted her notes. "Good news, everyone. I took samples from both wells last night, as well as several soil samples in a fifty-foot radius. The radiation levels are normal, and the water quality is consistent with previous readings. No sign of contamination or… anything out of the ordinary." A collective sigh of relief rippled through the room. "Excellent," David nodded. "Aidan, how are the pumps running?"

Aidan grinned. "Like a charm, Dad, good as new." David nodded, turning to Elena. "Elena, Brian and Junior, good work on getting the pumps switched out. Even though it was unnecessary, a little preventative maintenance is never a bad thing. Good initiative." Jennifer, leaning against the arm of David's chair, smirked. "Speaking of Junior, our little commando is officially on forced vacation today. No weapons maintenance, no patrol duty, no nothing. Go enjoy your day, son. Get your chill on, maybe even talk to a girl."

Little David, usually stoic and focused, furrowed his eyebrows. "Mom! Seriously? Who am I going to talk to? Everyone here is either taken, family, or underaged?" "Hey," David chuckled, "I'm sure you can think of something, Junior. You have my blessing." Little David leaned over to Aidan, whispering in his ear.

The conversation shifted to the ongoing tunnel excavation. Kayla provided an update. "The tunnel is progressing smoothly. As you stated, most of the soil we're digging through is backfill from the bunker construction. It's already churned up, so it's much easier to work with. We're filling the Hesco barriers and sandbags as we go. Should be done in a few weeks, at most." "Good work," David said, satisfaction evident in his voice. "Coordination is key, that's the kind of organization we need."

Suddenly, a cough broke the relative calm. Clarence, his brow furrowed, spoke up. "So, David, all this talk about family, and the future... how many folks are... uh... expecting?" A hush fell over the room, and all eyes turned to David. He surveyed his wives, a slow smile spreading across his face. "Well, Clarence," David said, drawing out the words for dramatic effect, "as of this morning, we have three confirmed pregnancies. Taylor here is about six weeks along. Alissa is about two and a half months along, and Jessica is due at the end of September."

A collective gasp rippled through the room, followed by a flurry of congratulations and excited chatter. Tanya rushed to Taylor's side, gently touching her stomach. Margaret, Lynn's perpetually quiet mother, spoke up. "Well, my goodness... that's... wonderful, David. You're certainly... building a strong family."

Clarence, however, looked utterly bewildered. "Three? All at once? Good heavens, David, you're a machine!" David simply chuckled, unfazed by Clarence's astonishment. "Just doing my part, Clarence. But, I'm not responsible for Alissa's pregnancy, that's Aidan's doing."

Margaret, ever practical, piped up again. "Perhaps we should convert one of the guest rooms in the garage into a nursery? We have a few that aren't being used. Plenty of space for cribs and such." "That's a wonderful idea, Mom," Lynn said, squeezing her mother's hand. "We can start clearing one out this afternoon."

As the women began to discuss nursery themes and color patterns, Little David tapped on David's shoulder. "Dad," he said, his voice low, "about that vacation..." David raised an eyebrow. "Yes, Junior?" "Well," Little David shifted his weight, "I was thinking… instead of just… chilling… maybe I could take the Beast out for a patrol? See if anyone needs help in the neighboring towns? Check for supplies, you know, 'scouting'?"

Jennifer groaned. "Oh, here we go. I knew relaxing was too much to ask." "It's smart thinking, Jennifer," Elena countered, "He's just thinking strategically. It has been a while since we had a good supply run. Plus, it'd be good to see how things are going?" "Maybe," David stroked his chin, considering. "It's not a bad idea, Junior, but I'm not letting you go out there alone. It's too dangerous, even for you. Someone has to volunteer to go out with you, and I mean volunteer, not be asked."

Little David's face fell. He scanned the room, his gaze landing on Aidan, then Josh, then even Seth, but they all skillfully avoided eye contact. Finally, a voice broke the silence. "I'll go." All heads swiveled to see Nicole standing near the doorway, her expression determined. "I could use a break from the ranch. Besides, someone needs to keep Junior from getting too excited. I wouldn't mind seeing what the towns look like, maybe we can even find a few more women to bring back here." Before David could respond, Jessica kicked him with her foot, shaking her head.

Little David's eyes widened slightly. "Seriously? You'd come with me?" Nicole nodded. "Someone's got to keep you out of trouble. Besides, it'll be good to stretch my legs. We can leave after breakfast." Jennifer smirked. "Well, isn't that convenient. You get to get out of the house, and get some alone time with Nicole. You're a smooth operator, kiddo."

Little David flushed slightly, but before he could defend himself, he caught David's eye. "Junior," David said, his voice unusually soft. "Are you comfortable with this? With Nicole going with you?" Little David hesitated, chewing on the inside of his cheek. "I… well, yeah. I mean, it's cool and all, but…" He struggled to articulate his unease. "No offense, Nicole, but… you're not exactly a… a hardened survivor type, you know? It's dangerous out there."

Nicole's smile faltered slightly. She stepped further into the room, her gaze meeting Little David's. "What do you mean by that?" Little David shuffled his feet. "It's just… you're… nice. You're sweet. You're… not like Mom and Elena, or Summer. No offense." He winced, realizing how clumsy that sounded. Nicole laughed, a genuine, warm sound that filled the room. "None taken, Junior. I get it. You think I'm all sunshine and smiles. But you forget, honey, I was in the military, too. Just like Elena, just like Summer. And your dad was my senior."

A murmur went through the room. "I… I'm sorry Nicole, I guess I forgot," little David said, apologetically.

Nicole waved a dismissive hand. "It's not something I advertise. But it's the truth. I know how to handle myself, Junior. I know how to shoot. I know tactics. I know how to survive. I just… I prefer being a mother now." She winked. "But don't think the sweet smile means I can't handle a weapon. Besides, you and David would never let any one of us skip training."

Junior looked at Nicole with newfound respect, his initial apprehension melting away. "Oh. Wow. Okay. I… I guess it's okay then." He ran a hand through his hair, a nervous habit he'd picked up from David. "So, uh… Goodfellow Air Force Base. Think it's a good place to scout, Dad?"

David, pulled from his inner musings, tilted his head. "Goodfellow? Potentially. It's a military installation, so expect security measures, potentially active resistance. But intelligence gathering is paramount. How long do you anticipate being gone?" Junior shrugged, his youthful eagerness shining through again. "Don't know, Dad. Maybe a day? Two, tops. I just wanna see what's left. Maybe there's some intel, some supplies… something useful."

David's brow furrowed slightly. "A day is optimistic. Prepare for the worst, Junior. Assume it will take several days. Take extra provisions, weapons, and fuel. And Nicole," he turned his gaze to her, a spark of concern flickering in his eyes, quickly masked by his usual stoic expression. "Are you certain you're comfortable with this? It's been a while since you've been off the ranch."

Nicole met his gaze, her expression softening. "David, honey, I appreciate the concern. But I could use some fresh air. Some perspective." She paused, her eyes twinkling mischievously as she glanced towards an imagined audience. "Plus, let's be honest, a little character development never hurt anyone, right?" The women chuckled, understanding Nicole's unspoken desire to reclaim a bit of her pre-motherhood identity. Even David couldn't deny his wives the need for some semblance of personal fulfillment.

As Junior started gathering his gear, weapons and ammo, Nicole followed him, a hint of playful energy in her step. "Alright, Mr. Future Apocalypse Explorer," she teased, bumping his shoulder playfully, "What are you really hoping to find out there? Besides intel, supplies, and… I don't know, a working gumball machine?"

Junior stopped, slinging a rifle over his shoulder, a serious look replacing his usual grin. "Honestly, Nicole? I want to see if there are any other survivor groups out there. Not just scavenging bands, but organized communities. People we could… work with." "Work with?" Nicole raised an eyebrow, intrigued. "As in…?" "As in, maybe bring back survivors." He gestured around the armory, implicitly referencing the fortified ranch and its well-stocked bunkers. "We have the resources, the security… hell, we have enough room in the apartment bunker for at least five or seven more families. It feels... wrong, being so self-sufficient while others are probably starving or fighting each other over scraps."

He paused, fidgeting slightly, his gaze drifting towards the floor. "Plus... and don't tell anyone I said this, okay? But... we're mostly family, right? I mean, yeah, you're all amazing," he quickly added, looking up at Nicole with genuine warmth, "but we're still basically an extended family.

That's not good for the future. We need to diversify the gene pool a little, you know?"

Nicole threw her head back and laughed, the sound echoing in the confined space. She hadn't expected such a pragmatic and, dare she say, responsible thought process from the young man. "Wow, Junior. You're thinking way ahead. Resource management, genetic diversity… You sound like a miniature David."

A small, almost imperceptible smirk tugged at the corner of Junior's mouth. For him, being compared to his father was the ultimate compliment. He straightened his shoulders, a newfound confidence radiating from him. "So, are you ready or what?" he asked, his voice regaining its usual playful tone. "Come on, let's see if we can find a group of people who aren't completely insane. It'll be like 'Survivor: Apocalypse Edition,' but with less backstabbing and more… well, hopefully more cooperation."

Nicole pushed herself off the doorframe, falling into step beside him as they headed towards the garage. "Alright, Mini-David, lead the way. But before we go full-on humanitarian mission, shouldn't we, you know… ask the David about this? I mean, it is his ranch we're potentially opening up to strangers."

Junior stopped dead in his tracks, his expression hardening. "No," he said firmly. "I'm not asking permission. Dad's got a lot on his plate right now. Between Taylor being pregnant, Jessica in a few months, and Margaret trying to coordinate turning that guest room into a goddamn nursery, he's already stressed. Plus, he's in the middle of that meeting.

We have a plan, we have the skills, and we know the risks. We don't need his permission."

Nicole stared at him, surprised by the vehemence in his voice. "Okay, okay, calm down. I just thought… you know, it's a pretty big decision. Potentially life-altering for everyone." "You're right," he mumbled, the playful tone gone. "I'm sorry. That came out wrong. It's just… I saw what happened with Kris. I saw the look on Dad's face after… after he had to deal with that. I don't want him to have to do that again. Especially now, with everything else."

He finally met her eyes, his own filled with a mixture of determination and a raw, underlying fear. "It's not about disobeying him, Nicole. I respect Dad more than anyone. But he can't do everything. We have to be able to take initiative, to protect what he's built here. And if that means making a decision without him breathing down my neck, then that's what I have to do."

"Alright, alright," Nicole said, her voice calm and reassuring. "I get it. You're right, we can handle this. We are capable. And David trusts us." She gave him a small smile, hoping to ease the tension etched on his face. "So, no permission slip required. Let's just… try to keep it a need-to-know situation, okay? Less for him to worry about." She turned and strode towards the armory.

Inside the armory, she grabbed her Beretta, checking the magazine and ensuring the chamber was clear. Then, she grabbed her AR-15. "Alright, partner," she said, turning back to Junior. "Weapon of choice?" Little David smiled, holding up his AR-10 and turning to show his father's P320 X-Ten. "Show off," Nicole teased, a small smile playing on her lips despite the seriousness of their mission. "Alright, Mr. 'I need the biggest gun.' Just try not to take down any low-flying aircraft, okay?"

As the Transit pulled onto the road, Nicole glanced at Junior, his brow furrowed in concentration as he gripped the steering wheel. "So," Nicole said, breaking the silence, "San Angelo… how long are we talking?" Junior blinked, momentarily distracted. "Uh, about three and a half hours, give or take. Depends on how bad the roads are." He tapped the gas pedal, the Transit rumbling as it skirted a particularly mangled sedan.

Instead of heading north towards Brownwood and the direct route to San Angelo, Junior turned south, towards Fredericksburg. Nicole raised an eyebrow, a playful glint in her eyes. "Going scenic on me? Thought you were all about efficiency, Mr. Weapons Expert." Junior shrugged, keeping his eyes on the road. "The southern route's a little longer, but the terrain is more open. We'll have better visibility. Less chance of… surprises." Nicole grinned, leaning back in her seat. "Surprises, huh? Well, I'm always up for a little excitement. Besides," she added, a twinkle in her eye, "we'll get to see more this way. Fredericksburg is supposed to be beautiful, even… well, like this."

A few minutes of comfortable silence passed, punctuated only by the rumble of the engine and the occasional crunch as the tires rolled over debris. "You know," Nicole began, breaking the quiet again, "I've been wondering something." Junior glanced at her, his brow furrowed slightly. "What's that?" "Being one of your dad's children, with so many wives... what's that like, from your perspective? I mean, you've kinda grown up with it," she asked, genuinely curious.

Junior thought for a moment, his hands tightening on the steering wheel. "It's... normal, I guess. I mean, it's all I've ever known. Sometimes it's chaotic, for sure. Especially when everyone's trying to get Dad's attention at the same time." He chuckled softly. "But mostly... mostly it's good. Everyone loves each other, even if it's in weird ways sometimes. And there's always someone there for you. Someone to talk to, someone to help you out. It's like having a whole team of moms." He paused, considering. "Not like the Lynn kind, though. I know it's probably strange for other people, but... it works for us. Dad has this way of rallying people together."

Nicole nodded, absorbing his words. "That makes sense. And your... feelings about it? No resentment? No weirdness?" Junior took a deep breath, his expression becoming a little more serious. "When I was younger... yeah, there was some weirdness. I was always waiting for the other shoe to drop, you know? Waiting for one of them to get jealous and try to tear everything apart, start some crazy in-fighting. I mean, you hear about that kind of thing all the time, right? Catfights, drama, backstabbing... I figured it was just a matter of time before it happened to us."

He glanced at Nicole, a wry smile tugging at the corner of his lips. "That's probably why I avoided relationships for so long. I didn't want to bring anyone else into that potential mess. I figured it was only a matter of time before the whole thing imploded. Then... well, it just never did." He shrugged. "They're weird, but they're our weird."

He paused, his gaze fixed on the long stretch of abandoned highway ahead. "I kind of see it like... like a solar system." Nicole raised an eyebrow. "A solar system?" "Yeah," Junior continued, warming to the analogy. "Dad's the sun, obviously. He's the center of everything, the source of all the energy and warmth. And each of his wives... they're the planets. Different sizes, different orbits, different compositions, but all revolving around him."

Nicole smiled. "You'll have to tell me which planet we all are, sometime." David chuckled. "Point is, they're all different, but they all work together. Some rotate counterclockwise, some even have rings, but none of them try to be their own sun." He glanced at Nicole again, his expression serious. "And after all these years, none of them have collided. That's the part that always surprised me. No cosmic explosions, no planetary wars. Just... a perfectly synchronized solar system."

Nicole was genuinely surprised by Junior's mature perspective. It was easy to forget that despite his age, he possessed an understanding far beyond his years. "Wow, Junior," she said softly. "That's... incredibly insightful. I wouldn't have expected you to see it that way." Then, Junior, without taking his eyes off the road, casually asked, "So, Nicole... what's it like, being one of Dad's wives?"

Nicole blinked, a little startled by the abruptness of the question. "What do you mean?" "I mean," Junior elaborated, "You joined the... the solar system, relatively late, right? After everything was already established. Plus, having kids right away. What was that like?" Nicole chuckled, a fond smile gracing her lips. "You don't miss much, do you?" She thought for a moment, considering how to articulate the experience. "Honestly, it was…surreal. Terrifying, exciting, confusing, and surprisingly… comforting, all at once."

She leaned forward, resting her elbows on her knees. "Being friends with Taylor definitely helped. We had each other's backs, no matter what. Going into it together made the whole thing less daunting. Less lonely, for sure" She sighed, thinking about the early days. "And yeah, I got pregnant immediately. So, a lot of the initial shock was overshadowed by baby preparations. It was…intense. Diapers and morning sickness became my reality pretty quickly."

Nicole sat quietly for a moment, watching the rusted scenery pass. "David has a way of making each of us wives feel like we're the only one. Not because he separates us, but because you never feel like you're getting a piece of David, it always feels complete and whole. Does that make sense?" "It actually does," Junior replied, nodding slowly. "He's like that with us as well. Never seems divided or distracted." He paused, then shifted gears, his voice taking on a more inquisitive tone. "So, what about my mom? What's your opinion of her?"

Nicole leaned back in her seat, considering the question. "Your mom… she's fascinating," Nicole began, choosing her words carefully. "She's the most unburdened of the wives, I think. She has no shame or regret about her love for David, or about any of us, really. She's just… happy. Comfortable in her own skin." Junior chuckled, a hint of fondness in his voice. "Yeah, that's Mom. Always been like that." Nicole continued, "And I think, and this is just my opinion, that Jennifer is much smarter than people realize. She's probably one of the smartest women I've ever met."

Junior's eyebrows shot up in surprise. "Really? You think so?" He seemed genuinely taken aback by the statement. "I mean, I know she's smart, but smarter than… Aunt Tiffany? Aunt Summer? Aunt Elena?" Nicole nodded emphatically. "Absolutely. Tiffany is strategic, Summer is perceptive, and Elena is brilliant in a very intellectual way, but Jennifer… she has this incredible emotional intelligence, this ability to read people and situations that's just uncanny. She understands motivations and dynamics on a level that's almost intuitive. Plus, she's a great gamer, you don't get to that level without excellent mental acuity."

She paused, thinking back to countless conversations with Jennifer, moments where she'd cut through the noise and zero in on the heart of the matter with laser-like precision. "She just doesn't always show it, if that makes sense. She's playful and sensual, and people tend to underestimate her because of that. But trust me, there's a lot more going on behind those eyes than most people realize."

Junior tapped his fingers on the steering wheel, mulling over Nicole's words. "I guess I never really thought about it that way. I always just saw her as…Mom. You know? Fun, loving, a little wild sometimes…" Nicole smiled. "Exactly. She embraces life, without reservation. But that doesn't mean she's not incredibly sharp. I think she's able to be so carefree because she's so intelligent. She knows what's important, she knows who she is, and she doesn't waste time worrying about what other people think." "Wow," Junior said softly, still processing the information. "That's… that's a new perspective, for sure. I'll have to pay more attention next time. See if I can pick up on what you're saying."

He glanced out the window, noticing the familiar green highway signs indicating they were nearing San Angelo. "Speaking of smart, we're almost there. Ready to see what this ghost town has to offer?" Nicole reached over and squeezed his arm reassuringly. "Ready as I'll ever be. Just remember what David said, we are not going to try and save the world. We are here to make contact, get information, and get back home."

As they approached the city limits, the Ford Transit rumbled over cracked asphalt, passing abandoned vehicles that were baking in the relentless Texas sun. The air hung heavy with the oppressive heat, broken only by the occasional gust of wind that stirred up dust devils in the deserted streets. San Angelo felt eerily silent, devoid of the usual sounds of traffic and human activity. "Damn," Junior muttered, his voice low. "He wasn't kidding. This place is a tomb." Nicole scanned their surroundings, her hand resting on her pistol. "Keep your eyes peeled. Just because it's quiet doesn't mean it's safe. We need to find a vantage point."

They drove slowly through the deserted streets, passing boarded-up storefronts and empty houses. The few cars they encountered were either stripped bare or had clearly been abandoned in haste, their doors left open and their contents scattered across the seats. "I'm betting most people bugged out," Junior said, his gaze sweeping across the desolate landscape. "Either headed west towards the lakes, hoping for water and fish, or east towards the Air Force Base, looking for some kind of organized response." Nicole nodded. "The Airforce Base is the logical destination for survivors here, agreed." She pointed to a four-story bank building in the distance. "That looks like a good spot to get a lay of the land. Let's check it out."

Junior steered the Transit towards the bank, carefully maneuvering around the abandoned vehicles. He parked in the shade of a nearby oak tree, its leaves already starting to brown from the heat. "Alright, let's gear up," he said, grabbing his go-bag from the back seat. Nicole mirrored his actions, adjusting her AR-15 and securing her Beretta in its holster. "Remember, we stay together. No heroics. If things get hairy, we pull back and regroup."

They exited the Transit and moved cautiously towards the bank building, their senses on high alert. The front doors were locked, but a side window had been shattered, providing them with access. Junior peered inside, his eyes scanning the dimly lit interior. "Looks clear. I'll go first." He carefully climbed through the broken window, landing silently on the dusty floor. Nicole followed close behind, scanning the street as Junior moved to clear the lobby. "All clear," he called out, gesturing for her to join him.

They moved through the deserted bank, their footsteps echoing in the cavernous space. The teller windows were empty, their computer screens dark and lifeless. Papers littered the floor, scattered by the wind that whistled through the broken window. They found the stairwell and began to ascend, their boots crunching on the concrete steps. As they climbed higher, the air grew warmer and drier, the oppressive heat of the Texas summer seeping into the building.

Finally, they reached the roof. The view was panoramic, stretching out across the desolate city and beyond. San Angelo lay before them, a ghost town baking under the unforgiving sun. Junior scanned the horizon, his eyes searching for any sign of life. "Not much movement," he said, his voice grim. "A few vehicles on the outskirts of town, but nothing organized. Looks like everyone really did clear out." Nicole nodded, her expression thoughtful. "Well, we accomplished our first goal. We got information. It's time to find some survivors, and get back to the ranch." She pointed to the east. "Let's try the road towards the base. Maybe we can find someone heading that way."

Junior took one last look at the desolate city, a sense of melancholy washing over him. "Alright," he said, turning to Nicole. "Let's do it. But let's be careful. This place gives me the creeps." Junior adjusted the AR-10 slung across his chest, the weight familiar and comforting. He wasn't entirely sure why San Angelo creeped him out. "Creepy and hot as hell," Nicole added, wiping sweat from her brow. "Let's move before we bake like potatoes in a microwave." She flashed him a grin, a touch of defiance in her eyes.

As they descended the stairwell, Junior couldn't help but analyze the situation. "You know," he said, "San Angelo was never exactly a booming metropolis to begin with. This close to the desert, water's always been a problem. Now, with no power to run the pumps, and everyone gone... there's not going to be anything left here soon." Nicole nodded, her expression sobering. "You're right. Anyone who stayed is probably long gone by now, searching for water. That's why we need to keep moving. If anyone's still out there, they're headed towards the rivers and lakes."

They reached the Ford Transit and climbed inside, the interior radiating heat. Junior cranked the windows down, letting the meager breeze wash over them. He started the engine, the rumble echoing in the silent streets. "Alright," Nicole said, consulting the map. "The base is east of here, just a few miles. We can swing by the base, see if anyone's holed up there. It's a long shot, but worth checking."

Junior nodded, putting the Transit in gear. "Roger that. But let's not get our hopes up. Military bases are usually the first places to get picked clean after something like this." "You think anyone even bothered to try and get backup generators running here?" Nicole asked, her voice cutting through the silence. Junior shrugged, his eyes scanning the surroundings. "Probably. But without fuel, parts, or skilled technicians, it's a losing battle. Plus, Goodfellow is strictly training. There won't be anyone with significant combat experience stationed here."

The closer they got to the Air Force Base, the more desolate it became. The once bustling streets leading to the base were now eerily quiet, devoid of any signs of life. As they approached the main gate, they could see that it was unguarded, the security booth empty and abandoned. "Well, that's not a good sign," Nicole commented, her voice laced with disappointment.

Junior drove the Transit through the open gate, his eyes scanning the deserted buildings and empty parking lots. The base looked like a ghost town, with tumbleweeds rolling across the cracked asphalt and dust devils dancing in the distance. "This is a bust," Junior said, his voice tinged with frustration. "Air Force bases are utterly useless after an EMP and as we said, Goodfellow teaches intel, it doesn't defend America." Nicole sighed, leaning back in her seat. "I guess we shouldn't be surprised. Like you said, military bases are usually the first places to get ransacked after something like this."

Junior parked the Transit in front of one of the main buildings, the silence pressing in on them. He turned off the engine, the sudden lack of noise making the emptiness even more profound. "Let's just take a quick look around," Junior said, reaching for his AR-10. Junior and Nicole stepped out of the Ford Transit, weapons at the ready, though their expressions betrayed more boredom than apprehension. The Texas heat beat down on them, making the abandoned base seem even more surreal. As they started towards the building, a chorus of shouts rang out. "Hold it right there! Don't move!"

Six figures emerged from behind abandoned vehicles and doorways, all wielding pistols with a few M4s. They looked tired, ungroomed, their faces a mixture of desperation and… something else. Something oddly pathetic. "Well, well, well," Junior drawled, his tone laced with amusement. "Looks like we've stumbled upon the Goodfellow Honor Guard." He exchanged a quick glance with Nicole, a silent agreement passing between them. Nicole smirked, raising her hands in mock surrender. "Don't shoot! We mean you no harm. Just checking the place out."

Chapter 38

The Benefits Package

"Alright, alright, easy does it," Junior said, his voice calm and even, as he carefully lowered his AR-10 to the ground. He made sure to do it slowly, deliberately, giving the frazzled airmen no reason to think he was making a sudden move. Nicole mirrored his actions, placing her AR-15 gently beside his. "No need to get your skibbies in a twist, fellas. We're just tourists, passing through."

One of the figures, a young Air Force Security Forces airman with a patchy beard and wide, bloodshot eyes, stepped forward, brandishing his M4 with more enthusiasm than skill. "Drop the pistols too! Now!" With a sigh that was almost theatrical, Junior reached down and unclipped his pistol, placing it on the ground near the rifles. "Happy now?" he asked, his tone laced with a hint of sarcasm. Nicole followed suit, setting her Beretta down beside his Sig. "There," she said, raising her hands again. "All clear. We're unarmed and utterly harmless. Unless you count charm as a weapon." She winked, flashing a disarming smile.

The airman didn't seem particularly charmed. He gestured with his M4 toward the building behind them. "Inside. Now. And no funny business." Junior chuckled softly. "Funny business? On a deserted Air Force base in the middle of nowhere? What kind of funny business did you have in mind? That is, if you don't mind me asking. And are you guys interested?" Nicole nudged him playfully with her elbow. "Behave yourself, Junior. They're just doing their job."

The senior airman with the patchy beard seemed to bristle at Junior's question, his grip tightening on his M4. "Just move it! Inside! Sergeant Miller will want to have a little chat with you both." He gestured inside with the barrel of his rifle, his face set in a grim line. Nicole rolled her eyes playfully, but complied, stepping past the airman and into the dimly lit barracks. "Lead the way, darling. We're all about a good chat." She winked back at Junior, who followed her with a low chuckle, shaking his head in feigned exasperation. "Honestly, some people just can't appreciate a good joke."

As they entered the barracks, the oppressive heat outside was replaced by a stale, musty air. The room was clean, but the general air of neglect that permeated the entire base didn't stop at the door. At a large desk, clearly meant for someone else, sat a young Air Force Sergeant, his face pale and drawn. He looked up as they entered, his expression a mixture of surprise and suspicion. "Well, look what we have here," Sergeant Miller said, his voice flat and devoid of any real enthusiasm. "Visitors. On a day like this. What brings you two to Goodfellow?" He leaned back in his rickety chair, studying them with a practiced gaze. "And who might you be?"

"Well, Sergeant Miller," Nicole began, her voice steady and professional, "It's Specialist Nicole Renado. Formerly with the US Army. I was an interrogator with the Army Reserves. I'm currently…between jobs." She offered another disarming smile, letting a touch of weariness creep into her tone.

Junior stepped forward, his expression polite but firm. "David Renado Junior, sir. My father is Retired Sergeant First Class David Renado of the US Army. The barracks' dimness seemed to accentuate Sergeant Miller's weariness. His eyes, shadowed and ringed, flickered between Nicole and Junior, trying to gauge their sincerity. "Former Army Specialist, huh?" he said, his voice tinged with skepticism. "And you, son of a Sergeant First Class. Quite the patriotic pair. Collecting intel, you say? For who, exactly? Seeing as how Uncle Sam's gone on indefinite leave."

Nicole suppressed a sigh. This was going to be a slog. "We're just trying to get a handle on the situation, Sergeant. See who's still out there, how they're managing. Assess the damage, maybe offer some assistance if we can." She chose her words carefully, painting a picture of benign exploration, not the covert mission she and Junior were really on.

Sergeant Miller's gaze hardened. "Assistance? Don't tell me you're one of those do-gooder types, coming in here trying to 'fix' things. We're doing just fine here, managed to keep things running, albeit barely." He gestured around the barracks with a weary wave of his hand. "We don't need your help."

Junior, so often a volcano of wit and playful sarcasm, remained impassive, his focus locked on Sergeant Miller. He noticed the minute details, the way the Sergeant rubbed his temples, the tremor in his hands, the subtle twitch in his left eye. He was exhausted, stressed, and deeply distrustful. "You two…a couple?" Sergeant Miller asked abruptly, his eyes narrowing. Nicole chuckled, almost amused by his impromptu question. "Actually, Sergeant, Junior's father… is my husband." Junior, unfazed by the direction of the conversation, merely nodded. "Yes sir. Nicole here, is my stepmom, known her since I was five," he said flatly.

Sergeant Miller blinked, clearly amused by the information. He ran a hand through his thinning hair, the skepticism in his eyes warring with a flicker of… something Junior couldn't quite decipher. "Right…stepmom. And your dad…married to a former interrogator. That sounds convenient." Junior interjected. "My father was also an interrogator, as well as a lot of other things." Sergeant Miller shifted uncomfortably. "So what 'other things' is your dad, kid?"

Little David's face remained unchanged. "It doesn't matter what my father is. As far as you're concerned, he could be the devil, or an envoy of God himself." He paused, letting his words settle. "If I wanted anything from you, I wouldn't have to ask. I could take anything I want, anyone I want, and there is nothing you or any of your desperate rabble could do to stop me." Little David smiled again. "But I'm not here for that, I am a vanguard, a representative of my father, and I'm here to talk like men, not squabble."

Nicole bit back a laugh, impressed by Junior's audaciousness. The kid had a way of cutting through the bullshit, and she had to admit, this "vanguard" approach was certainly… unexpected. She leaned against the cool metal wall of the barracks, letting Junior take the lead. Let him be the charismatic, slightly terrifying face of their little expedition. She was there to provide the backup, the experience, and the occasional sanity check.

Sergeant Miller stared at Junior, his expression a mixture of disbelief and something akin to… respect? Fear? It was hard to tell. "The devil, huh? Or an envoy of God? You got a high opinion of your old man, kid. And you, Miss… Stepmom-Interrogator. You just let him talk like that?" He seemed genuinely bewildered.

Nicole pushed off the wall, stepping forward slightly. "Sergeant, let's be clear. My husband, Junior's father, is a… unique individual. He has skills and resources that are, frankly, beyond your comprehension. But Junior's right. We're not here to conquer, or to steal. We're here to see if we can help. To see if there are others out there who are trying to rebuild, just like we are." She kept her tone even, professional. "And," she added, a hint of a smile playing on her lips, "we're trying to keep him from getting bored."

Junior chuckled, a low rumble in his chest. "Boredom is a dangerous thing, Sergeant. Especially for someone with my father's… skillset." He let the thought hang in the air, unspoken.

Sergeant Miller's eyes darted between Nicole and Junior, clearly trying to assess the situation. He was a seasoned soldier, but this was… different. These two weren't playing by any rules he recognized. "Alright," he said finally, sighing heavily. "Let's cut the crap. You said you're here to help, but also to see who's rebuilding. What do you want to know? What's the real agenda here?"

Junior stepped forward again, his expression shifting from subtly threatening to disarmingly earnest. "Sergeant, there's no hidden agenda. We're not spies, we're not scavengers. We're looking for people. People who are tired of scratching out a living, people who want something more than just survival. People who are willing to follow."

Nicole watched Junior with a mixture of amusement and pride. The kid was a natural. A little too natural, maybe. She was used to dealing with weak minded people, but it was something else dealing with people like this who spoke with natural authority.

The senior airman with the patch beard, a wiry guy with a sneer permanently etched on his face, scoffed. "Follow? Follow who? You? You're barely old enough to shave. And your 'unique' dad? Probably some doomsday prepper holed up in his garage, thinking he's King of the World. Don't try to sell us that garbage."

Junior's eyes narrowed, but his voice remained calm, almost conversational. "You doubt my sincerity, Airman?" He paused, tilting his head slightly. "You doubt my abilities? You think you know what I'm capable of?" A dangerous spark ignited in his eyes, a stark contrast to the boyish face. Nicole bit back a smile. Here it comes.

"Look, kid," the airman spat, stepping closer, puffing out his chest. "This ain't some video game or a movie. This is real life. You and your... stepmom... came strolling in here with your fancy weapons and your tall tales. You think you can just waltz in and take charge?" He gestured dismissively. "You're just a kid playing soldier."

Sergeant Miller pinched the bridge of his nose, a weary sigh escaping his lips. The airman, whose name tag read "Davis," was clearly itching for a fight, and Junior... well, Junior was more than capable of delivering one. Miller didn't need any more trouble. He had enough on his plate, trying to keep a semblance of order in this chaotic new world.

"Hold on," Nicole interjected, placing a hand lightly on Junior's shoulder. Her voice was calm but firm, a subtle warning. "Let's not resort to theatrics. Airman Davis, with all due respect, you're making assumptions based on... appearances. We understand your skepticism. We're outsiders. But we're not here to challenge your authority or start a war. We're trying to offer something, a chance for a better life."

She turned her attention back to Sergeant Miller, her gaze direct and unwavering. "Sergeant, we appreciate you hearing us out. Perhaps instead of debating hypotheticals, we could see the people you're responsible for? Let them decide for themselves if what we offer is something they're interested in. We're not recruiters, we're simply extending an invitation."

Miller studied her for a long moment, his eyes searching for any sign of deception. He saw only sincerity, tempered with a quiet confidence that was both intriguing and unsettling. He glanced at Junior, who, despite the simmering intensity in his eyes, stood patiently, respecting Nicole's intervention.

"Alright," Miller conceded, slowly. "Fine, you can talk to them. But under my supervision. And no pressure tactics. They're free to make their own choices." He cast a warning glare at Davis. "Davis, stand down. You're on perimeter duty. Go."

Davis grumbled under his breath but grudgingly complied, shooting one last venomous look at Junior before stomping off. Miller watched him go, then turned back to Nicole and Junior, who smirked inwardly. "Theatrics," Nicole had called it. He preferred to think of it as a persuasive demonstration of potential. Still, Nicole's approach was undoubtedly more diplomatic, and in this situation, diplomacy was key. As they followed Sergeant Miller to the abandoned dining facility, Junior took in the surroundings, his senses heightened, cataloging every detail. The heat was oppressive, even in the shade, and the air hung heavy with the scent of decay and desperation.

Inside the dining hall, the atmosphere was thick with a mixture of apprehension and hope. Young faces, weathered beyond their years, stared back at them, a kaleidoscope of emotions swirling in their eyes; fear, uncertainty, and a flicker of something that might have been eagerness. Sergeant Miller cleared his throat, his voice echoing in the cavernous room. "Alright, listen up! This is… Nicole, and this is David or… Junior. They say they have an offer for you. I've made it clear they're not forcing anyone to do anything. You can choose to listen, and you can choose to walk away. Understood?" A murmur of assent rippled through the room.

Nicole stepped forward, her presence calm and disarming. "Thank you, Sergeant. As I mentioned outside, we're not here to recruit you. We understand you're in a difficult situation, and we are simply here to offer an alternative. My… my husband… has a ranch, about three to four hours away, where we have power, water, food, and protection. We're self-sufficient and welcome those willing to contribute."

Nicole smiled gently, her gaze sweeping across the tired faces. "We aren't promising paradise," she continued. "Life is still hard. But it's safe, and we work together. We have farmers, teachers, and people who know how to fix things. More importantly, we have a community. A family."

"What kind of work would we be doing?" a young woman asked, her voice laced with apprehension. "It depends on your skills and what you're willing to learn," Nicole replied. "We need people for everything: farming, repairs, cooking, security, teaching the kids, helping with the animals. My husband believes in matching people with jobs they can be passionate about and that benefit the community."

Another voice piped up, this one a little louder, a little more assertive. "What about supplies? Are we just expected to work for free?" Nicole nodded, anticipating the question. "You'll be provided with food, shelter, clothing, and access to medical care. Beyond that, we operate on a resource-based economy. Everyone contributes, and everyone benefits. There's no money involved."

Junior finally spoke, his voice low and even but carrying an undeniable weight of authority. "And we have a well-stocked armory. Everyone is expected to learn how to use a weapon and help defend the ranch. Which shouldn't be an issue for most of you." "Okay, I'll bite," a lanky young man with a freshly shaved head said, shifting his weight nervously. "What's the catch? This all sounds… well, too good to be true."

Nicole nodded, unfazed. "There isn't a catch, per se. But there are realities. Life on the ranch is structured. David, my husband, believes in order and efficiency. He's…

particular, about things." She paused, choosing her words carefully. "He has… high expectations. He's autistic, brilliant, and sees the world in a way most people don't. That means rules are rules, and he expects them to be followed. He's also incredibly fair and compassionate. But he does not suffer fools gladly."

Junior chuckled softly. "Yeah, Dad's got a nose for bullshit like a bloodhound after a squirrel. Try to pull a fast one, and you'll regret it." He pushed off the wall, his eyes scanning the room. "Also, there's chores. Lots of 'em. We all pull our weight. No freeloaders allowed. And, you'll be expected to learn new skills. Dad's a firm believer in continuous improvement. He'll find something for you to do, even if that something is learning how to castrate a goat." A ripple of nervous laughter spread through the room.

A young airman, practically still a boy, hesitantly approached them. "Ma'am? Sir? I... I have a question." Nicole immediately softened her expression. "Of course. What's your name?" "Airman Carson, Ma'am." "What's on your mind, Carson?" Carson shuffled his feet, avoiding eye contact. "What... what happens if you don't follow the rules? I mean, everyone messes up sometimes, right?"

Junior crossed his arms, his gaze steady. "Dad's not unreasonable. He understands mistakes happen. But deliberate disobedience, laziness, or anything that puts the community at risk? That's a different story." Nicole added, "David believes in restorative justice. If you make a mistake, you fix it. You learn from it. If you hurt someone, you make amends. The punishment fits the crime, focusing on education and repair, rather than just retribution." "But what if it's a big mistake?" Carson pressed, his voice barely audible.

Nicole placed a comforting hand on his shoulder. "Then you face the consequences. David doesn't shy away from tough decisions. But he always strives to be fair, even when it's difficult. He's a leader, Carson, a true leader. And leaders do what's best for the group, even if it's not what's easiest." Another airman, a young woman named Thompson with intelligent eyes and a weary slump to her shoulders, spoke up. "What about... relationships? I mean, is there dating? Are there... expectations?" A blush crept up her neck as she fiddled with her tattered uniform.

Nicole met her gaze with a reassuring smile. "As for relationships, David believes people should be free to form connections naturally. There are no arranged marriages or anything like that. But," she emphasized, "anyone who disrespects those bonds, who violates trust or consent, will face consequences. David protects his family fiercely."

Junior, who had been leaning against a nearby table, straightened up, a mischievous glint in his eyes. "So, Airman Thompson," he said, a wide grin spreading across his face, "got a boyfriend here somewhere? Or are you just curious about the talent pool we've got back at the ranch? 'Cause, I have to warn you, I'm the only eligible bachelor your age. Unless you prefer them really young or much older." He winked. Nicole rolled her eyes good-naturedly. "Junior! Behave yourself."

Junior raised his hands in mock surrender. "Hey, just saying! Besides, gotta be honest. Life on the ranch ain't a dating game. It's more like... one-and-done. Everyone's working together, living together, surviving together. If things go south with a boyfriend or girlfriend, you can't just go to different schools or move to a new town. You're stuck seeing them every day, at dinner, during chores. Awkward exes aren't something you can escape on the ranch. So, most people tend to be careful about getting involved. It's serious business." He sobered slightly. "But when it works, it really works. Family is everything to Dad. And he expects us to treat each other like family, good times and bad."

Nicole nodded in agreement. "He's right. Relationships, especially romantic ones, are viewed with a certain... gravity. David fosters an environment of open communication and encourages couples to work through their issues. But drama and pettiness? He has very little patience for it." She looked back at Airman Thompson, her expression softening. "The most important thing is honesty, both with yourself and with others. Don't enter into a relationship out of desperation or loneliness. Choose someone because you genuinely see a future with them, someone you respect and trust. Because on the ranch, relationships aren't just about love, they're about survival."

The atmosphere, once thick with apprehension, had eased slightly, replaced by a hesitant curiosity. A young soldier, his face barely out of adolescence, fidgeted beside a young woman who looked equally nervous. He cleared his throat. "Uh, ma'am? Sir?" He addressed both Nicole and Junior, then glanced at the woman beside him. "What about... kids? Are kids... welcome?" The woman squeezed his hand, her eyes downcast. Her stretched uniform hinted at the secret she carried.

Junior's easy grin faltered. He exchanged a quick, almost imperceptible glance with Nicole, who nodded. This was a question they hadn't anticipated, a vulnerability they hadn't considered. He stepped forward, his voice losing its playful edge, becoming gentler, more measured. "Is this your girlfriend?" he asked, placing a hand on his shoulder. The young soldier nodded, still avoiding eye contact. "She got pregnant right before the base shut down, and I'm afraid of taking her anywhere." Junior looked at the young woman, she looked almost as pregnant as Jessica. "Do you love this woman? Are you willing to look after her?" he asked, assessing his response. Junior knew how young soldier couples were, but times have changed. "I… I do," he muttered.

Nicole leaned forward, taking the young woman's hands. "We have several pregnancies on the ranch, so you aren't alone. Even my best friend just found out she's pregnant," Nicole said, reassuringly. "Yeah, and my brother's wife too," little David blurted. Junior, ever the blunt speaker, continued, "Dad loves kids, but he doesn't sugarcoat things. Raising kids in this new world? It's hard. Damn hard. It's not like when he was a kid and played outside til the street lights came on. We teach our children how to live, how to survive, and how to fight." Junior took a breath before continuing. "Look, we have some committed and smart people at the ranch; a nurse, a pharmacist, ranchers, farmers, engineers and between me and my siblings, we know seven foreign languages."

He pointed a thumb back towards Nicole. "She's got a pair of twins that will knock your socks off, and you won't find two better-trained or more fiercely loyal kids anywhere. They carry their weight, and then some."

Junior took a deep breath, his expression softening slightly. "Look, we ain't saints. Life on the ranch ain't a picnic. Dad's got rules, and he enforces them." He stepped forward abruptly. His tone changing, devoid of the previous charm. "There are no resources here. We have some on the ranch. End of story. I'm not here to brief you on benefits packages." He crossed his arms, his eyes scanning the group with a detached intensity. He was done with the pleasantries.

Nicole stepped forward, placing a reassuring hand on his shoulder before addressing the group. "Newcomers always have difficulty adjusting. It's not something you can just fall into. Think of it like a solar system," she said, winking at Junior. "Junior's father, my husband, is the patriarch, the star in the center. People either get caught in his orbit, or they shoot through the system like an asteroid. Maybe they make it out, maybe they collide with someone else. The point is, it will change you, and it's a lot to handle in the beginning." Nicole paused before continuing. "So if you aren't prepared for that possibility, there's no reason for you to ask any more questions."

Junior watched as silence blanketed the mess hall, the air thick with unspoken questions and, surprisingly, a hint of apprehension. He had expected more pushback, more insistence. Maybe the apocalypse had knocked some sense into these trainees. Or maybe, he thought with a cynical edge, they were just too scared to ask the wrong question.

He turned to Nicole, a silent question in his eyes. She gave a slight nod, a tiny smile playing on her lips. "Alright," he announced, his voice regaining its earlier, more neutral tone. "We're heading out. Anyone who wants to come, gather your things. The van only has room for ten more. We're leaving in fifteen minutes." After Leaving the dining facility, sergeant Miller met him outside with their weapons. "I hope you know what you're doing," he said before turning and going back inside.

"Think anyone will actually come?" Junior asked, squinting against the glare. Nicole shrugged, adjusting her Beretta in its holster. "Hard to say. The pregnant couple Sara and Marvin seem pretty desperate. Kathy too. The older girl with the blonde hair, she kept glancing at me like I was her last hope of getting a decent latte." Junior chuckled. "Decent latte? I doubt Dad even remembers what a latte is."

They leaned against the side of the Ford Transit, the metal already hot to the touch. The air shimmered around them, distorting the already desolate landscape. The silence was broken only by the distant drone of insects and the occasional gust of wind rustling through the parched grass. Ten minutes stretched into an eternity. Junior tapped his foot impatiently, scanning the entrance to the mess hall. "Come on, people," he muttered under his breath. "Time's a-wasting."

Finally, the door creaked open. Sara and Marvin, the expecting couple, emerged first, their faces etched with a mixture of hope and uncertainty. Behind them came Kathy, clutching a battered backpack, followed by Carson, and Thompson, with six more Soldiers, half male, half female. Junior counted them quickly, eleven, exactly.

"Well, butter my biscuits," Junior drawled, pushing himself off the van with a theatrical sigh. He clapped his hands together, a gesture that bordered on mocking. "Looks like someone didn't pay attention in math class." He tilted his head towards Nicole, who simply raised an eyebrow, completely unfazed.

"Okay, people," Junior continued, his tone shifting to a brisk, borderline insensitive, efficiency that mirrored his father's own. "We got a problem. A numbers problem. A ten-is-less-than-eleven problem. This fine piece of American steel only seats twelve comfortably. And by comfortably, I mean packed like sardines in a can of Texas heat." Sara's face crumpled. "But... you said..." "Shut it preggers!" he interrupted. "You and your boy toy stand aside, you two get to cut the line. It's the rest of you that have an issue.

Junior watched, a faint smirk playing on his lips, as panic rippled through the group. He knew this moment was coming. He'd inherited more than just his father's combat skills; he had a knack for controlled chaos. "Hold on now," Kathy spoke up, her voice trembling slightly. "There's got to be another way. We can't just leave anyone behind." "Unless," Junior said, his tone laced with mock innocence, "someone here is particularly… unpopular. You know, the kind of person who always eats the last donut, or leaves the toilet seat up. Maybe someone who sings horribly in the shower? I'm just spitballing here." He paused, letting his words sink in. "We could, theoretically, vote someone off the island."

"Woah, woah, woah, hold your horses, Junior," Nicole interjected, stepping forward with a sigh. "Seriously?

Vote someone off? We are not turning this into some twisted, post-apocalyptic reality show. Besides, I doubt 'bad shower singer' is a valid reason to condemn someone." She shot him a stern look. "Pull yourself together. You're acting like a teenager with a video game addiction."

Junior rolled his eyes. "Alright, alright, fine. No tribal councils. You always ruin my fun, Nicole." He turned back to the group, the mock innocence gone, replaced with a keen, assessing gaze. "How about this. Other than Sara and Marvin here, is anyone else here an exclusive or unexclusive couple? Speak now, or forever hold your peace."

A hand slowly went up. It was Olivia Thompson, her expression a mixture of fear and defiance. "I... I'm not with anyone," she stammered, her voice hesitant. "But nobody here likes me. I'm kind of... the shower singer you were talking about." She blushed crimson. Junior smiled. "Olivia, I like your honesty. You can stay." He gestured to the side. "So, no more couples?" he asked, scanning the group.

A beat of silence hung in the air, thick and heavy with the weight of the unspoken. Finally, a lanky kid with a mop of brown hair, who identified as Andrew, shuffled his feet. "Uh... me and Susan are kinda..." He trailed off, glancing at Susan, a girl with kind eyes and a nervous smile. "Kinda what, Andrew?" Nicole prompted gently. "Kinda seeing each other? Kinda just friends? Kinda contemplating the meaning of existence together?" Andrew squirmed. "Kinda... together. I guess."

Junior's face was unreadable for a moment, then he sighed. With lightning speed, he drew his X-Ten. The sound of the slide racking echoed in the sudden silence. The weapon pointed not at Andrew, but at Susan. Gasps rippled through the group. Nicole's eyes widened in disbelief. "Junior! What in the hell do you think you're doing?!"

Junior didn't flinch. His gaze remained fixed on Andrew. "The apocalypse has a funny way of stripping away the bullshit, wouldn't you agree, Nicole? No more pretending. No more maybes. Just raw, unfiltered truth." He turned his attention back to Andrew. "I asked if you two were a couple. You said 'kinda.' Kinda isn't good enough, sounds to me like you're using her, or maybe you're going to bring drama to my home. Is she a convenience for you Andrew?" He paused, letting the weight of his words sink in. "The problem with convenience, Andrew, is that somebody always ends up used." He took a step closer, the gun never wavering. "So, I'm asking you again. Are you with her?"

Andrew swallowed hard, his Adam's apple bobbing nervously. He looked at Susan, his eyes searching hers. He saw fear, yes, but also a desperate plea. "I…" He started, his voice cracking. Junior cut him off. "No thinking. No 'I thinks.' No 'I feels.' This isn't sensitivity training, soldier. Just a damn yes or no. And if you can't give me that much, then I already have my answer." He shifted the Sig slightly, the muzzle now pointed directly at Susan's chest.

Nicole gasped, taking a step forward, but Junior held up a hand, stopping her. "Stay out of this, Nicole. This is between him and her." Andrew's eyes widened in horror. "No! Don't!" He lunged forward, placing himself between Junior and Susan. "Don't shoot her! Shoot me! Please, just don't hurt her!" Junior didn't move, his expression unchanged. The silence stretched, punctuated only by Susan's ragged breathing. Then, slowly, deliberately, he lowered the Sig.

Junior holstered his pistol, keeping his eyes locked on Andrew, a faint flicker of something unreadable in their depths. He then turned to Susan, his expression softening marginally. "Susan," he said, his voice surprisingly gentle. "Can you sit on Andrew's lap?" The question hung in the air, absurd and out of place after the preceding threat. A collective murmur rippled through the small gathering. Sara, her face pale, clutched Marvin's arm. Olivia, her eyes wide, stared at Junior with a mixture of fear and confusion.

Susan, her face streaked with tears, blinked in disbelief. "What? Sit… on his lap?" "Yes," Junior confirmed, his tone unwavering. "It's a simple request. Can you sit on his lap?" He glanced pointedly at Andrew, who was still trembling slightly. Andrew stared, Dumbfounded, his protective instincts warring with complete bafflement. "Uh… what? Why?"

Junior, unblinking, tilted his head slightly. "Just answer the question, Susan. Can you, or can you not, sit on his lap?" He glanced at Nicole, a small, almost imperceptible twitch at the corner of his mouth. Was he actually enjoying this? Nicole, despite Junior's earlier warning, couldn't help but step in. "Junior, maybe we can explain what we're trying to find out…" "Nope!" Junior cut her off, holding up a hand. "Still between them. She needs to make a decision, Nicole. We don't have time to coddle." He turned back to Susan, his voice losing some of its gentleness. "Time is of the essence Susan."

Susan, still bewildered, looked at Andrew, then back at Junior, then to the ground as if the answer was painted there. Tears still welled in her eyes, but a flicker of understanding seemed to dawn. "I… I guess I can. If it helps." She shuffled hesitantly towards Andrew, her movements stiff and awkward. Little David smiled. "Then with you sitting in his lap, we might just have room for all eleven of you."

Chapter 39

The Desperate Survivors

Susan, her face a mask of confusion and residual fear, carefully lowered herself onto Andrew's lap. Andrew, still reeling from the near-death experience, instinctively wrapped his arms around her, a protective gesture that felt strangely natural. The interior of the Ford Transit suddenly felt even more cramped, the air thick with a mixture of apprehension and relief. Junior beamed, clapping his hands together. "Excellent! See? Teamwork! Now, everyone else, find a spot. Kathy, you're next to Riley. Noah, squeeze in by Caleb. Olivia, hop in next to Sara and Marvin. Darrel, climb in the back, and try not to look so scared."

With Junior's surprisingly cheerful prodding, the remaining survivors began to clamber into the van, a chaotic mess of shuffling limbs and muttered apologies. Nicole watched the scene unfold, a mixture of amusement and concern swirling within her. Junior's methods were definitely… unorthodox, but undeniably effective.

Once everyone was crammed inside like sardines in a can, Junior slammed the side door shut. "Alright, Nicole," he said, turning to her with a grin. "Let's get these folks back to the ranch. And try not to drive too fast. Remember, pregnant lady on board!" Nicole chuckled, shaking her head. "Pregnant ladies and… well, whatever that was back there. You handle the entertainment, I'll handle the driving." She put the Transit in gear and left the base, back towards San Angelo proper.

"First stop," she announced, "we are hitting the department store!"

A chorus of confused murmurs arose from the back. "A department store? Why?" Darrel asked, his voice cutting through the murmurs. "Because," Little David explained, turning around in his seat, "you all look like you've been sleeping in your clothes for a week. Which, I guess, you probably have been. We're getting you some new clothes. At least four sets each." "But...we don't have any money," Sara pointed out. Little David waved a dismissive hand. "Don't worry about that. Aint nobody going to be there anyway."

The remaining ride to the department store was filled with deafening silence and heavy breathing. Nicole pulled the Ford Transit into the deserted parking lot of a large department store. The windows were dusty, and several cars lay abandoned nearby, grim reminders of the world they now inhabited. "Alright, everyone out!" she commanded. "Stay close, and follow Junior's instructions. He's surprisingly good at this sort of thing."

Little David hopped out of the van, rifle slung casually over his shoulder, and surveyed the group. "Okay, listen up," he said, his voice surprisingly authoritative. "We're going in, grabbing clothes, and getting out. No dilly-dallying. Stick together, watch each other's backs, and if you see anything…or anyone…suspicious, let me or Nicole know immediately."

He pushed open the doors of the department store, the hinges groaning in protest. The interior was dim, dust motes dancing in the shafts of sunlight that pierced through the grimy windows. Racks of clothes stood silent and still, a stark contrast to the bustling activity that would have filled the space just a few months ago. "Alright," Little David announced, clapping his hands. "Let's split up into groups. Women with Nicole, men with me. Find what you need, and meet back here in thirty minutes. And remember, no stealing anything fancy. We're here for survival, not high fashion."

Nicole led the women towards the ladies' section, while Little David guided the men in the opposite direction. The trainees, still slightly shell-shocked, moved with a hesitant caution, their eyes darting nervously from shadow to shadow. In the women's section, Nicole surveyed the racks with a practiced eye. "Alright ladies," she said. "Prioritize comfortable, durable clothing. Jeans, t-shirts, hoodies, that sort of thing. And don't forget socks and underwear. We're not exactly running a laundromat back at the ranch, so you'll want plenty."

The women began to browse the racks, their initial apprehension slowly giving way to a sense of purpose. Sara, still clutching her stomach, carefully selected a few sets of maternity clothes, her face softening with a hint of a smile. Olivia, her eyes wide with wonder, cautiously reached out and touched a soft, brightly colored sweater.

Little David surveyed the men's section. It was a chaotic jumble of discarded mannequins, fallen displays, and scattered garments. He grabbed a shopping cart, the wheels squeaking in protest as he pushed it forward. "Right, listen up," he said, his voice brooking no argument. "We're not here to browse. We're here to equip ourselves for survival. Think practical, think durable. Jeans, work boots, thick socks, and layers. And no, Andrew, that sparkly disco shirt does not qualify as essential survival gear."

Andrew hastily dropped the offending garment. Little David sighed, pinching the bridge of his nose. He knew these kids were scared, disoriented, and probably overwhelmed by the sudden shift in their lives. But he didn't have time for hand-holding. "Alright," he continued, softening his tone slightly. "Think about the Texas weather. It's brutally hot right now, but winter's coming. Grab a few light t-shirts, but also look for something warm, like a hoodie or a flannel shirt. And don't forget gloves and a hat. You'll thank me later when you're chopping wood in January."

He demonstrated by grabbing a stack of plain, sturdy denim jeans and tossing them into the cart. Then, he added several pairs of thick wool socks, a couple of thermal shirts, and a heavy-duty work jacket. He then grabbed a box of heavy-duty trash bags and a roll of thick rope from the hardware section.

"Alright, everyone gather 'round!" Little David commanded, clapping his hands together. The group, laden with their bagged clothing, shuffled towards him. "Nicole, could you grab a ladder from the automotive section?" Little David asked, pointing towards the back of the store. Nicole nodded and effortlessly navigated the debris-strewn aisles, returning moments later with a sturdy aluminum ladder. "Here you go, Junior," she said, handing it over. Little David grinned. "Thanks, Nicole. You're the best." He turned back to the group. "Okay, so we're going to tie these bags to the roof rack of the van. It's gonna be a tight squeeze, but we need to keep the inside of the van clear. Andrew, you're up first. Grab your bags and let's get you loaded."

Andrew, still looking slightly dazed, hesitantly approached with his bulging trash bags. Little David demonstrated how to secure the bags to the roof rack using the rope. He showed Andrew how to tie a taut line hitch, ensuring the bags wouldn't shift or slide during the drive back to the ranch. "Got it?" Little David asked, giving the rope a final tug.

Andrew nodded, his eyes widening slightly as he realized the weight and importance of the task. "Yeah, I think so." "Good. Now, everyone else, line up and let's get this done. Nicole, can you keep an eye out and make sure no one tries to sneak anything?" Nicole chuckled. "Consider it done, Junior." She positioned herself near the entrance, her hand casually resting on the grip of her Beretta. "Kathy, make sure you double-knot that one! We don't want your unmentionables ending up on the Highway," he called out, earning a blush from the young woman and a snicker from Marvin. "Alright, alright, I got it," Kathy mumbled, yanking the rope with unnecessary force.

Suddenly, Nicole stiffened. Her eyes narrowed on the distant horizon. "Junior," she said, her voice low and serious. "Company coming. Looks like trouble." Little David's head whipped around, his playful demeanor instantly replaced with razor-sharp focus. "How many?" he barked, already scanning the horizon himself. He hefted his AR-10, the movement smooth and practiced. "Six, maybe seven. Hard to tell at this distance. Definitely armed, and they don't look friendly,"

Nicole replied, her eyes still fixed on the approaching figures. "They're moving fast."

Without missing a beat, Little David turned towards a beat-up, abandoned sedan parked haphazardly between them and the approaching threat. "Okay, everyone, Just keep working, I'll take care of this." Then, with a grunt that surprised even Nicole, Little David gripped the edge of the sedan. Muscles bulging in his arms and shoulders, he lifted. The sedan groaned under the impossible strain, the suspension screaming in protest. With a final, Herculean effort, he heaved the entire vehicle onto its side, creating a makeshift barricade between his group and the rapidly approaching figures.

The collective jaws of the rescued trainees dropped. Susan, mid-knot, stared with wide-eyed disbelief, the length of rope dangling forgotten from her hand. Even Marvin, usually quick with a wisecrack, was speechless, his mouth agape like a landed fish. "Uh… Junior?" Caleb finally stammered. "Did you… did you just flip a car?"

Little David, oblivious to the stunned silence he'd created, shrugged. "Yeah? Needed something to slow them down. What? You guys never flipped a car before?" He glanced back at Nicole, a hint of a playful smirk tugging at his lips. "I thought that was standard procedure in the apocalypse survival guide."

Nicole shook her head, a genuine smile gracing her features. "They're not used to someone actually being the apocalypse survival guide, Junior. Just give them a minute." She subtly adjusted her grip on her carbine, her gaze unwavering as she swept the horizon. "They're almost here."

With a smile, little David stepped into the open, his hands raised slightly. But before he could open his mouth, a shot was fired.

The sound cracked the air, sharp and violent. A bullet whizzed past Little David's ear, kicking up dust from the asphalt behind him. The trainees screamed, scattering like startled pigeons. Nicole swore under her breath, leveling her AR-15 towards the origin of the shot. "Junior, get down!" she yelled, already squeezing off a couple of rounds in the general direction of the unseen shooter.

Little David, however, remained standing, seemingly unperturbed. He calmly reached up and touched his ear, examining his fingertip for blood. "Well, that wasn't very polite," he said mildly, more annoyed than frightened. "I was just trying to have a conversation." "Conversation? They just tried to turn your head into a Jackson Pollock painting!" Nicole exclaimed, firing another burst. "Get behind the damn car!"

David sighed dramatically, a puff of air ruffling his already slightly disheveled hair. "Alright, alright," he muttered affectionately, but made no move to seek cover. Instead, he raised the AR-10, his movements fluid and impossibly fast. In less than five seconds, six shots rang out, each perfectly placed. He lowered the rifle, a faint wisp of smoke curling from the barrel.

Nicole lowered her rifle, her keen eyes scanning the area, confirming what she already suspected. "Well, that's… taken care of," she stated, a mix of relief and exasperation in her voice. Little David just shrugged again, the epitome of nonchalance. "It's efficient. Besides, I didn't want them to ruin my good shirt." He gestured to his button-down, meticulously clean despite their journey.

Caleb, finally regaining his composure, croaked, "Did… did you just… six shots?" "Yup," Little David replied cheerfully. "Headshots. Saves on ammo. Plus," he added with a wink, "it's cleaner that way." Marvin, ever the comedian, found his voice. "Cleaner? Dude, there's probably brain matter splattered all over the highway!" "That's their problem," Little David retorted, his tone light but firm. "We offered peace. They chose violence. Now, can we get back to loading the van? I'm starting to sweat." The group, still reeling from the sudden and efficient display of deadly force, slowly began to gather themselves and resume loading the Ford Transit.

Darrel, his face pale and sweat-streaked, approached Little David hesitantly. "Um… excuse me?" he stammered. "Are… are you always like that?" Little David tilted his head, considering the question. "Like what? Efficient? Resourceful? Annoyingly calm in the face of mortal danger?" He paused, tapping a finger against his chin. "I suppose so. It's generally expected of me." "No," Darrell said quickly, "like… like that. Headshots in five seconds? Flipping a car with your bare hands? Is… is everyone at the ranch like that?"

Little David looked at Nicole, a playful glint in his eyes. He knew what she'd say. Before he could answer, Nicole spoke up, her voice laced with amusement. "Kinda." Darrel's eyebrows shot up. "Kinda?" Junior stepped in, sensing Darrel's confusion, "It means we don't fuck around. But that doesn't mean we can't enjoy ourselves. We have standards but we still have fun." He clapped Darrel, maybe a bit too hard, on the shoulder, smiling. "Don't worry, you'll fit right in! We'll teach you everything you need to know to survive… and maybe a few things you don't, heh!"

Nicole expertly navigated the Ford Transit around the flipped sedan, the faces of their newly acquired companions a mixture of awe and terror still plastered on their features. The 90s rock anthem blasting from the speakers seemed oddly juxtaposed with the recent violence, but it served to diffuse the tension, replacing it with a hesitant, almost surreal, sense of normalcy.

Junior bounced in his seat, humming along off-key to the music. He caught Darrel's bewildered expression and grinned. "See? Told ya we have fun! Just gotta roll with the punches, literally sometimes." Olivia, who'd been unusually quiet since the… incident, leaned forward from her seat behind them. Her voice, still a little shaky, cut through the music. "Um, David? I mean, Junior… what do you do at the ranch? Or are you just, the leader's son?"

Junior snorted. "Being the Patriarch's son is mostly being everyone's punching bag for jokes," he said, winking at Nicole. "I'm not the oldest, nor am I the tallest. But seriously, I got a couple of gigs. My main thing is weapons and combat. I train tactics and firearms. I'm also one of two gunsmiths, make sure everyone's got the right tools for the job and knows how to use 'em."

He puffed out his chest a little. "My brothers, sisters and I can teach you anything from hand to hand combat, sword fighting, a variety of foreign languages and even how to sew a nice pair of pants. But we all have different personalities and styles, so if I'm too much to handle, my younger sister could teach you. Oh, and Kyle, my sister Grace has dibs on him." Nicole chuckled, glancing at Olivia in the rearview mirror. "He's being modest. 'Weapons and combat' translates to 'he makes sure no one messes with our family, ever.' And he's really good at it. The whole family is."

She paused, considering her words. "Think of it this way: David, that's Junior's dad, he's the architect. Plans everything, sees the big picture. We all fill in the details. Aidan's the mechanic, Brian's our tech guy, Lily's a badass, Seth's our scout, and Grace… well, Grace is just terrifyingly good at stealth. You don't want to play hide-and-seek with her."

Junior grinned, his earlier somber mood completely evaporated. "Exactly! We ain't just surviving, we're going to be the future of the human race! And it's gonna be a race that can handle whatever this new world throws at it." He thumped his chest. "Strong, smart, and ready to rebuild!" He turned in his seat again, addressing the group directly. "Look, what happened back there with those scavengers? That's the kind of stuff we deal with. But we don't just hunker down and wait to die. We train, we prepare, we adapt. We learn from everything. And we have fun doing it!"

Olivia, still staring out the window, spoke up again. "So, Nicole's married to your dad? What about your mom, is she still around?" "Okay, deep breath," Nicole said, flashing a smile in the rearview mirror that she hoped was reassuring. She caught Junior's eye and saw him give a curt nod, understanding the signal. "Remember that solar system analogy? David's… well, he's our sun. And trust me, nobody, nobody, is immune to David's gravity. You either get caught in his orbit, or you…" She trailed off, making a small hand gesture suggesting a violent explosion.

Junior chuckled. "Yeah, pretty much. Dad attracts people. That's just how he is. He's... complicated." "Complicated is an understatement," Nicole agreed, then took the plunge. "So, Olivia, to answer your question directly: yes, I'm married to Junior's dad. And so are… eight other women."

A stunned silence filled the Ford Transit. Andrew coughed awkwardly. Darrel looked like he was about to pass out. Riley's jaw dropped. Only Kathy maintained a neutral expression, though Nicole suspected she was just very good at hiding her surprise. Nicole held up a hand. "Hold your fire. I know what you're thinking. It sounds crazy. It kinda is crazy. But it works for us. Think of it like... our solar system. We have nine planets, right? All orbiting the same sun, each with their own purpose, their own strengths. David's... a big sun. And we're all orbiting peacefully."

She glanced at Junior, who was stifling a laugh. "Maybe not always peacefully. We have our moments. But we're a family. A very large, very unconventional family. And we stick together." Marvin, ever the literalist, piped up from the back. "Um, actually, Pluto isn't considered a planet by most people anymore. They downgraded it to a dwarf planet." Junior groaned dramatically. "Marvin, really? Now? Of all times? You had to bring in planetary classification?"

Junior raised a finger. "Consider this, Pluto is a dwarf planet, but a planet nonetheless. Taylor is the nanny, but she's still bearing his child and is his wife, just the same." He turned his body back to the front. "Everyone has their reasons and each relationship is unique. You'll see that yourself, but don't underestimate them. They helped build our home, and my dad will show no mercy to anyone who disrespects them."

The Transit continued its journey, the initial shock slowly giving way to a nervous curiosity. Nicole could sense the questions bubbling beneath the surface. She decided to address them head-on. "Look, you're joining a community that prizes honesty and respect. So, if you have questions, ask. But be polite. My husband deserves your respect. And so do his wives and children. We've built something special out there, and we're willing to share it, but not at the cost of our peace."

Olivia, cautiously raising her hand, spoke up. "I... I guess I'm just wondering... how does it work? Day to day? Is there like, a schedule? For... for everything?" Junior and Nicole exchanged amused glances. "There's no schedule, Olivia," Junior answered, his voice laced with affection. "Dad isn't exactly operating on a nine to five, especially not after the EMP. Each of the women have their own roles and responsibilities, they each run something for the group.

"They all share a bedroom with one of the others, but David's is at the top. They can be very... vocal. At all hours." Nicole smirked, causing a few faces to redden. "Point is, David makes sure all the needs of his wives, the children, and the group are met. That's all that matters, and he's very good at it." Andrew ventured, "What about... intimacy? Is there... competition?" Junior snorted. "Unless you have some vested interest in being a part of it, just know they're all taken care of."

The Transit rumbled to a stop just outside the ranch gates. The white plantation house stood sentinel against the Texas sun, a stark contrast to the chaos they'd left behind. He took a deep breath and announced to the new arrivals, "Alright, everyone. Time to meet the family. Remember what Nicole said: respect. And try not to stare. Especially at Jessica. She bites." He chuckled, but there was a definite glint of warning in his eyes. He glanced at the house, then to the back. "Dad doesn't know I brought you, so just try to look apologetic, I'll handle the backlash."

As they pulled up in front of the house, David emerged, a striking figure even in the harsh sunlight. Summer was on one side, her face etched with concern, and Josh on the other, leaning slightly, a silent bodyguard. David's expression was unreadable as he scanned the group, his eyes sharp and assessing.

The new soldiers didn't know what to expect, but remained quiet. They were a motley crew, fresh-faced and wide-eyed. Junior hopped out of the Transit, flashing a sheepish grin at his father. "Hey, Dad. Surprise!" David didn't return the smile. He folded his arms across his chest, his posture radiating authority. "Junior. Explain." His voice was calm, but there was an undercurrent of steel that made the recruits shift nervously. "Well, Nicole and I were scouting, and we found these guys at the Airforce Base. They were... stranded. Thought they might be useful." Junior spread his hands, trying for nonchalance. "Didn't seem right to leave them behind."

David looked at the new arrivals for a minute, his gaze lingering on Sara, then Darrel, who seemed particularly nervous, then the others. He looked back at Junior. Nicole approached David, who pulled her into a hug, kissing her soundly. "Welcome home, love," he murmured, then, without breaking the embrace, "Tiffany needs to know about our guests. Get her up to speed." He released her, a playful glint in his eye. Nicole grinned. "Will do, hon." She winked, then headed inside, her gait purposeful.

David turned back to Junior, patting him on the shoulder. "Good initiative, son. I'm proud. But now, they're your responsibility. Indoctrination starts now." He gestured towards the recruits. "They need to understand the rules of this house, the structure, the expectations. They need to know what we offer, what we require, and what we don't tolerate." Junior straightened, a new sense of purpose hardening his features. "Yes, sir. I've already started."

David's gaze softened slightly. "Good. Now, introduce me to my new guests." He walked over to the group, his eyes meeting each of theirs in turn. "Welcome to our home. I'm David. And this," he gestured towards Summer, who offered a warm smile, "is one of my wives, Summer. Josh there is our son-in-law." He paused, letting that sink in. The new soldiers exchanged glances, a flicker of confusion and curiosity in their eyes.

"Alright," little David began, clapping his hands together. "Let's get introductions out of the way. These fine folks," he gestured to the new arrivals, "are the, uh… the Goodfellow bunch. Recruits, fresh from training. Guys, this is my dad, David, and this is Summer. Also, that's Josh, he's married to my sister Lily." David nodded as each recruit mumbled their name and a brief introduction. He noted their anxiety, their eagerness to please, and their underlying exhaustion. He also noticed the pregnant girl, Sara. He'd need to speak with her privately later.

"Darrel Carson, sir. From Mississippi." Darrel stammered, his eyes darting nervously around the property. David held up a hand. "First name is fine, and don't 'sir' me. We're all family here." "Olivia. I'm... thank you for taking us in." Olivia's voice was quiet, but sincere. "Marvin, this is my girlfriend, Sara." Marvin stated, his arm wrapping protectively around Sara's shoulders. "Sara," she added, offering a weak smile.

"Andrew," said a young man with a mop of dark hair, then he reached around and took Susan's hand. "Susan," the young woman stated shyly. David held up a hand, ceasing the introductions momentarily. "Andrew, are you and Susan a couple?" he asked, looking at Susan. "Yes! He responded enthusiastically, as he looked at little David. David nodded his head. "Good, take good care of her." "Kathy Martin," a young woman offered, her voice a bit stronger than the others. "Riley," a girl stated, her voice quiet. "Noah," a young man stated, looking around. "Sophia," a young woman said, looking nervous. "Caleb," a young man introduced himself with a nod.

David smiled, the corner of his mouth twitching upwards in a way that Summer recognized as genuine amusement. He clapped his hands together, startling a few of the recruits. "Alright, folks. Enough standing around in the Texas heat. My house is your house. Come on inside, cool off, and get something to eat. We've got plenty." He ushered them towards the wide, welcoming porch, Summer falling into step beside him.

As they crossed the threshold, the recruits visibly relaxed, the oppressive heat instantly replaced by the cool, conditioned air. The stark contrast between the outside world and the inside of the house was jarring. The gleaming, tiled floors, the comfortable furniture, and the soft hum of electricity were luxuries they hadn't seen in months. They gawked upwards at the ceiling fans as Olivia giggled. "Wow," Marvin whispered, his eyes wide as he took in the spacious living room. "This is... incredible."

David chuckled. "I try to keep things comfortable. Summer, could you show them to the dining room? We have some brisket left over from lunch." Summer nodded. "Of course, Darling. This way, everyone." She guided them through the living room, towards a large dining room table laden with food. Plates piled high with smoked brisket, potato salad, coleslaw, and beans awaited them, along with pitchers of iced tea and lemonade. "Dig in," Summer encouraged, gesturing towards the feast. "There's plenty for everyone."

The recruits, hesitant at first, quickly succumbed to the aroma of smoked meat and the promise of a full stomach. They fell upon the food with a quiet desperation, their initial awe replaced by a ravenous hunger. David watched them, a mixture of compassion and amusement on his face. As they ate, David turned to Junior and Nicole, his voice low. "They seem... shell-shocked. More than I expected."

David listened intently as Junior explained the situation. The amusement that had flickered across his face earlier was replaced by a steely resolve. He absorbed the information, processing it with the speed and efficiency that defined him. "So," David said, his voice calm despite the undercurrent of anger he felt. "They were just abandoned. Left to rot." He hated the thought of people suffering through no fault of their own, especially those who had sworn an oath to protect others.

Nicole nodded, her expression mirroring his own. "Pretty much. The officers were gone, the buildings were locked up, and the food was running out. They were scared and desperate." Junior chimed in. "Honestly, Dad, they were about to turn on each other. The situation was getting hairy. I figured some young, able-bodied volunteers would be a good addition to our community." He paused, then added with a shrug, "Besides, I was bored."

David suppressed a smile. "I appreciate the initiative, Son. But you should have told me first. We need to be careful about who we bring into the fold." He glanced at the recruits, who were now devouring the brisket with gusto. "I know, Dad, but I figured you'd say no. You're always so cautious." Junior countered, a hint of defiance in his voice. "Caution is what has kept us going," David retorted, his tone firm but not unkind. "Now that they're here, we'll make the best of it. But this is a learning opportunity for both of us. Next time, talk to me first."

Nicole placed a hand on David's arm, her touch grounding him. "They seem like good kids, David. Just scared. And Junior's right, they could be a real asset. We can use all the help we can get, especially with things on the horizon." David looked at Nicole, his eyes softening. "I know. It's just… difficult. I want to protect all of you, all of our community. But sometimes, I feel like I'm playing a never-ending game of chess, trying to anticipate every possible threat." "That's why we're here, David," Nicole said, squeezing his arm gently. "We're your Knights, your Rooks, your Bishops. We're here to help you, to protect our King."

Appendix: 3

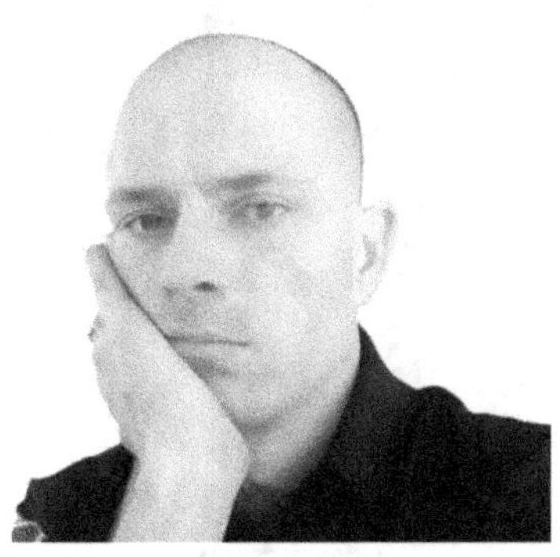

David

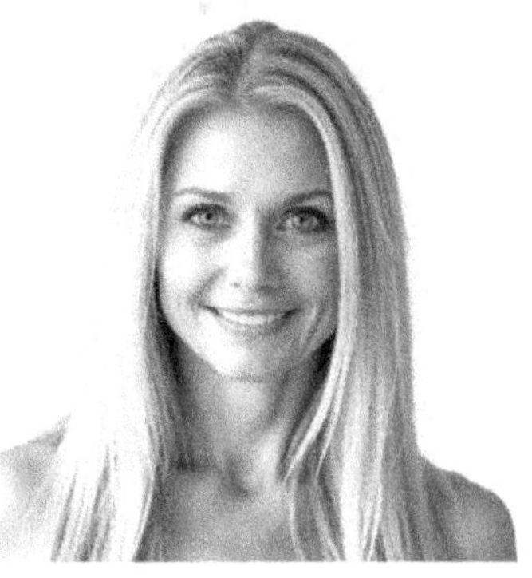

Tiffany

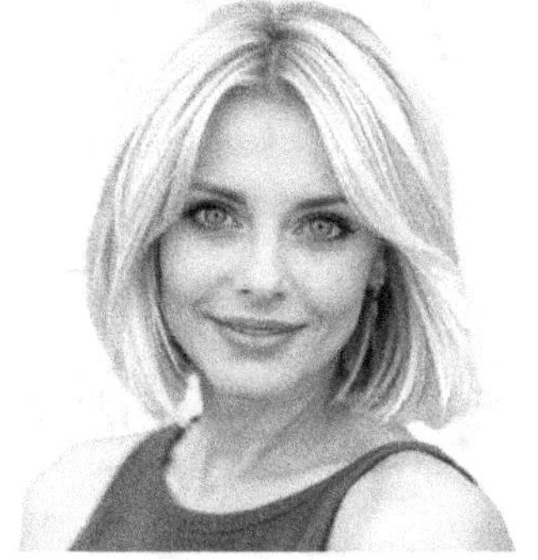

Jennifer

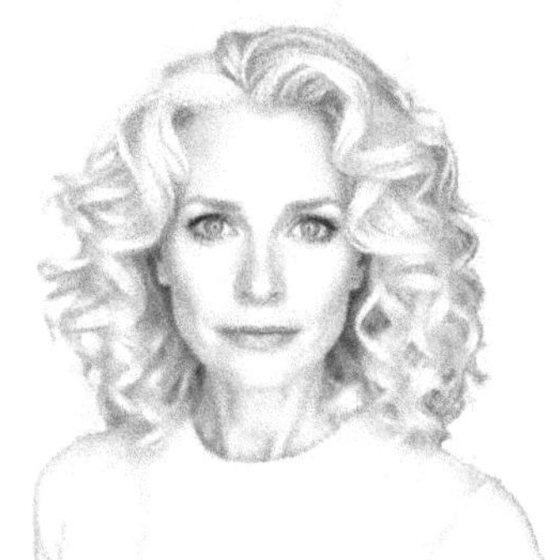

Summer

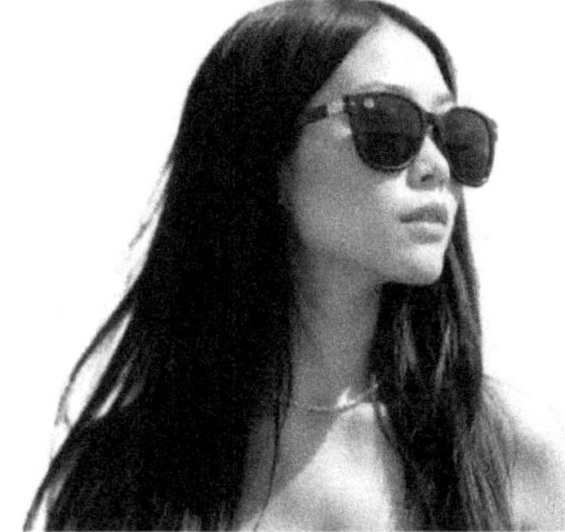

Elena

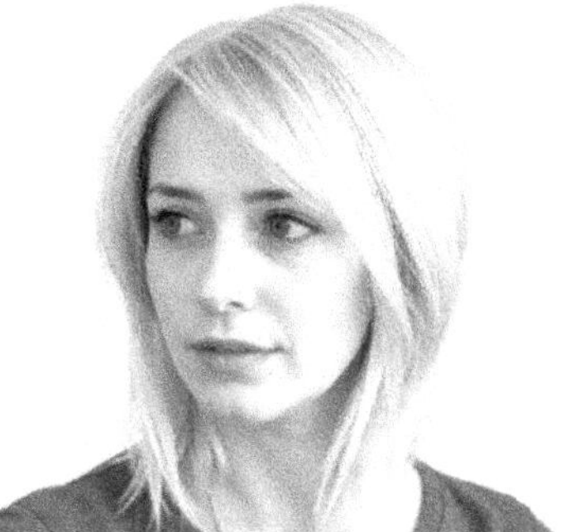

Nicole

Taylor

Jessica

Kayla

Tanya

www.ingramcontent.com/pod-product-compliance
Lightning Source LLC
Chambersburg PA
CBHW070501300726
48975CB00007B/2279